DOC HOLT

42 ✓

C.J. PETIT

Printed in the United States of America

First Printing, 2018

ISBN: 9781092964845

TABLE OF CONTENTS

C.J. PETIT

PROLOGUE

Double L Ranch
Comanche County, Texas
May 16, 1876

"The only damned mudhole for a whole damned mile around and that dumb critter has to go and find it," Doc snapped as he readied his rope.

Joe Sheraton laughed and shouted, "Hell, Doc, he just wanted a drink."

Doc whipped his lasso through the air, watched it settle over the steer's horns then snapped it tight before it could settle around his neck, although he thought if it had, he might be doing the stupid animal a favor.

"A drink of what? Mud?" Doc yelled back as he tightened his rope around his saddle horn and began walking Trapper backwards.

Joe just sat grinning as he watched Doc Holt's big pinto gelding's haunches bulge as it began to stretch the rope.

The steer had been struggling for almost an hour and was exhausted, but the torque provided by the power of the horse pulled his hooves out of their muddy prisons and it began to struggle to free itself.

It took almost another two minutes of Trapper's assistance to finally liberate the steer from the mudhole.

Doc patted Trapper's neck as he walked the horse over to the steer, leaned down and removed his rope then coiled it before replacing it on his saddle.

3

"Let's get this idiot back to the herd before he decides that goin' in there wasn't such a bad idea in the first place," Doc said to Joe.

Joe turned his horse around and began moving the steer back south to where the main herd was grazing about a mile and a half away.

As he and Doc walked their animals behind the muddy critter, Joe asked, "You comin' tonight, Doc? It's gonna be a lotta fun."

Doc looked over at Joe and replied, "I ain't been on one yet, Joe, so what makes you think I'm goin' this time? What you do is your business, not mine. Besides, what you boys call fun doesn't exactly sound like fun to me. Seems to me that you boys should just make the ride down to Comanche and spend some time at The Shotgun and blow off your steam down there."

"The boss kinda expects us to go, Doc. You gotta come along. I think he's gettin' kinda riled with you stayin' behind."

"He's payin' me to take care of the herd and if he wants me to do other things that I don't cotton to then he can just send me packin'."

"Aw, c'mon, Doc. You don't gotta do nothin'. Just ride along and watch. The boss won't even care that much as long as you ride along."

Doc shook his head and replied, "I'll care."

———

That night just after sunset while Doc laid on his bunk reading a two-day-old copy of *The Comanche Chief*, the boss, Charlie Lynch, rode out with his sons, his son-in-law and the rest of the hands…ten men out to do no good.

4

CHAPTER 1

July 27, 1876

Doc was moving the strays back to the herd when he spotted a rider coming toward him from the south. It didn't take him long to identify the foreman, Rex Crenshaw. He kept the steer moving and let the foreman get close enough to tell him what he wanted. He wasn't in a good mood after another do-nothing job.

"Hey, Doc, they need you back at the house," Rex shouted when he was within fifty yards.

Doc didn't reply, but just nodded and kept the steer moving. He was headed that way anyway and didn't see the reason to hurry, but his foreman thought otherwise.

"He wants to see you right away, Doc," he repeated as he drew closer.

"What about?"

"Smitty got hurt. Caught a horn in his right thigh. I'll drive the cows back."

Doc just nodded and set Trapper to a medium trot. He supposed that Rex expected him to gallop the three miles back to the Double L ranch house, but he wasn't about to stress his horse for Ned Smith, the boss's son-in-law. That man was the laziest son-of-a-bitch ever to set foot on a ranch in Texas, but his blonde hair, blue eyes and big smile had won over the only Lynch daughter, so he'd won his personal lottery and moved into the house. Besides, if he'd been stuck by a horn and wasn't already dead then a few extra minutes wouldn't matter.

The Double L had been a good place to work until the boss fell in with a group of like-minded men that felt the South shouldn't have surrendered or Texas should have told the Confederates to go to hell and become independent again. They thought they could make things right, at least the kind of right as they saw it, by making their night rides. They visited former slaves who had the audacity to homestead some land, folks that didn't support secession, some of the hated Yankees who had moved into the area and, of course, any Jews if they could find them.

He had expected some form of repercussion for not going along on any of the 'visits' by the boss and the boys, but his stay-in-the-bunkhouse policy hadn't earned him any real retaliation yet other than assigning him to the simple jobs that all seemed to be on the north or the western reaches of the ranch. He suspected that the boss wanted to fire him, but Doc figured that he hadn't done it yet because he was too good at what he did with the added benefit that he could provide emergency medical help which was an almost weekly occurrence on a large working ranch.

He arrived at the ranch house twelve minutes later and spotted Beth Smith, the aforementioned lone Lynch daughter as she stood on the porch. Doc pulled Trapper to a stop in front, stepped down and tossed the reins over the hitching rail before walking onto the porch of the big house.

"Doc, Ned managed to get himself cut by a longhorn," Beth said unsympathetically, "and he wasn't even working with the bull, he was trying to ride him."

"I'll take a look at him, ma'am," Doc said as he followed her into the house.

He didn't bother removing his hat when he spotted Ned Smith lying on the brocaded couch with his right thigh wrapped in a towel. Doc walked toward the moaning man, looking for the expected pool of blood but not seeing much more than a silver-dollar-sized patch.

"What happened, Ned?" Doc asked as he took a knee next to the couch, removed his hat, set it on the carpeted floor and pulled back the towel.

"I got throwed by a bull and caught his horn on my leg. I was damned lucky he didn't stomp on me or stick me in the gut with one of them horns."

Doc looked at the wound and almost laughed but held back and turned to Beth, who was standing behind him, and said, "Ma'am, I'll need a sewing kit and a bottle of whiskey."

"I'll get them, but only if you stick him with the needle, Doc." she said before she left to get the kit and the bottle.

While he waited, Doc asked, "Why were you ridin' a bull, Ned? Seems like a stupid thing to do. That's why God gave us horses."

"Eddy challenged me to do it. He said he could, and I figured it wasn't so bad."

"You are lucky that you weren't trampled. Fifteen hundred pounds of pissed off bull can ruin your day, and I don't think that Beth is all that happy with you, either."

Ned ignored the Beth side of Doc's comment and replied, "I kinda figured that out after. Is it gonna hurt when you fix it up, Doc?"

"Yup. Can't help that unless you wanna drink some of that whiskey your wife is bringin'."

Ned was thinking about it when Beth came hurrying back into the room with the sewing kit and a full bottle of Kentucky bourbon. Not exactly the rot-gut whiskey the ranch hands were familiar with down at The Shotgun, not that Doc could tell the difference even if he did drink.

Doc took the bottle, uncorked it and handed it to Ned before taking the sewing kit.

Ned upended the bottle and drank almost half as Beth looked on with wide eyes. She had never seen Ned drink out of a bottle before and she was surprised when he'd downed so much liquor without hesitation.

Ned handed the bottle back to Doc, who'd been surprised by the quantity as well, then leaned back and closed his eyes.

Doc stood and walked to a nearby chair and took a seat as Beth followed him and sat down in the adjacent chair.

"Doc, why aren't you sewing him up?" she asked.

"Just waitin' for the whiskey to make him happy enough that he won't notice what I'm doin', ma'am."

"Oh," she said as she turned to look back at Ned, "I don't really care if you started right now, Doc. He earned some pain."

Doc was surprised at her comments as he looked at Beth Smith, and knew that many of the hands, including him, had set great store in her when she was Beth Lynch. Doc knew he was too old, but he still wished she had made a better choice in husbands than Ned. There had been a few broken hearts in the bunkhouse when Ned bounced in and announced that Beth had agreed to marry him and more than a few jealous stares.

Doc was neither broken-hearted nor jealous but felt bad for her because Ned was just an empty shell. Beth was sweet, easy on the eyes and deserved better. Doc had always thought of Beth as the little sister he never had.

When Doc figured that the bourbon had worked its magic, he stood, pulled a straight-backed chair over to the couch and opened the sewing kit. He threaded some black silk thread through a needle, then splashed some whiskey on the wound, causing Ned to grunt and begin to shed tears before Doc started to sew up the wound. It wasn't deep or even very wide, considering it had supposedly been made by a bull horn, but it still took sixteen sutures to close properly. After it was done, Doc used the same towel that had been wrapped around it before as a bandage.

Without looking at Beth, he said, "Mrs. Smith, I'll need some strips of cloth to hold the towel in place."

"I'll be right back," she said before she disappeared down the hallway.

Doc then looked at Ned and asked, "What made that cut, Ned? It sure wasn't no bull horn."

Ned was already feeling loose tongued from the bourbon, so he replied, "Don't go tellin' Beth, but Juanita kinda threw a knife at me," then he giggled.

"Is Eddy gonna cover for that bull story?" Doc asked, intending both uses of the adjective.

"Sure. Me and Eddy are compadres. Boy, that Juanita sure is a firebrand! Beth ain't nothin'."

Doc was about to severely correct Ned's opinion of Beth when she returned with some unused fabric with a pink floral pattern and handed it to Doc.

He smiled at her selection of a suitably feminine design wondering if it was intentional for some form of retribution for her husband's stupidity or infidelity if she knew. He began ripping strips of the cotton cloth, tied off the bandage, then stood and replaced the straight-backed chair and turned to Beth.

"He'll need to have the bandages changed once a day, Mrs. Smith. I'll remove the sutures in a couple of weeks."

"Thank you, Doc."

Then after a pause she asked, "Doc, why are you calling me Mrs. Smith or ma'am? You called me Beth since you first got here."

"I know, ma'am. That's when you were just a young filly, but you're a married woman now, and that wouldn't be proper."

"I don't mind, Doc," she said, "you were always special to me."

"Well, ma'am, I appreciate that, but I'm kinda particular about not offendin' anybody if I can avoid it, and callin' you by your Christian name might upset your husband."

"I suppose you're right. Ned does seem sensitive about things like that," then asked softly, "Doc, does he drink whiskey like that when I'm not around?"

Doc replied, "Ma'am, it's just not my place to say. What another man does ain't my business as long as he leaves me be. Keep an eye on him for the next few days for signs of infection. If he starts gettin' feverish, or it starts hurtin', let me know. Okay?"

She smiled at Doc, nodded and replied, "I will. Thank you again, Doc. You're a real treasure."

Doc smiled at her, reached down and picked up his hat then said, "I've been called many things, Mrs. Smith, but it's a first for that one."

He turned and walked out of the house onto the porch, stopped for a few seconds, then pulled on his Stetson, stepped down the stairs, mounted Trapper and rode back to the pastures to resume his now expected unimportant jobs.

After he'd gone, the boss, Charlie Lynch, walked out of his office to where Beth was sitting next to Ned in the same straight-backed chair that Doc had used.

"How is he, Beth?" he asked.

"Doc said he'll be fine. We need to change his bandages, watch for a fever, and Doc will have to take his stitches out in two weeks."

"Good. I don't know why he tried such a foolish stunt. Eddy is still a little boy inside and Ned should have known better than to pay him any attention."

Beth snapped, "Why should you expect that from Ned? He's not a real man himself. He's just a prettier boy than Eddy."

Charlie was well aware of Ned's shortcomings but didn't comment as he walked over and picked up the half-empty bottle of bourbon before asking, "Did Doc use this much, or did he drink some himself?"

"No, Papa. Ned drank most of it, and Doc poured some on his wound. Doc didn't have any at all. You know he doesn't drink whiskey."

Charlie grunted, turned and walked back into his office then took his seat behind his desk to go back to his books. He lifted his pencil, stared at the ledger then tossed the pencil to the desk and leaned back, locking his hands behind his neck.

He had heard bits and pieces of what had transpired, but not Beth's question about Ned's drinking habits. He knew that Ned, like most of the cowhands and his sons, drank as a man should. Doc was the exception, and he wished that he did imbibe some to bring him off his high horse. It was bad enough that he refused to go along with everyone else when they went for one of their nighttime visits, but when he went into Comanche with the boys after payday, he didn't pal around with them at The Shotgun Saloon or visit the ladies on the second floor. It wasn't like he was a Bible-thumper or anything, he just was so damned stand-offish. If he wasn't such a good hand or such an invaluable asset because of his medical skills, then he would have fired him months ago when he refused to go on the night visits.

He thought that assigning him to those meaningless jobs in the north and west and keeping him away from the second herd on the east would drive him to quit. If it wasn't for Beth and Martha, he would have fired him after that first refusal, regardless of how valuable he was to have around.

————

That night the other ranch hands all pressed Doc about what had happened to Ned, but all he'd tell them was that he had a wound to his leg from a longhorn tip and he'd sewn it up. It wasn't because he liked Ned, he just didn't think it was any of their business.

With no good gossip coming from Doc, they launched into their favorite topic after the ladies at The Shotgun Saloon; their after-dark visits to unacceptable neighbors, some more than twenty miles away.

Doc knew what they were doing, and he was ashamed of himself for even knowing about it. Rationally, he could tell himself that it was none of his business, but it just didn't feel that way inside. They were hurting and sometimes killing innocent folks just because the boss felt that they didn't belong in Texas.

Charlie Lynch hadn't always been that way, at least as far as Doc knew. For the first five years he'd been with the Double L, he'd been the best boss he'd ever had. But then he got chummy with Bill Wheeler at the Bar W and he must have inspired him to go down that dark path of making this part of Texas for only their kind of Texans. Either he'd been infected by Bill Wheeler's talk or it just awakened the demon inside him, but whatever had been the match that lit the fuse, the boss had bought whole hog into the idea and began to use violent ways to make it happen.

The night rides had only started a few months ago, though, and Doc almost went on the first one until Carl Henson told him to get a torch. Once he knew the purpose behind the nighttime excursion, he'd just returned to the bunkhouse and laid on his bunk until they returned all giddy and excited a few hours later. The torches only had been used on that first raid when they realized it raised the alarm for other prospective victims for miles around, so they stuck to six-shooters and rifles after that.

What bothered him even more than the boss's conversion was the surprising willingness of his fellow ranch hands to go along with it. The boss's three sons and Ned he understood, but the boys all seemed to enjoy themselves as if it was a big party. They'd even brag about it, and each time they went out, it seemed to be getting worse. He knew that he had to leave soon as he could sense the growing hostility from the boss and a wall being built around him to shut him out.

But they still talked, and as they talked, he wanted to tell them to shut up, but he just laid there and tried to think of something else…anything else.

His dream, like all the hands, was to own his own place. He'd been saving up for it since he returned to civilian life after the failed war for Confederate independence. Granted, it was hard, but he was up to almost two thousand dollars after eight years of denying himself any pleasures or the slightest of luxuries.

He'd just banked his pay every month except for ten dollars, and the only big expenses he had allowed himself was when he bought Trapper, his pinto gelding three years ago, a new Colt Peacemaker firing the .45 Long Colt a year later, and a Winchester '73 to replace his '66 last year. He had kept the Yellowboy because it still shot well, and the gun smith had only offered him two dollars in trade. It was worth more than that to him, so he'd kept it. He rode remuda horses most of the time, except when he rode to the far reaches of the ranch and Trapper needed the exercise.

Everything else he owned could fit into his saddlebags, just in case he decided to make the break and leave the Double L. He knew that it was coming soon and maybe it was time to call it quits today. He just couldn't see things getting any better.

———

Eleven miles northwest of where Doc was resting, Rhonda Byrne was huddled in the corner of the bed, not knowing how much longer she could hold on. She still had nightmares about what had happened that dark night in May when the night riders had come, killed her husband and their two ranch hands, driven off their small herd and taken their five horses. She'd been

14

raped by several of the men, how many she couldn't remember, and left for dead, but she hadn't died, at least not yet.

For three days after the attack, she had just crawled into bed, cried and wanted to die. She had been severely beaten before and after being raped and the bruises and cuts hurt badly, but the drive to stay alive was still there. She didn't want to face her maker if it wasn't her time, so despite her injuries and her despondent mood, she had finally gone out into the kitchen and eaten. There hadn't been much food even before the night riders had come because the monthly supply run was two days away, but she thought she could manage.

Over the next six weeks, her physical injuries had mostly healed, but the damage to her mind was always there. The first few nights, she was in so much pain that she just slept dreamlessly, but as the pain subsided the nightmares began.

They went beyond simple nightmares as she relived that horrible night over and over each time that she entered the dreamworld. In those sleeping horrors, the attack was even worse than it had been that dreadful night because in her dreams she was fully conscious as they struck her and raped her while they laughed as if it was a game. Rhonda came to fear the night as much for the coming of the resurrected assault even more than the very real terror of the fanged creatures that lurked just outside the house.

She knew that she wasn't pregnant from the attack, which had surprised her because she had believed that God was punishing her and becoming pregnant would have been the final proof of just how much He hated her. It would have been the ultimate irony for a woman who'd given birth three times and never had a chance to suckle her child. She had lost two daughters and one son and only one of the girls had even taken a breath. Each loss had devastated her, fueling her guilt and hardening her belief that God was punishing her in the cruelest possible way.

The food in the pantry had been gone for two weeks now, and she had been reduced to eating the oats in the horses' feed bins and even that had run out four days ago. Rhonda was now desperately hungry. She'd lost almost twenty pounds and knew she couldn't hold out any longer if she stayed in the house.

As she sat huddled on the bed, she could hear the creatures of the night searching for her. The coyotes, and even a cougar had come into the yard over the past few nights but hadn't entered the house, at least not yet.

Now they were getting bolder and had been scratching at the door, trying to gain entry to sink their sharp teeth into her. If the thought wasn't so hideous to her, Rhonda thought that maybe she should just walk out into the night and be done with it. She knew that they weren't coyotes out there. They were demons sent by an angry, unforgiving God. But even in her deep despair, her upbringing still wouldn't allow her to actively end her own life. If she died, it would be from something out of her control, whether it was the hungry carnivores or a return visit from those bastards from the Double L.

So, tomorrow she decided she had to leave the ranch to find something to eat but didn't know anywhere else to go but to follow the road south to Comanche. It would be a long, devastating walk and she wasn't sure she had the energy to make it. Even if she did, she had no money to buy anything. She would have to beg or do something worse if she wanted to eat. But as she sat in the corner with her arms wrapped around her, she could feel her ribs and knew that even if she had to offer herself for sale to survive, she'd be lucky to get a dollar.

She guessed she was probably down to around a hundred pounds now and had almost no energy left at all, but she knew she had to make one last desperate attempt to find food. Tomorrow, she'd walk to Comanche and if she didn't make it, God would have his final revenge. She'd be in hell and her nightly dreams of horror would become permanent.

———

Morning assignments were being handed out and Rex almost cringed as he spoke to Doc. He knew what the boss was doing, but he was the boss and Rex couldn't change the orders.

"The boss wants you to head up to the northwest corner again, Doc. He says that we're losin' too many critters. They're wandering off the ranch, and he wants 'em back."

"Okay, Rex," Doc replied, "but we both know there ain't any beeves up there. This is just a waste of my time, but I'll head up there anyway."

Rex just shrugged then walked away feeling worse than usual.

The other ranch hands had all gone to their jobs, but as Doc had expected, he was being sent off on his lonesome to the far reaches of the spread.

He turned and led Trapper toward the chow house, stopped at the entrance and caught sight of the cook.

"Fred, I won't be stoppin' back for lunch. They're givin' me another do-nothin' job."

"Need some chow to take with ya?" Fred Richards asked.

"Yeah, Fred. I'm headin' out to the great beyond to hunt for wanderin' cows that ain't even there."

"You sure seem to get all the good jobs, Doc," the cook said as he snickered and began putting together a bag of food for Doc to take with him.

"It looks that way, doesn't it?" Doc asked with a grin.

"That's 'cause you're so damned persnickety, Doc," he replied as he handed Doc the bag.

Doc took the heavy bag and said, "Thanks, Fred. I appreciate it. You know this is a lot more food than just lunch. I can't eat this much in two whole days."

"Sure, you can, Doc. And I appreciate you bein' the only one who doesn't call me Cookie."

Doc grinned, hung the food bag over his saddle horn, mounted Trapper and before he turned the pinto away, replied, "Your mama didn't name you Cookie, Fred."

He waved to the cook and set Trapper off to the northwest. It was another worthless job that meant nothing, and Doc figured that it was time to ride on. He had to feel useful and riding around in the Texas heat without any reason wasn't useful.

———

Rhonda had started walking just after sunrise, keeping a slow pace to conserve her remaining energy but it was still hard. Her stomach had stopped growling at her two days ago, apparently having given up any expectation of results from its constant complaints.

She kept her eyes trained forward as she walked south. She'd be crossing onto Double L land in another two hours or so if she kept going, but then she'd have to swing wide to avoid the ranch house. If she saw a rider, he'd be one of those Double L ranch hands who had raped and beaten her, so she'd need to drop to the ground and hope that she hadn't been spotted, but she knew that in her faded yellow dress, there wasn't much chance of being overlooked. Then she felt like laughing at the absurdity of trying not to be seen. *What more could they do to her?*

––––––

An hour later she was still moving, but she already knew that she wasn't going to make it. She was already hideously thirsty in the hot Texas sun and her legs felt like rubber bands as she shuffled one foot in front of the other.

She finally closed her eyes but kept her feet moving, each step more and more difficult. Why she persisted, she couldn't understand. Maybe she didn't want to die because she knew that God hated her and would send her to hell for what she'd done. She believed that God was the one who had sent those night riders as a message that more pain was to come, and Rhonda believed that she deserved it. She had sinned and had never truly repented. Instead, she had stopped going to church at all, and she was sure that her unholy decisions had cost her husband and the Clancy brothers their lives.

––––––

Doc had crossed the northern edge of the Double L twenty minutes earlier and was scanning for any stray cattle. He'd done it just a week ago and was reasonably certain that there weren't any more wandering beef critters this far off the ranch and wondered if the boss just intended for him to keep riding.

He stopped Trapper, pushed the brim of his Stetson back on his head, pulled out his canteen and after pulling off the cork, took a long drink of the lukewarm water. He lowered his head and as he was ramming the stopper back in place, he spotted movement about a mile northwest, but it wasn't big enough to be a steer or a rider. He didn't think it was a coyote, either. It was moving much too slowly.

Curiosity more than anything else made him hang his canteen and nudge Trapper into a trot heading in the direction of the movement. It was simply something to do other than just wandering around aimlessly.

After another minute, he knew it was a human on foot, then watched as the figure collapsed to the ground. He kicked Trapper into a canter which ate up the remaining distance, and when he was within a hundred yards, he saw that she was a woman with bright red hair wearing a barely yellow dress.

He pulled Trapper to a stop when he was fifty feet away, grabbed his canteen and hopped to the ground, jogged to where she lay on her face in the dirt and took a knee believing that she was already dead.

He rolled her carefully onto her back, saw that she was still breathing then opened the canteen and poured some water on her forehead as he said, "Ma'am? Are you with me? Can you hear me?"

Rhonda heard the voice and didn't know whether she wanted to answer the question or not. She knew he had to be one of those night riders from the Double L and had probably been one of those that had killed the men then beaten and raped her.

"Ma'am, you need to drink some water. I'm going to lift your head a little bit, so it doesn't go into your lungs."

She still didn't reply, so Doc lifted her head and tipped the canteen slowly to let the water flow into her mouth.

Rhonda couldn't resist drinking the incredible cooling water as it spread across her tongue. As more water slipped past her lips, she felt such relief that she would have cried if she had the moisture.

As he watched her swallow, Doc was pretty sure that she was Mrs. Byrne, the wife of a small rancher northwest of the Double L. It had been visited by the Lynch boys and the ranch hands about six weeks ago, and he'd heard some of them talking about the red-headed bitch who had fought like a puma. He felt worse now that he could put a face on one of their victims…much, much worse.

"Ma'am?" he asked, "What can I do to help you?"

Rhonda whispered, "Let me die. God hates me and wants me to die so He can send me to hell where I belong."

"No, ma'am. He doesn't hate you, or He wouldn't have sent me here to help you."

"That's not why God sent you. He sent you to punish me again. Go ahead, do your worst." she said hoarsely as she spread her legs apart.

Doc was stunned by her response, but replied, "No, ma'am. I'm not here to hurt you. I'll do whatever you need."

"Then just go away."

"Yes, ma'am," Doc said as he lowered her head to the ground, then stood and walked back to Trapper.

Rhonda was surprised that he had gone so quickly but felt the sun on her face as she laid quietly in the heat and imagined how much hotter it would be in hell. Five minutes later she faded away and darkness overtook her.

Fifty feet away, Doc looked at Mrs. Byrne as he held Trapper's reins. Once he was sure that she was asleep or passed out, he led Trapper back to where she lay, slipped his arms under her and lifted her easily from the ground. He took two strides to his horse then stepped into the stirrup, lifted himself and her listless body into the saddle then began walking Trapper to the northwest, following her tracks back to her ranch.

When he spotted the ranch buildings, he was surprised to see that they were still intact and not burnt to cinders. He also had expected to find the remains of some bodies somewhere nearby, unless Mrs. Byrne had buried them, and he doubted if she had the strength. The only possible answer to the question was that the buzzards and night critters had done what their nature drove them to do.

He reached the ranch house, carefully dismounted, carried her into the house through the front door, turned at the first bedroom and laid her gently onto the quilts. Again, he was surprised that the furniture all seemed to be undamaged and even the bedding seemed untouched. There were a few bullet holes in the walls and the floors, but they hadn't ransacked the place.

He let her sleep and after a quick inspection of the pantry and finding it empty, he walked back outside to get the suddenly important bag of food that Fred had given him.

Ten minutes later, he had the cookstove fired up and while it was heating, he left the house through the back door to hunt for those remains that had to be somewhere. There should at least be some skeletons as the critters wouldn't have carried off all the bones. He'd seen some blood stains in the wood in the main room along with the bullet holes in the floor, so someone had died there, and he believed that it must have been Mrs. Byrne had moved that body outside with the others.

He stopped by the barn, found no horses, which didn't surprise him, but there were four full sets of tack and a wagon and harness still inside. After the barn, he walked slowly to the bunkhouse, its door wide open. As he drew closer, he could see the bullet holes through the walls all lower than four feet from the ground. But when he looked inside, he spotted four bunks, two without any bedding and blood on the floor nearby. Obviously, no attempt had been made to clean the blood as it had been in the ranch house, *but where were the bodies?*

He had his answer when he found a grave behind the bunkhouse, but it wasn't as big as he expected, unless all three bodies had been dumped into one deep grave, which would be a lot harder to dig. He would have dug a wider, but shallower hole for all three corpses. He'd done it a few times during the war.

Doc's search over, he headed back to the kitchen to cook something for Mrs. Byrne, even more troubled now than he had been when he had first spotted her. At least three men had been killed in that 'visit' six weeks ago, and from what Mrs. Byrne had said to him as she lay on the ground, they had all raped her afterwards. All this pain and suffering caused by men he worked with, and even after hearing them joke about it, he had done nothing.

As he cooked, he stewed in his own thoughts. Even as he had heard them talking about what they had done, he didn't believe that they were evil men. Their boss wasn't some heartless, cruel man who loved killing, either. *How could apparently normal men like them do such evil things and not feel so incredibly guilty?* He hadn't done anything himself, and had initially believed he could live with it, yet the longer it went on, the guiltier he felt for not stopping them. Now, after witnessing first-hand the unjustified evil that had been committed, his guilt became overwhelming. He hadn't even told them what they were doing was wrong. He had just stayed apart from what they were doing, telling himself that it wasn't his business.

It was a code he had lived by since he was a teenager. As long as he was left alone, what happened wasn't his business. It had become ingrained into him over the years, but now that rule was thrown into his face as a coward's way of allowing evil to thrive. That woman sleeping in the other room was the face of his failure to do what was right.

He knew he couldn't do anything to make things right for Mrs. Byrne, but as he dumped the can of beans into the frypan, he made up his mind. He would provide for her and what the riders from the Double L and the other like-minded groups did on those visits would become his business and he'd do whatever necessary to stop them.

———

Rhonda returned to consciousness, wondering why she wasn't roasting in hell. It was hot, but not nearly as bad as she had expected. This was Texas hot, not Hades hot. Maybe this was purgatory, and they had gotten it all wrong about eternal damnation in the first place. Maybe you just stayed uncomfortable for a while before God let you into heaven.

But then her nostrils flared as she smelled food cooking. It was only then that she realized that she was still alive. She strained to pull her eyelids open and when her eyes could take in her surroundings, she realized that she was in her own bed, and her mouth was incredibly dry.

She turned her head to the left and saw a glass of water on the small side stand and tried to sit up to drink some of that life-giving water but her head spun, and she kept falling back.

Doc heard sounds coming from the back bedroom, so he set down the wooden spoon, slid the frypan from the hotplate back to the warming area, then quickly walked down the hallway to the bedroom and stepped inside.

"Ma'am, do you need some help sitting up?" he asked when he saw her struggling.

"Why didn't you let me die?" she asked hoarsely as she dropped back to the bed.

"I can't watch any of God's critters die, much less His greatest creation," Doc replied as he walked to the bed, sat down on the edge and picked up the glass.

"What are you a priest or something?" she croaked.

"No, ma'am. Just a cow hand. Let's sit you up."

He put his right hand behind her back and helped her into a sitting position then held her stable as she took the glass in both hands and quickly drank the water in big gulps.

Doc took the glass from her thin hands, returned it to the stand and let her back down.

"I'll be back in a few minutes with more water and something to eat. Okay?"

Rhonda didn't reply but just watched him leave with the empty glass and wondered if he had done anything to her while she was asleep or passed out, whichever it was. She quickly checked and found that he hadn't removed any of her clothing, so unless he dressed her again, he hadn't taken advantage of her.

She thought that he must not be from the Double L at all, but must have just been passing through, and Rhonda felt a rush of relief once she reached that conclusion. She was going to eat soon and wouldn't be hurt again. The man seemed thoughtful too, which was something new and different for her.

Doc spooned his creation into a bowl and knew it wasn't great as he wasn't a cook and never claimed to be, but it was food, and she needed it badly.

He refilled the glass at the pump, walked back down the hallway to her bedroom and set the bowl of beans and smoked beef on the table with the glass of water.

"Can you sit up now, ma'am?" he asked.

"I think so."

Doc just watched her eyes as she tried to sit up to make sure she wasn't going to fall over, but she was able to make it to a sitting position without too much difficulty, so he picked up the bowl and held it out to her.

"Now, this may not taste very good, but you need to get some food into you. It's kind of hot, so be careful."

Rhonda looked at his face as she accepted the bowl. It was a rough, but kind face with caring blue eyes, but lighter than her own dark blue.

She kept her eyes on his face as she took a bite of food and then had to close her eyes when her tongue felt the nourishment. He said it may not taste good, but he was oh, so wrong! It was manna from heaven as she began to chew the beans and beef. There was so much flavor after her last few meals of dry oats.

26

Rhonda began taking bite after bite almost forgetting to chew when Doc said, "Ma'am, don't eat so fast. Your stomach is going to fight back, and you might throw up. Just slow down and let the food take its time gettin' down there."

She almost laughed at the thought of her stomach rebelling but did slow down. When she finished, Doc took the empty bowl and gave her the glass of water.

After drinking half of the glass, she handed it back to Doc, then slowly laid back down to the bed, closed her eyes and sighed.

"Now, ma'am, as much as you might want to eat, you gotta take your time and not eat right away. I'll bring you another bowl in a few hours. You can sleep now."

Rhonda didn't reply but let herself relax with something in her stomach that belonged there and an unexpected, yet incredibly welcome sense of security. But she was still exhausted from the walk and let herself drift into a thankfully dreamless sleep.

Once she'd closed her eyes, Doc stood, walked back out to the kitchen and washed the empty bowl before leaving the house, walking out to Trapper and stepping into the saddle.

Doc then wheeled Trapper south and headed for the Double L to tender his resignation. As he rode, he thought of different reasons he could provide the boss for his decision to leave the ranch. Part of him wanted to rant about what he'd found, but he knew that it wouldn't do anything but alert the boss that his ex-ranch hand was now a problem and that Mrs. Byrne was alive. He'd have to use a much more reasonable reason for his departure to keep them away from the Byrne ranch until Mrs. Byrne was stronger but didn't have any idea of what to do after that.

He was well onto Double L land when he spotted the foreman talking to Lou Robinson and Whitey Smith, so he angled that way.

When he drew close Rex shouted, "Back so soon, Doc? You find any strays?"

Doc didn't reply until he was close and replied, "Nope. Not a one. I don't think there's any up there at all. To tell the truth, Rex, I'm gettin' tired of all this useless work. I been sent on jobs any greenhorn could handle. I can guess why the boss ain't happy with me, so I reckon it's time I pulled up stakes and moved on."

"Aw, c'mon, Doc! The boss is just a bit outta joint 'cause you seem to think you're better'n the rest of us, includin' him. Tell him you're sorry for bein' the way you are, and he'll let it go."

Doc shook his head and said, "I never thought I was better'n anybody, Rex. I'm a lot worse in the things that matter. I'm gonna head over to ranch house to pick up my pay and head out."

Rex was going to argue, but Doc wheeled Trapper to his right and trotted away toward the ranch house.

Whitey glanced over at the foreman and said, "Rex, I got a feelin' that somethin' bad is gonna come outta this."

"It already has, Whitey. Losin' Doc is a bad thing for all of us."

Doc reached the ranch house fifteen minutes later, stepped down and tied off Trapper before climbing the stairs onto the porch and knocking on the door. He removed his hat and a minute later, the door was opened by Martha Lynch, the boss's wife.

"Why, hello, Doc. What can I do for you?" she asked pleasantly, which was her nature.

"I'd like to see the boss, ma'am."

"Of course, he's in his office," she replied as she waved him into the house.

"Thank you, ma'am," he said while crossing the threshold.

Mrs. Lynch returned to whatever she was doing in the kitchen as Doc walked to the office door, but before he could knock on the door jamb, the boss said, "Come in, Doc."

Doc nodded and stepped to the front of his desk as he twisted the brim to his Stetson, then said, "Boss, I think it's time I moved on. You're payin' me top hand pay and you just ain't gettin' your money's worth."

Charlie Lynch was relieved that it had happened and saddened at the same time. Doc was his best hand and his medical expertise had saved several lives over the years, but he was now a risk and it was better that he left.

He pulled open the top drawer of his desk and counted out three twenty-dollar bills and handed them to Doc, saying, "Here's this month's pay and a twenty-dollar bonus for helping Ned. We're going to miss you, Doc."

Doc just took the cash, stuffed it in his pocket then nodded, turned and left the office without comment before crossing the large main room floor and going out the door.

After clearing out his things from the bunkhouse, which took all of ten minutes, he rode out of the Double L and headed for Comanche.

————

Rhonda awakened just as Doc was arriving in Comanche and slowly sat up, then remained sitting on the edge of the bed for a minute to collect her balance and her thoughts. *What if the man who had brought her back to the house and given her food was from the Double L?* The odds of a lone rider heading north of the Double L towards her ranch were very slim.

What if God sent the rider from the Double L? What if he was one of those that had killed Jamie and the Clancy brothers and then beaten and taken her? Maybe his conscience had bothered him so much, he was riding to the ranch to ask for forgiveness. But that made no sense. *Why would he suddenly decide to ride to the ranch after six weeks, especially when he thought that everyone was dead?*

She knew that the men who had abused her thought she was going to die from her injuries or lack of food because she had vague memories of that discussion. None of them had wanted to shoot a woman, but whoever was in charge had said that she was going to die anyway, so let her get taken away by the night critters. They had washed their hands of her death yet had buried her husband and the Clancy brothers. Everything about that raid, aside from the very real fact that it had happened, made no sense at all.

Now she suspected that she had a rider from the Double L who would be returning soon. But why he would be returning, if he did, made no sense at all. If he was going to do anything to her, he would have done it already.

Rhonda had no answers, so she finally stood, walked slowly out of her room and headed for the kitchen to see if there was more food. Even though he had told her not to eat right away, it had been at least three hours, and she was still very hungry, so she didn't think it would matter.

———

After a stop at the Comanche State Bank and withdrew three hundred dollars, Doc had gone to the livery, where he bought one horse and two mules, along with a pack saddle for one of the mules.

The horse wasn't exactly what he would have chosen if he'd wanted another horse for himself, but it was for Mrs. Byrne, so he'd selected the smallest horse the liveryman had for sale, a young tan filly with a black mane and tail and a white star on its forehead. She was a pretty thing and he thought she was perfect for a woman to ride.

Then he led the trio to Miller's Dry Goods and bought four panniers for the pack mule. He then filled them with sacks of flour, sugar, coffee, salt, potatoes, onions, and lots of tins of food. He added two slabs of bacon, a ham, two smoked briskets, four dozen eggs, some butter, lard, and other necessities before selecting six pairs of socks, a pair of boots that looked about right, four dresses, two camisoles, and two nightdresses, as well as four pairs of bloomers, which raised Pat Miller's eyebrows. He picked up a spool of cord, a can of coal oil and two boxes of matches before lugging them to the front of the counter.

"Okay, Pat, that'll do it for now. I need four more boxes of .44s for my Winchesters and two boxes of the .45 Long Colts for my pistol."

"Okay, Doc," Pat said as he turned, pulled open a drawer and began removing the boxes of cartridges.

As he was stacking them onto the counter, Doc said, "Give me one of those twelve-gauges too, will you, Pat? I'll need a couple of boxes of birdshot shells and a couple of #4 buckshot, too."

Pat didn't miss a beat as he then closed the cartridge drawer and opened the one beneath it and picked out the requested shotgun shells. After he'd put them on the counter, he took down one of the new Remington twelve-gauge shotguns and laid it beside the boxes of cartridges.

"Pat, is that a Sharps you got hangin' there?" he asked as he pointed at the carbine.

"Yes, sir. A Model 67 carbine. Fires the .50-70 cartridge. It's been used, though. I'll make you a good price if you want it, but I only got two boxes of cartridges for it."

"How good a price, Pat?" he asked.

"With the cartridges, I'll let you have it for twenty dollars. The cartridges themselves are two dollars a box."

"Let me take a look at it."

Pat removed the carbine from the wall and handed it to Doc. It was a lot heavier than the Winchester, and he'd never used one before, but the extra range and power of the gun might be necessary.

He examined the receiver, the chamber and then the barrel. The rifling was excellent and there was no sign of corrosion anywhere.

"Okay, Pat, add that to my order. Just give me the damage and we'll get this all loaded up."

Twenty minutes later after a stop at Dodson's Feed and Grain for two bags of oats, and a second at the butcher where he picked up two steaks and some sausages that he liked, Doc led his heavily-laden pack mule along with the horse and second mule out of Comanche and turned north to return to the Byrne ranch.

———

Rhonda was lying on her bed in pain. She had eaten too much, too quickly and her stomach was hurting something fierce. She had vomited most of the food but had managed to run to the back porch before regurgitating onto the dirt. After rinsing her mouth out, she had crawled back into her bedroom and curled up in a ball hoping she hadn't ruptured something inside her thin gut. She wished she could fall asleep again, but it was no use. The stomach pain wouldn't let her do anything but suffer.

———

Doc didn't expect to see any of the Double L hands out when he passed the buildings because it was chow time. He hadn't eaten since breakfast, so his mouth began to water as he passed close enough to pick up the aroma of whatever Fred was cooking for the boys.

An hour later, he spotted the Byrne ranch house in the distance and assumed that Mrs. Byrne was awake by now. He still had no idea of what he was going to do after he dropped off the supplies and the animals. She probably wouldn't want anything to do with him or any other man after what had happened to her, and that went double for a man from the Double L. He thought the best thing he could do would be to just leave the food and animals with her, give her the shotgun and some money and then leave if that's what she wanted.

But even though it may have been the best option, he didn't want it to be that way. He wanted to protect her and let her get better before he left. He felt he owed that to her at least because he had done nothing to prevent what had happened to her.

In the end, it wouldn't matter what he wanted, only what she did.

———

Twenty minutes later, he pulled up to the back hitchrail of the ranch house, stepped down, then picked up the sour smell of Mrs. Byrne's vomit on the ground. He knew what she'd done, so he didn't knock but walked into the kitchen and then headed directly for the bedroom, hoping she wasn't really hurting.

He stopped outside the open door, tapped on the jamb and stuck his head inside.

"Ma'am, are you okay? I reckon you ate more food too fast and too soon."

Rhonda didn't turn away from the wall that had been the focus of her attention for four hours when she replied, "My stomach hurts badly. Is it ever going to feel better?"

"Yes, ma'am. But it'll take a few more hours, then you'll be able to eat again, but you'll have to take it slow and easy this time."

"Why? I was so hungry."

"'Cause your stomach kinda shrunk and you forced it to get too big, too fast. Once it relaxes, you'll be able to eat and if you take it nice and easy, it'll go back to the way it was before. It'll take a few days, though."

Rhonda then asked quietly, "Who are you? What's your name?"

"My name's John Holt, but everybody calls me Doc. It's been so long that I can't recall the last time anyone called me anything but Doc."

"Are you a doctor?" she asked.

"No, ma'am. My father, he was a country doctor, and I picked up a lot from him. When I went off to war, I was a regular soldier for a few months, then they found out about my knowin' about medicine, so they made me a corpsman. When the war was done, I started tendin' cattle, and had to help some of the other fellers when they got hurt, so pretty soon, everybody started callin' me Doc."

"Why were you riding north of the Double L?" she asked still facing the wall.

"I used to work there. I drew my last pay a few hours ago."

Rhonda suddenly turned to face him, forgetting about her stomach pain as rage filled her.

She shouted, "You did this! You were here and killed my husband, the Clancy brothers and then joined the others and beat me then raped me until I was almost dead! You, heartless bastard!"

Doc felt he deserved every word of the accusation as he replied, "No, ma'am. I wasn't here, but that's no excuse. I knew what they were doin', and I didn't stop 'em, and I'll never forgive myself for that. Those boys hurt a lot of folks and I didn't do a damned thing to stop what they were doin'.

"I kept tellin' myself it wasn't my business, but that was wrong, ma'am. It was real wrong. I know you'll never forgive me for what I shoulda stopped, and I understand that, but all I can do is to help you as much as I can. If you want me to leave right now, I'll understand that, too. I bought you a horse, a pair of mules and some food that I can bring into the house. I'll leave you a shotgun and some shells, so you can protect yourself and some money to help you get along for a few months."

He looked down at her and said, "I am really sorry, Mrs. Byrne. I'll go and bring the food and things into the house and then put the horse and mules in the barn now."

Rhonda didn't reply but saw the pain in his light blue eyes and knew that he was deeply disturbed by what had happened. *But how could any decent man know what was going on and do nothing about it?*

Doc quickly left the room, walked down the hallway and out of the house, his guilt almost overwhelming. He knew that every word that Mrs. Byrne had screamed at him was well-deserved.

––––––

Rhonda didn't know what to think or what to do. His offer to give her food, a horse and mules and even a shotgun would mean she would be able to fend for herself for a few months at least, *but did she want to do that? What would happen after that or if those riders came back?* She'd never fired a gun before and didn't know if she could shoot a man even if she had.

Just a few hours ago, she was preparing herself to die and now she had a glimmer of hope and it was because of the guilt of the man who had brought her back to the ranch house and fed her. Her recently acquired sense of security was dissipating, and she wanted it back, and the only one who could restore it just left the house.

It came down to a question of trust. *Could she trust a man who had been a rider from the Double L?*

———

"Papa, why did you fire Doc?" asked Beth as she put the bowl of boiled potatoes onto the table.

"I told you, Beth, I didn't fire him. He just quit. It's not the same."

She took a seat next to Ned and said, "But why did you let him go? Who is going to take out Ned's stitches?"

"I hadn't thought about that, but I'm sure anyone can take them out."

Beth fumed as she began to eat her steak while her husband suddenly wished that Doc had waited two weeks.

"Why did he quit, Charlie?" asked Martha.

"I think he just thought it was time to move on, dear."

"After six years, Doc just decides out of the blue that he wants to leave and simply rides off?" she asked.

Charlie took a sip of his coffee then replied, "A man's got to do what a man thinks he's got to do. I can't read the man's mind, Martha."

None of the men at the table commented, leading to almost a minute of silence before Joe asked for someone to pass the potatoes.

———

Doc settled the mules, Trapper and the filly into their stalls, then returned to the house and began moving the supplies he had already left on the porch into the kitchen.

37

The last thing he carried inside were the shotgun, his two Winchesters, and the Sharps.

He spent another half an hour putting everything away in the cold room or the pantry before he fired up the cookstove again and filled the coffeepot with water.

While he waited for the water to boil, he examined the Sharps more closely. He thought he'd never need another rifle after he bought the '73, but here he was with an older, single shot weapon in his hands just because it had a much longer reach than the Winchesters. He pulled out one of the Sharps .50 caliber cartridges from the box and stood it on its end, then pulled one of the Long Colts from his gunbelt loop and stood it next to the Sharps cartridge. Finally, he took one of the .44s and put it in the line. It was a progressive set of three steps, beginning with the short .44 and ending with the .50 caliber Sharps. Then, he picked up the .44 and stood it on top of the .45 Long Colt and it still wasn't as tall as the Sharps cartridge.

After replacing the cartridges, he thought he'd fix something for himself and see if Mrs. Byrne could manage to eat something. It should ease her stomach pain.

———

Rhonda was feeling better, but her stomach still wasn't happy. She could hear Doc Holt out in the kitchen as he brought things inside and was curious about what he was bringing into the house.

She was also seriously engaged in an internal debate about what to do about him. She believed him when he had said that he hadn't been involved in the attack, and she could tell that he really was contrite about not stopping them, *but was it enough to trust him?* And then there was the whole character issue. The

38

man may not have been involved, but he was a coward for not standing up to them, and Rhonda couldn't abide cowards.

But then there was the memory of the overpowering fear that she felt just last night when she was scrunched up in the corner of her bed, waiting for the four-legged invaders to come into the house and didn't think she could go through that again.

Rhonda decided that the only way to get an answer was to go and talk to Mister Holt again, so she slowly stood, let out a deep breath and shuffled out of the room.

She walked so quietly that Doc didn't hear her coming as he cut up some potatoes to put into the pot of hot water.

"Mister Holt," she asked as she entered the kitchen, almost making him slice off a finger, "Why?"

She was taking a seat when he turned to her and asked, "What do you mean, ma'am?"

"Why did they do this and why didn't you do anything to stop it?"

He set the knife down and leaned against the counter before replying, "You don't sound like you're from around here, ma'am. Where were you raised?"

"New York, but what has that got to do with it?"

"Everything, ma'am. Was your husband from New York, too?"

"No, he was from County Clare in Ireland."

"Can I guess you're both Catholic?" Doc asked.

Rhonda flared a bit as she snapped, "What I believe and which church I attend doesn't matter!"

"Maybe it doesn't matter in New York, Mrs. Byrne, but it sure matters to some folks around here. You have three things goin' against you before you even said 'howdy'. You're a Yankee, you're Irish and you're a Catholic. Those men and others in the area are tryin' to drive out anybody that ain't white, Protestant and a supporter of the Confederacy and Texas independence."

"The War Between the States is over and they lost."

"A lot of folks down South don't see it that way, ma'am. Texas has a double dose of anger because a lot of Texans thought we shoulda just gone back to bein' a country of our own again and tellin' the Confederates to do their own fightin', but after they voted to secede, and there was a lot of funny things about that vote, Texans dove into the war with their rifles loaded.

"When the Confederates lost, a few men around Comanche County and in other places that believe that Texas needs to be independent again figured they should do something about it. They think that those that don't think like they do are the problem, and those boys aim to fix it."

"And you just stood back and let them do it?"

Doc exhaled sharply and said, "Yes, ma'am. I did, and I'll burn in hell for doin' it, too."

"Why did you let them do it? It was a cowardly thing."

"Yes, ma'am. I'll agree to that, too. It was cowardly and just plain wrong. I followed one rule since I was an almost-man that if folks left me alone, they could live their lives and it wasn't my business what they did. That worked for all my life until those boys began takin' those night rides. I figured it wasn't my business what they were doin', and let it go on too long.

"But I was wrong, ma'am. I was just about as wrong as a man can be. It shoulda been my business. I shoulda at least tried to talk 'em out of doin' it, but I didn't. It's my shame and I'll have to live with it for the rest of my life. All I can do is try to make it right.

"But for right now, I'm going to get you back on your feet whether you want me to or not. Then when you're okay, which should be a week or so, I'll leave and do what I have to do to make sure that they don't do it anymore."

"How are you going to do that?"

"I haven't figured it out yet, ma'am. I just know I gotta do it."

"You think that will get you into heaven, then?"

"No, ma'am. I ain't aimin' that high. I'm just gonna try and stop 'em from hurtin' any more folks."

Doc turned back to his cooking, feeling that he had said all he wanted to say, and began to cut up an onion.

Rhonda asked, "Can I call you Doc?"

"Yes, ma'am. That would be fine," he replied without turning from his onion-chopping.

Then he slid one of the two steaks to the cutting board and began cubing it and tossing the pieces onto the fry pan.

"Who were the men that came here that night?" she asked quietly.

Without stopping his beef cutting, he answered, "My boss, Charlie Lynch, his three sons, his son-in-law, and the five other ranch hands."

41

"There were ten of them?"

"Yes, ma'am."

She almost whispered, "Do you know how many of them took me?"

Doc stopped cutting, looked down at the cubes of meat and replied, "No, ma'am. But I don't think you oughta be thinkin' about that. It ain't gonna help to go through it again in your head."

Rhonda snapped, "You don't want to tell on your friends. Is that it?"

Doc let out a breath and said, "I know it was at least the five ranch hands, but I can't see the boss doin' that kinda thing. I can't say that for his three sons or his son-in-law, so it could be as many as nine."

Rhonda closed her eyes and recalled that night.

"Do you have any idea how horrible that was for me? First, I saw them shoot my husband, then they killed our two ranch hands before they beat me and raped me until I was unconscious. Do you really have even the slightest hint how terrified and ashamed I was? *Do you?"* she asked, finishing in a voice rising almost to a screech.

Doc finally turned slowly to look at Rhonda and answered quietly, "No, ma'am. I don't think any man can have even the slightest idea of how bad that would be for a woman. I've watched thousands of men die, some in so much pain that they screamed for almost an hour before they passed on. But dyin' released 'em from their pain. You and other women who had that happen gotta live with the pain inside. I can't imagine how bad that is."

42

"Trust me, it's the most horrible thing I could imagine. I've spent six weeks afraid to go to sleep and face my nightmares. Those men are animals and I wanted them all to die horrible deaths."

Doc returned to cubing the last of the steak as he said, "They will die, ma'am, but I can't say it will be in a horrible way. But whether they die soon or years from now, they'll have to face God and answer for what they did to you and the others. You weren't the only woman who suffered from their hands, and your husband wasn't the only man to die. It's why I gotta stop 'em."

"It's too late to help me, though, isn't it?" she snapped.

"Yes, ma'am. It is. I can't say I'm sorry anymore 'cause you must think I'm not serious about it, but I am. Now I've gotta do some thinkin' about how to do what I gotta do."

Doc began to stir the sizzling beef, browning all the sides.

After almost a minute of silence, Rhonda glared at Doc, and asked sharply, "What do you think about us Yankees and Irish Catholics invading your precious Texas?"

"Did you do somethin' wrong by comin' here?" he asked.

"No, we did not!" she answered quickly, knowing that she wasn't being totally honest.

"Then I ain't got a problem with it, ma'am. People oughta be allowed to go where they wanna go as long as they don't take it from somebody else."

"So, how do you feel about us taking Texas from the Mexicans, or taking this country from the Indians?"

Doc put down the wooden spoon, turned to face Rhonda and said, "Now, ma'am, you seem to think I'm the devil himself. What governments do ain't the same as what folks do. The Spanish took Texas from the Indians, the Mexicans took it from Spain, and the Americans took it from the Mexicans. Even the Indians do the same thing to other tribes. It's always been that way and I don't have no say in it. I won't hurt anybody or take somethin' that's not mine, and that's the best I can do.

"Now, I'm gonna try and stop those men from hurtin' other folks because I finally figured out that it's my business after all. You can hate me until you die, and if it makes you feel better, you go right ahead. I'll leave you set up, so you can take care of yourself, but I'm still gonna try and stop what's been goin' on."

Then an angry Doc turned back to the counter, dumped the frypan of seared steak cubes into the pot with the potatoes and onions, and stuck his fingers in the poke of salt and sprinkled some into the stew. *Was she going to accuse him of being a cannibal next?*

Rhonda then asked, "Why did your friends bury my husband and our two ranch hands after shooting them and doing what they did to me?"

Doc still didn't turn to look at her as he replied, "I've been thinkin' about that, and I figured there could only be two reasons. First, they didn't want flocks of buzzards flyin' overhead to let anyone know what had happened out here. The other reason, believe it or not, was because they believe they're good Christian men tryin' to make things right again. Now, don't get all mad again. I'm just tellin' you what they think."

"How in God's name could they believe that they were good Christians after killing three men, raping and beating me then leaving me to die?" she asked sharply, ignoring his request not to get mad again because she hadn't stopped being angry in the first place.

"I got no idea what they're thinkin', ma'am. It's like the Spanish Inquisition back in the Dark Ages. Those priests all thought they were doin' good to convert those Jews into good Catholics. Every one of 'em thought God would thank them when they arrived at the Pearly Gates.

"These men think they're doin' somethin' that will help Texas, even though they're committin' horrible crimes. I'll be honest with you, ma'am, even after they told me what they did, I still thought they were good men inside. They'd give you the shirt off their backs if you needed it, but that doesn't seem to match up with what they're doin'.

"The boss was a good man until he met up with some other ranchers who convinced him about what they believed. He bought into every word and took it along even farther. I wish I could take a look into their heads and hearts to figure out why they think it's okay, but I can't. Only God can see into their souls and know what they're thinkin'."

"Can't you go to Comanche and get the sheriff to stop this?"

"No, ma'am, I can't. He's their shield. He doesn't go out on any of the raids, but he protects the ones that do. Besides, your ranch is in Eastland County, not Comanche, so he wouldn't have any jurisdiction out here, anyway. Eastland doesn't even have a town, much less a sheriff."

"Do they know I'm alive?" she asked quietly.

"No, ma'am. They think you're dead."

"Why didn't they shoot me or bury me?"

"They couldn't shoot a woman, which don't make much sense, does it? They can beat her and abuse her, but heaven forbid if they point their Colts at her. I'm guessin' that they didn't bury you 'cause you were still alive in the house and figured some critters would come and take you away at night."

"That's what I recalled them saying and it didn't make any sense to me at all."

"No, ma'am," he said as he stirred his stew.

"How do you know about the Spanish Inquisition?" she finally asked.

"I may sound ignorant, ma'am, but I ain't stupid. I used to read a lot when I was a boy and history was a lot better than those dime store novels that the other kids read."

Rhonda's anger finally began subsiding then she spotted a pannier still sitting in the corner, pointed and asked, "What's in that one?"

Doc glanced where she was indicating and replied, "Oh, I bought some clothes and things for you when I was in Comanche. That dress you're wearin' seemed kinda thin. You don't have to wear 'em if you don't want 'em."

She then saw the boxes of ammunition stacked next to the rifles in the corner.

"Why so many bullets?"

"Cartridges, ma'am. A bullet is what comes outta the business end of a gun. A cartridge has the powder, the bullet, and the primer all in one shiny little brass can. I got 'em 'cause I figure I might need 'em."

"Do you think they'll come back?"

"No, ma'am. They won't come back here."

He looked down into his pot of stew and saw it beginning to thicken as it boiled. He guessed it needed another twenty minutes or so of simmering.

Then he turned back toward Rhonda and asked, "Ma'am, do you mind if I sit down? The stew ain't gonna be ready for a while."

"Of course, you can sit down. Why are you even asking?"

Doc stepped over to the table and sat opposite Rhonda before answering, "Just bein' polite, ma'am. This is your home, not mine."

"Yes, I suppose it is now."

Doc then asked, "Mrs. Byrne, do you have any family that can help you?"

"No, my family is all back in New York," she replied.

Doc scratched his chin and said, "Ma'am, if you'd want, I can take you to Comanche where you can take the stage to Waco and pick up a train to New York. It'll take a few days, but I can give you enough money for the trip."

"That doesn't matter. I don't believe they would welcome me back with open arms."

He wasn't about to ask why because it was none of his business. That was between her and her family.

"Well," he said, "if you're plannin' on stayin', then you're gonna need help, at least 'til you're stronger. I'll stay out in the bunkhouse for a few days until you're strong enough and then I'll leave. But if you'd feel better if I wasn't around, and I can understand why you would, and I'll just move on. You'll still have the horse and two mules and the shotgun and shells, just don't let anybody else know you're here."

Rhonda didn't reply as she thought about his offer.

While she was thinking, he asked, "Mrs. Byrne, how many head of cattle and horses did you have before they came?"

"We had five horses and I think it was forty cattle. Do you know where they are?"

"Yes, ma'am, I believe I do, at least where the beef critters are. The boss had a smaller herd that he was keepin' over on the eastern pastures that I don't think he wanted me to see, but I spotted it about a month ago and rode over and checked it out on a Sunday when the boys were all in their bunks after spendin' their pay in The Shotgun Saloon in Comanche. I found a lot of different brands in that herd, and some of 'em already had been rebranded with the Double L. What was your brand?"

"The Circle B."

"Okay. Now the horses in the remuda were all Double L animals, I'm sure of that. They couldn't just let your horses loose, 'cause they'd most likely wander back to their corral, and they sure didn't kill 'em. I didn't see any in Comanche, either. So, I'm guessin' they're somewhere else, maybe with another rancher that rides with 'em."

"Are you going to get them back?" she asked.

"Do you want 'em back, or would you rather get the money?"

"How much would that be?"

"Around twelve hundred dollars or so."

Rhonda thought about it. She knew she couldn't run the ranch, but what would she do with the money?

"How much is this ranch worth without the cattle?"

"Not too much, maybe eight hundred, but findin' a buyer would be tough. It's only one section and not close to a town, but you got good water in Wayne's Creek, so that's a plus, and you've got enough grass to handle a herd up to maybe a couple of hundred head."

Doc stood and walked back to the cookstove, stirred his stew and pushed it off of the hot plate onto the warming side of the stove, then took down two bowls from the shelf and spooned in a full bowl of stew for himself and a half a bowl for Mrs. Byrne, then put a spoon in each bowl.

He walked to the table and placed her bowl before her and his on the opposite side of the table before filling two cups with coffee and bringing them to the table.

"Can I eat?" she asked as she looked at the stew.

"Yes, ma'am. Just take it slow this time and listen to your stomach and not your head. If it says its full, even after three bites, then stop."

"Alright.", she said as she filled her spoon, then blew on the hot stew.

Doc watched as she took her first bite, then began to eat himself. He'd forgotten how hungry he was but still ate slowly as he kept one eye on Mrs. Byrne to make sure she didn't eat too much or too quickly. She must have learned her lesson, because she did neither.

When they were done, Doc took both bowls to the sink, washed them and put them in the drying rack.

"I'm gonna take my rifles and ammunition out to the bunkhouse, Mrs. Byrne, but I'll leave the shotgun. I'll load it first, though. I'll be doin' some practice shootin' with the Sharps 'cause I never shot one before, so don't be scared."

"I won't."

Doc nodded and walked to the corner where the empty panniers were, dropped all the ammunition except the shotgun shells into one, then opened the shotgun, took out two of the buckshot shells and slipped them into the tubes before snapping it shut.

"Now, ma'am, if you need to shoot this thing, just pull back one of these hammers, then point it and pull the trigger. You can do that twice. You could do both at once, but the kick would be pretty bad, so I'd suggest you don't try it. Okay?"

"I understand," she replied.

Doc nodded, opened the back door, picked up the pannier of ammunition, slid the strap over his shoulder, then grabbed his two Winchesters and the Sharps before walking through the doorway and kicking the door closed.

He headed for the bunkhouse with his heavy loads still trying to get a full grasp on the situation, but knowing he had time to come up with some kind of plan to put an end to all this. *But would he have to punish those who committed the crimes? If he did, how much punishment should he give himself for not trying to stop them?* Then he doubted he had the moral authority to do either. He was just a cowhand, and an out-of-work cowhand at that.

He reached the bunkhouse, set his Winchesters on one of the naked bunks and the Sharps and ammunition on the other. All of them were carbines, not rifles, so their accuracy at range wasn't as good as the longer-barreled rifle or musket versions, but they could be fired from a horse easier and were more popular. The Sharps, even though it was a carbine, still had a longer barrel than the Winchesters and would take care of the range issue.

He opened up one of the Sharps cartridge boxes, removed six of the long .50 caliber monsters and then picked up the Sharps and left the bunkhouse.

He wasn't concerned about anyone from the Double L hearing the sound, not at ten miles. He only had another hour or two of daylight but was anxious to try the Sharps.

Doc found a suitable target at about four hundred yards, a small, head-sized rock sitting all by its lonesome.

He opened the breech and slid in the first of the cartridges, closed the breech and set the sliding cursor to four hundred yards. The wind was negligible, the altitude was about a thousand feet, but the temperature was still almost ninety degrees, so he knew that the air was thinner and backed the sliding rear sight down to three hundred and sixty yards.

He cocked the hammer then brought the sights in line with the rock a quarter of a mile away. He blew out his breath, held it, and began to squeeze the trigger. The big carbine rammed into his shoulder as it blew out a large cloud of gunsmoke and the fifty-caliber slug of aerodynamically shaped lead.

Doc saw the ground explode about three feet behind the rock, then brought the Sharps back down, opened the breech, removed the spent brass and after putting it in his right pants pocket, pulled out a fresh cartridge and slid it home, closed the breech and cocked it again.

He didn't make any adjustments to the sight, but worked off the first shot, aiming to a point just below his first hit. Again, the Sharps boomed and this time the rock exploded when the massive amount of kinetic energy was released into the stone.

Doc whistled at the amount of destruction wreaked by the heavy round at that distance, then blew out the smoke from the barrel and decided he was comfortable enough with the gun and that he didn't need to waste any more of the expensive cartridges.

He returned to the bunkhouse, set the Sharp back on the bunk, then shook the one lamp inside and found it still contained kerosene. So, he lit the lamp, then sat down to clean the Sharps.

———

In the ranch house, Rhonda had moved the pannier to her bedroom and began to unpack its contents. She was surprised to find the four dresses, but much more surprised when she found the camisoles, nightdresses and underwear. *What kind of man would even consider buying such female things?* Most men would turn three shades of red if a woman even mentioned them.

Then she found the boots, socks and the bars of scented soap, shampoo, toothbrush and powder, privacy paper, and even a hairbrush. She hadn't had scented soap or used shampoo since she'd left New York. They didn't have a bathtub in the ranch house, just a large metal washtub, but she wished she had enough strength to lug the water from the pump to the washtub.

It had been too long since she'd had a bath, just over six weeks, for some reason. She imagined that she had a foul odor, and that Mister Holt probably smelled better than she did. He did seem amazingly clean for a ranch hand, and was even smooth shaven, which was unusual.

She sat on the bed with the bottle of shampoo in her hand, wondering what to make of Mister Holt. He seemed to want to help her and had certainly done that and more. He'd saved her life, but she still wasn't sure that it was a good thing.

Rhonda sighed, set the shampoo down, and not bothering to lock the doors because there weren't any locks anyway, she stood and closed the door to the bedroom. She then removed her faded yellow dress, donned one of the two nightdresses before she walked to her bed and just laid on top of the quilts because of the heat. She was asleep in minutes.

———

Doc Holt didn't get to sleep for a while. After he finished cleaning the Sharps, he returned to the barn and picked up his saddlebags, carried them back to the bunkhouse and set them on the other bunk.

He removed his towel and bar of white soap, left the bunkhouse and headed for the creek that ran just a few hundred yards east of the barn.

An hour later, he returned to the bunkhouse in the dark walked inside and put his things away then stripped, leaving his pants on and, as Rhonda had done, just laid atop the blankets, locked his hands behind his neck and stared at the ceiling.

He knew he couldn't just go to the Double L and start blasting away. The sheriff and probably a big posse would trail him back to the ranch and hang him on the spot. Besides, it wouldn't stop the others from doing what they were doing.

Doc Holt finally decided that the best thing he could do would be to lay low for a couple of weeks until he was forgotten then he'd put the fear of God into them.

Just as he was drifting off, a bone-chilling scream erupted from the house, and Doc's eyes shot open. He quickly pulled off his Colt's hammer loop, grabbed the revolver and sprinted barefoot out of the bunkhouse into the moonlit yard.

He didn't see any horses in the front of the house, so he raced to the back and after not seeing any tied up in back either, slowed down, stepped up onto the small back porch and swung the door open slowly.

He tiptoed inside, then stopped and listened, not hearing any voices, just movement from Mrs. Byrne's room. After a minute of silence, he didn't believe there was anyone inside.

He called out in a normal voice, "Mrs. Byrne? Are you okay?"

There was a short pause before she replied, "Yes. I just had a nightmare."

"I'm sorry to intrude, ma'am," he said before turning and leaving the house, his heart slowing down after the false alarm.

He returned to the bunkhouse, replaced his Colt and as he returned to the bunk, wondered if this was a nightly occurrence. He wouldn't have been surprised if it was, either. He couldn't imagine the horrors that awaited Mrs. Byrne every night after she closed her eyes.

It took him longer to go to sleep the second time, finally drifting off just before two o'clock.

CHAPTER 2

It was the first day of his new self-created job, but Doc still woke up in a bunkhouse as the sun broached the horizon as he had almost every waking day since the end of the war. The difference this time was that there were no other snoring men in the bunkhouse with him.

He left the bunkhouse, walked around behind it rather than use the privy just in case Mrs. Byrne was inside the small house, but more because of the convenience.

After returning to the bunkhouse and getting dressed, he ran headlong into what was a totally different experience for him when he thought about breakfast. There was no chow house, no cook, and no chow line to join. He didn't know if he was supposed to cook or Mrs. Byrne would handle it. Neither of them had thought of it yesterday.

So, he just walked to the barn to feed the horses and the mules. There was some hay in the loft, so it wasn't urgent that he go to Comanche for more. He guessed that there was about a month's worth, but they could graze out in the fields, too.

He had to climb into the loft to drop a bundle of hay onto the ground then once it was down, he dragged it into the barn.

He pumped the long trough full of water for the two horses and two mules before checking on the condition of the wagon. The harness looked in good shape and there was a half-full can of grease underneath with a spare axle. There was even a spare wheel in the corner of the barn along with a good set of tools.

He walked in front of the wagon and began to pull it along to see how the wheels were and found that it rolled easily enough.

How he could manage to get the cattle back or have them paid for was going to be difficult, but not impossible. He couldn't use the threat of going to the law for obvious reasons, but there was another way he might be able to get that issue resolved.

He was almost sure that Mrs. Lynch had no idea what her husband was doing on the raids. They weren't that frequent, and Doc was sure that the boss had a good excuse for not being home once every few weeks and was just as sure that none of the hands or the sons would have mentioned it to her or Beth either.

But if he threatened to tell the women if the cattle and horses weren't returned, then he'd be setting himself and Mrs. Byrne up for a deadly attack instead.

Yet he felt if he could somehow exploit that weakness in the boss's armor then he could put a stop to the raids without anyone else dying, including himself.

―――

At the Double L, the big topic of conversation in the chow house was Doc's sudden departure.

"Why do you think he left, Rex" asked Lou Robinson before he shoveled a forkful of scrambled eggs into his mouth.

"You know the boss wasn't happy with him for not comin' on our night rides, so he was sendin' him out on easy jobs and he had me keep him away from the other herd on the eastern pasture. He kinda figured out that his time was comin', I reckon."

"I don't know, Rex. It'll be kinda hard for Doc to hook up with another outfit for a while," said Carl Henson.

"Nah, he's a top hand. He'll just have to ride east to where there are more spreads."

Lou then asked, "But why so sudden, Rex? He was okay a couple of nights ago."

"Beats me, but at least we'll be able to mix that other herd in with the main herd now that we don't have to hide 'em anymore."

"What about them horses over at the Wheeler's?" asked Whitey Smith, "We gonna bring 'em back here to the remuda?"

"Nope. That was the deal with Bill Wheeler. We get the cattle and he gets the horses."

"Oh. I didn't know there was a deal," Whitey said.

"Now, you know."

"When are we goin' out again?" asked Lou.

"How the hell should I know? The boss will tell me when. We're kinda runnin' low on places to go now anyway."

"There's always the Adler spread," offered Joe Sheraton.

Rex had a piece of bacon poised in front of his mouth, stopped and asked, "The Adler spread? Why would we care about them?"

"I heard they were Jews. Got a whole Jew-church set up in the house," Joe replied.

"No kidding? Are you sure?" he asked.

"It's what I heard. We never seen 'em in church. Not once."

"Hell, you ain't ever seen half of us in church, either. That don't mean nothin'," Rex replied before he rammed the bacon into his mouth.

"Yeah, but I caught sight of Lenny Adler once at the creek, and he was, you know, trimmed."

That did get Rex's attention, so he said, "I'll mention it to the boss."

Joe grinned and took a big drink of coffee, satisfied with his accusation. He had never seen Lenny Adler naked, but had seen him sitting with Irene Spencer in Comanche making eyes at each other, and Joe didn't like it. He didn't like it one bit.

———

Rhonda was almost shocked when she realized how late it was when she opened her eyes. After her nightmare last night, she had slept for eight or nine restful hours, the first time that had happened since that night.

She rubbed her stomach and attributed the sleep to having eaten normal food then slid out of bed, quickly walked down the hallway, crossed through the kitchen and left the back of the house walking to the privy. She didn't care that she was wearing the nightdress because its flannel was thicker than her yellow dress. She had two other dresses, but the yellow was the one in the best condition. The four that Mister Holt had bought were all much better than her three even when they were new.

As she stepped toward the privy, she glanced around quickly to see where Mister Holt was and didn't see him anywhere. A flash of panic ran through her as she thought he might have gone, suddenly realizing why she had slept so long. For the first time since the attack, she had felt safe.

When she exited the privy walking back to the house, she scanned for Mister Holt in a less rushed fashion and saw his shadow in the barn as he forked hay into the stalls.

She exhaled and continued walking to the house at a faster pace.

Doc caught sight of Mrs. Byrne out of the corner of his eye but continued his work, taking advantage of the less than scorching hot temperatures that would arrive later in the day. He had decided to wait for her to invite him in for breakfast, but if she didn't, he'd skip breakfast entirely. He'd surely miss his morning coffee, though.

Rhonda started a fire in the cookstove and quickly returned to her room to dress. She still wished she could take a bath, yet she was already tired just from walking to the privy and back, but she was feeling better.

Fully dressed for the first time in almost a year, she walked to the kitchen and filled the coffeepot with water, set it on the cookstove, then used some of the scented soap to wash in the sink. She really needed to shampoo her hair, too. It was naturally curly, as most redheads were but it felt so dirty that she wasn't about to start trying to brush it out until she'd had a chance to wash it.

After setting the coffeepot on the stove, she had to sit for a few minutes to regain some energy, but soon had one of the two slabs of bacon on the cutting board and several slices sizzling on the large steel frypan. When she went into the cold room and saw the stack of eggs, she almost began to cry as she took out six and returned to the stove.

Doc has seen the smoke from the cookstove pipe, so he knew that Mrs. Byrne had started the cookstove, but he wasn't about to go and knock on the back door. He had felt so uncomfortable with her understandable interrogation that had reminded him of his failure, he thought it might be better if he just rode back to Comanche, bought some more food he could keep in the bunkhouse and just stayed out of the house altogether.

He did decide that it would be worth his time to go and check the pastures and see if there weren't any cattle still out there that the riders had missed. It was night when they drove away the small herd and some might have strayed, but he was sure the horses were all gone.

So, he quickly saddled Trapper, mounted, and walked him out of the barn. He stopped at the bunkhouse, stepped down before he went inside, picked up his '73 then remounted and rode back past the barn heading north.

The tall pinto ate up the short distance to the northern edge of the small ranch, but Doc kept riding expecting that if there were any strays, they'd be further out. He followed the creek, knowing that any strays would gravitate toward the only water in the area.

He rode another two miles before he was rewarded when he found five cattle making up their own small herd. When he was close enough to read their backsides, he found the Circle B brand, or what he assumed was the brand on their hind quarters. It wasn't a very clean job of branding and it looked as if the brand itself was handmade, but he'd found five animals that belonged to Mrs. Byrne and that was something.

Doc pulled off his rope and began calling to the beeves to get them moving back south, feeling better about doing something he was comfortable doing. The animals weren't happy about leaving the water, but they started to head back south anyway.

It took him two hours to get them back to their own pastures and grazing where they belonged.

———

Rhonda had finished cooking breakfast ten minutes after Doc had ridden off to the north and had walked out of the house to tell him that it was ready, but this time she wasn't able to find him at all. When she looked in the barn, she saw the one horse and two mules, but his horse was gone. He had said he would leave her and suddenly realized that he was really gone.

She turned and raced back to the house in almost a panic, forgetting to go into the bunkhouse to check if his things were still there. She sat down and tried to calm herself, feeling so alone and vulnerable again after just a few hours of security. She was stunned to realize how quickly she had been accustomed to the security of having him nearby.

She looked over at the shotgun, which she now believed was her only protection and closed her eyes, knowing why he had gone. She had punished him for her sins. She had made him responsible for things he hadn't done, called him a coward, and simply belittled him. If she had been in his boots, she would have ridden off, too. She probably wouldn't have stayed as long as he had either, much less cooked her food.

Rhonda looked at the plates sitting on the table and wanted to hurl them against the wall but knew that it wouldn't help. The only thing that would make things better would be if Mister Holt returned, and that was unlikely.

She took some scrambled eggs and bacon, set them on her plate, poured herself a cup of coffee and began to slowly eat, taking heed of Mister Holt's advice to eat slowly.

As she chewed on the bacon, she wondered what she would do now that she was alone again and was hard pressed to come up with an answer. She had a horse now but had never saddled one before. When she had ridden, which wasn't often, either Jamie or one of the Clancy brothers saddled it for her.

She felt so damned useless. All she could do was cook, clean the house, sew and do laundry. It had been all that had been expected of her and now, she'd never get the opportunity to learn anything else.

Rhonda finished her two strips of bacon and her scrambled eggs, then sat sipping her coffee, wondering if she could figure out how to saddle the horse. Then she almost laughed when she realized that even if she did, where could she go? A woman riding alone and unarmed was an inviting target for any man who happened to see her, and with her red hair, any Double L rider would know that she hadn't died and would soon correct that oversight.

She stood, carried her plate and cup to the sink, washed them and set them in the drying rack before walking back to her bedroom.

When she entered her bedroom, she saw the clothes that Mister Holt had purchased for her and felt terrible. He had only wanted to help. Granted, he felt guilty for not stopping what they had done, but it was a sin of omission, unlike her own sins. *Who was the greater sinner?* He hadn't hurt anyone, but she had. She had hurt her parents, Jamie, and had offended God.

She stepped over to the stack and lifted the edge of a bluebell patterned dress and let the fresh cotton slide across her fingers. It was such a pretty dress, and she believed that she didn't deserve to wear it.

Then she turned and walked back to her bed, and like she had when she was a little girl, she went to her knees, put her hands together, closed her eyes, and for the first time in more than ten years, Rhonda prayed. It had been so long that she wasn't sure that God would even listen to her anymore, but she begged God's forgiveness for her sins, including her latest sin in blaming a good and thoughtful man for things he hadn't done.

She also beseeched God to send him back and that she would no longer be so selfish and thoughtless. Then she asked for one more thing. Rhonda Byrne asked that God to ask Jamie to forgive her for what she had done, knowing that only God could intervene on her behalf and tell him that she was truly sorry.

When she had finished her long confession and conversation with God, she began to recite her favorite prayer, "Hail Mary, full of grace…"

When she finished, she bent at the waist, put her chest and face on the bed and began to softly weep.

———

Doc walked Trapper back into the barn, stepped down and began to unsaddle his friend. When he was devoid of tack, Doc brushed him down and let him drink and munch on some oats before he left him in his stall and walked back out into the Texas sun.

He headed for the back of the ranch house feeling happy to be able to give Mrs. Byrne some good news for a change. Five sullen critters weren't much, but it was a start.

He walked with a lively step as he quickly crossed the dirt yard and hopped up onto the back porch without touching the steps, knocked on the back door and waited.

———

Rhonda had been lying on the bed waiting for a reply to her prayers for more than two hours and was close to drifting off to sleep when she was startled by the knock coming from the back door. She had no concern about the possibility of it being anyone else other than Mister Holt. God wouldn't punish her again, not after her sincere repentance. So, she swung her legs out onto the floor and almost ran down the hallway, across the kitchen floor and threw open the door.

"Mrs. Byrne, I…" Doc said, but was stunned into silence when Rhonda flung herself at him, locked her arms around him and began to sob.

"You're back! You're back! God sent you back to me! I'm so sorry! I'm so very sorry! Forgive me, please!", she begged as she held onto him tightly and the tears or complete relief flowed down her cheeks.

Doc was overwhelmed with the sudden change but had no choice but to put his arms around her thin body and let her unburden herself.

"It's alright, ma'am. I don't hafta forgive you for anything. It's alright," he said softly.

"Please call me Rhonda. Please?" she said in a shaky voice.

"Okay, Rhonda. I'll do that, but I don't need to forgive you. You didn't do wrong. They did it to you."

"But it was because of my sins that they did this. Then you came, and I blamed you for things that you didn't do and that wasn't right."

He released her from his grasp, then led Rhonda into the kitchen, leaving the door open and guided her to a chair before he managed to sit her down. He'd noticed the cold scrambled eggs and bacon still sitting on the stove and felt bad about not coming over to the house earlier that morning but then, he wouldn't have found the cattle, either.

Once she was sitting, he pulled a chair over, and sat down in front of her. Her head was still down, and she was still crying, but she seemed happy, which mystified Doc to no end, especially with his limited experience with women.

"Rhonda, will you be okay?" he asked.

She nodded, then began wiping the moisture from her face as she looked at him and smiled.

"Where did you go, Doc?"

"I rode north a few miles to see if I could find any of your cattle that might have strayed before they took your herd. I found five of the critters a few miles north along the creek and brought 'em back to your ranch. There were two steers and three cows, but one of the cows was carrying a calf, so even if I don't find your other cattle, you'll have something."

She continued to smile as she said, "It doesn't matter, Doc. All that matters is that you came back. I was so afraid that you'd left me. I was so very frightened of being left alone that I asked God to send you back, and he did."

"Now, Rhonda, I know this sounds kinda sacrilegious and all, but you can't keep blamin' or thankin' God for everything. What

65

happened to you wasn't 'cause God was angry with you. It was because a bunch of wrong-thinkin' men set out to hurt you. I didn't come back at all because I never left except to go and look for those critters."

Rhonda nodded, but didn't believe a word of it. God had finally forgiven her for her sins and so had Jamie. Doc Holt was the proof of that forgiveness and she would never drive him away again.

"Doc, I made you some breakfast, but it's cold. Did you want me to make you some more?"

"No, Rhonda, this looks really good. You just stay there, and I'll take care of it, okay?"

"Okay," she replied as she smiled at him.

Doc smiled back, still totally confused by the incredible transformation in Mrs. Byrne, or Rhonda as he had to remember to call her. She seemed to place great stock in calling her by her Christian name, although he had to admit that he liked to hear her call him Doc rather than something less hospitable.

He spooned out the scrambled eggs, tossed on four strips of bacon and then felt the coffeepot. It was still warm enough, so after he put the plate on the table, he filled a cup with coffee.

"Would you like some more coffee, Rhonda? It's still warm."

"Yes, please, Doc," she answered, still smiling as her dark blue eyes gazed up at him.

Doc poured another cup of coffee and set it down before her.

He moved his chair back to the table and before he took a bite, said, "Rhonda, I gotta apologize again. I shoulda come over and let you know I was headin' out to look for those cattle. I didn't know it would get you so scared."

"No, that's alright, Doc. Whatever happened this morning or yesterday is in the past. Things are much better now."

Doc smiled at her again, still wondering what had happened, but began to eat his eggs and bacon, a bit unnerved at having Rhonda sitting there just looking and smiling at him. Granted, he liked her much better in her current mood than she had been yesterday, but the sudden change did leave him concerned that she might return to her previous hostile persona at any moment.

Then Rhonda said, "Doc, while you were gone, I realized that all I could do was womanly things in the house. I can't saddle a horse, shoot a gun or do anything else that I should know what to do on a ranch. Could you show me how to do those things?"

"Of course, Mrs. B...I mean, Rhonda. I'd be happy to help you. You'll feel a lot better when you know you can do those things without havin' to depend on one of us big lummoxes to do it for you."

"When can we start, Doc?" she asked as she continued to smile.

"As soon as I finish eatin', if you'd like."

"I'd like that. And, Doc, I didn't thank you for the dresses and other things you bought for me. That was very thoughtful. I was surprised to find that you had even bought some underwear and nightdresses. Men don't usually think of such things."

"You're welcome, Rhonda."

"You know, Doc, not many men would have been willing to suffer the embarrassment of buying them, even for their wives."

67

"I wasn't embarrassed any. It's just cloth, Rhonda, just like this shirt or the dress you're wearin'. It's just cut different, that's all. If Pat Miller thought I was kinda sick in the head for buyin' 'em, he's entitled to his opinion, but it doesn't bother me any."

"I ran out of soap just before that night and had added them to the supply list, but things happened. I hope I didn't offend you because I hadn't bathed in so long. I was going to take a bath this morning and use the scented soaps and shampoo you bought, but I wasn't strong enough to pump the water."

"Don't give it a thought, Rhonda. I'm a cow hand. I lived around some nasty-smellin' critters all my life. If you'd like, I'll fill your tub with water for you."

"Would you? I'd be very grateful."

"I'll do that shortly," he replied before polishing off his bacon and eggs.

Rhonda felt immensely relieved by his return and began to see him in a totally different light now that she had stopped blaming him for what had happened to her. She knew he was a good seven or eight inches taller than her five feet and six inches, but it wasn't his height that marked him as a man.

His face was almost hard, but his blue eyes were so soft and told her much more than what he said. He wasn't traditionally handsome as Jamie or Will Clancy had been, but it was a good face and it marked him as a man to be respected. He may have told her not to blame or thank God for everything that happened, but at that moment, Rhonda Byrne thanked God profusely for returning Doc Holt to her ranch house.

Doc had noticed her silent inspection of him before he stood up with the plates and added that to the list of things he'd probably never understand. It was still making him uncomfortable, but felt it was the least form of punishment he deserved for allowing her to be as hurt as she had been.

After setting the plate and cup in the drying rack, he turned back to Rhonda and asked, "Do you have a bathtub, Rhonda?"

"No, I have to use the washtub. It's in the spare bedroom on the right."

"Is that where you want me to carry the water?"

"No, because I have to be able to dump it out. I usually take a bath in the barn."

"Well, you can take it in the bedroom if you'd like. I can empty the tub when you're done and don't concern yourself about the water spillin' on the floor. It'll just go out through the cracks and it'll be all dry in a few minutes."

"That would be wonderful. My feet always got dirty when I took a bath in the barn."

"Okay, then I'll start pumpin' the water," Doc said as he reached beneath the counter, picked up the wooden bucket and began filling it.

Rhonda just sat and watched, which unsettled Doc, but he still managed to get the washtub filled. The water was already lukewarm after just a few minutes, so when it was about two thirds full, he returned the bucket to where he had found it and turned to Rhonda.

"I'll be outside in the barn, Rhonda. When you're all done, you can find me there. Okay?"

Rhonda stood, beamed at him and said, "Thank you, Doc."

"You're welcome, Rhonda," he said before smiling at her then turned and left the kitchen.

Rhonda sighed, then headed back to her bedroom to get the soaps, shampoos and a towel before returning to the second bedroom for her long-awaited bath.

Doc Holt was still off-balance by Rhonda's sudden shift. He thoroughly enjoyed talking to the new Rhonda, but aside from the concern about what had precipitated the change was a new worry that she might go to the other extreme and not want him to leave the ranch at all. He could understand her strong need for protection after what they had done to her and her husband and ranch hands, but he didn't want her to become obsessive especially as he wasn't sure he'd survive for very long.

Under normal circumstances, he wouldn't have objected to having her pay attention to him. Rhonda Byrne, despite her lost weight, was still a handsome woman. He didn't know how old she was, but he guessed somewhere between twenty-five and twenty-eight. Her deep red hair and blue eyes marked her as much an Irishwoman as any living back on the Emerald Isle. He'd known quite a few Irishmen during the war, and it seemed that one out of three of them had the same red hair and blue eyes that adorned Rhonda.

But he still knew he'd have to do what he thought had to be done. Those nightriders had to be stopped and made to see the errors of their ways. Texas didn't belong to just white Protestants who were born and raised here. There was enough land in Texas to take in the entire country, including the Indians, and probably all the Canadians and Mexicans too, and still leaving enough room for all the cattle.

Doc knew he'd have to talk to Rhonda, so she'd understand that he had been serious when he had told her that he had important work to do in Comanche County.

———

"They're Jews?" asked Charlie Lynch incredulously.

"That's what Joe Sheraton told me. He said he'd seen Lenny Adler at the swimmin' hole, and he was, well, trimmed, if you know what I mean."

"No kidding! Well, that's news to me. I always figured his family was German or something. He even lost his oldest boy at Gettysburg fighting with General Hood."

"It's up to you, boss. I'm just passin' along the word."

"Okay, Rex. I'll talk to Bill Wheeler and see what he thinks."

The foreman stood, then left the boss's office before heading out of the house to return to the bunkhouse.

———

Rhonda took her time as she stood in the tub, luxuriating in the suds and the sweet scent of the soap. When she finished bathing, she knelt beside the tub and shampooed her hair. It took even longer to get her hair clean than it did to take the bath, but when she stood, she felt immeasurably better.

She tiptoed back into her bedroom to dress, using the towel to dry her hair and letting the hot, Texas air dry the rest of her.

———

Doc had to guess which of the saddles was Rhonda's, not having a clue as to her husband's or either of the Clancy brothers' height. As it turned out, it really didn't matter as all them were within an inch of each other.

He saddled Trapper and then set out a set of tack for Rhonda's horse. After he had moved everything over, he began to rethink his timing for stopping the night raids.

There weren't a lot of ranches and farms in the county or in the neighboring counties that belonged to the 'undesirables'. There had already been five of the raids since they started, and that only left three that he could classify as belonging to potential targets: the pro-Unionist Jackson farm, just across the border in Brown County, the Double M ranch owned by the Northerner Millers in eastern Comanche County, and the Mulligan ranch just across in Erath County. Ironically, the Mulligan ranch was just north of the town of Dublin, Texas, which was close to becoming a ghost town now.

Maybe the boss would want to get their cleansing work done before returning to their normal lives as good citizens. Doc decided he'd begin doing some night riding of his own down to the Double L to keep an eye on the comings and goings of the ranch hands. It would mean less sleep, but it wouldn't be too bad. They always left the ranch just after sundown, which at this time of year would be around nine o'clock. If no one rode out by ten, he'd return to the Circle B.

He didn't even think about the Adler ranch. Like Charlie Lynch, they had a German heritage and should have fit right in with the rest of the 'good' people. The Adler family spread, the Slash A, was just eight miles due west of the Double L.

Doc had just finished with his new plans when Rhonda walked into the barn wearing her new clothes with her smile seemingly implanted permanently on her face now.

"I feel wonderfully clean again, Doc," she announced as she stepped closer.

"Glad to hear it, Rhonda," he replied, "I've already saddled Trapper, my horse, and I'll show you how to saddle your horse. Okay?"

"Alright. Do you want me to do anything?"

"Not yet. I'll show you how to saddle and unsaddle her, then I'll help you saddle her again before we go out for a short ride."

"Okay," she said as she leaned against the nearby wall.

She paid attention as Doc went through the process step-by-step, explaining the purpose of each part of the saddle and how it all worked together. Then he began removing the tack from the filly with less explanation, but she still watched closely.

Doc felt he was under her intense scrutiny as he had earlier and began to feel uncomfortable again. It wasn't the same type of discomfort he'd felt yesterday when Rhonda had grilled him about what he had failed to do about the raids, but having a woman watching him was still disconcerting. He just wasn't that comfortable around women because he'd spent so little time with them.

When he finished, he turned back to Rhonda and said, "Did you want to try, Rhonda?"

"I don't think I'll be able to pick up the saddle yet, Doc," she said as she took two steps to where he stood.

"I didn't think you'd be able to handle it yet, so I'll take care of that," he replied already picking up her flowery scent even with the more powerful horse smells nearby.

"Okay, I'll get started."

After the horse blanket was in place, Doc tossed her saddle onto the filly and let her tighten the cinches, but Doc had to show her a trick to get them tighter that he had neglected to mention earlier.

With her horse saddled, Doc asked, "Rhonda, do you have any riding clothes? You're not exactly dressed for sitting astride a saddle."

"Oh, I forgot about that. When I used to go riding before, I'd just wear some of Jamie's britches, but they're all gone. I was so angry that I burned them all. I almost burned down the house, too."

"I'd let you wear some of mine, but they're too big, I think."

"Yes," she said as she looked at his lower half, "I could make a riding skirt out of one of my old dresses later today. Can we go riding tomorrow, then?"

"That's fine. I'll unsaddle your horse and then I'll go inside and empty the tub."

"I'm sorry, Doc. I should have thought about that before I asked you to show me how to saddle a horse."

"It's alright, Rhonda. Before we go back, I gotta tell you about somethin' I just come up with. Startin' tomorrow night, I'm gonna head down to the Double L just before dark and watch the ranch house to see if they go out on one of their visits. I'll leave here around eight o'clock and if they don't go anywhere, I'll be back by eleven o'clock. I figured at first that I could just go and come back and not let you know 'cause you'd already be in the house anyway, but then I thought you'd get scared if you knew I was gone, so I'm just lettin' you know."

"I thought you weren't going to do anything until I was strong again. What if something happens to you, Doc?"

Doc grimaced and replied, "I'll be okay. I just don't want them goin' out hurtin' folks, and me findin' out about it later. I can't let it happen again, Rhonda. I just can't."

Rhonda nodded but still worried as Doc began unsaddling her filly.

"What are you gonna name this lady?" he asked as he worked.

"I never had my own horse. Do you have any suggestions?"

"Well, she's a pretty young lady, almost four years old, so that makes her just about marryin' age for a human, if that helps."

Rhonda walked up to the filly and put her hand on her neck.

"She is pretty, isn't she? Can I call her Bride? She hasn't foaled, has she?"

"No, she's still a filly."

"Did you pick her out for me?"

"Yes, ma'am, I'll admit that I did. She was the shortest horse they had for sale, and with her bein' a filly and all, I thought she'd become your good friend."

"Thank you, Doc, that was very thoughtful."

Doc just nodded and after he finished putting the tack where it belonged, he said, "Let's go back to the house and I'll empty out the washtub."

"Okay," she replied, then as they began walking, she asked, "Did you want to use the tub before you empty it, Doc?"

"No, ma'am. I took my bath last night in the creek. It's a lot easier."

Rhonda nodded but flushed at the image her mind created.

When they entered the house, Rhonda asked, "Doc, I've been thinking about you riding out at night to go to the Double L, and I have a request."

Doc was almost afraid to ask, but as they entered the kitchen, he did.

"What is that, Rhonda?"

"Could I come with you?"

Doc had expected her to ask him not to go, at least for a week or so, but her question had taken him totally by surprise. He picked up the bucket and they continued down the hall.

"Why would you want to do that? You'll be safe here."

"I'd feel safer if I were with you, Doc."

As they turned into the bedroom, Doc said, "Let me think about it. Okay?"

"Okay, but please don't leave without talking to me first."

"I won't," he said as he dipped the bucket into the washtub.

Rhonda had taken a seat on the bed because she was tired already but watched as he left the room with the water and returned a minute later for another scoop. She continued to watch as the water level dropped wondering what his decision would be about letting her come along.

She had made the request because she was worried that if something happened to him, she wouldn't know and not knowing was much worse than being there. Besides, she wanted him to show her how to shoot one of the Winchesters.

Once there were only a few inches of water, Doc picked up the washtub and carried it out to the front porch and dumped it over the edge before returning it to the bedroom and setting it down, not having come any closer to deciding about what to do about her request.

————

"I kinda suspected Adler was hidin' somethin'," Bill Wheeler said as he and Charlie Lynch walked out to the Wheeler barn.

"How could he hide something like that for as long as we've known him, Bill? He's been on that spread for fifteen years now."

"Jews are like that, Charlie. Now that I think about it, if you look at his nose and those beady eyes, it all makes sense. He doesn't go to church, either."

Charlie didn't think that Ben Adler had beady eyes or a funny nose at all, but he wasn't about to argue the point.

"I think we need to pay Adler a visit soon, Charlie. He's closer to your spread, so do you and your boys want to handle it?"

"Okay, Bill. But it's pretty soon after the last one, so I'll probably wait a couple of days."

"That's okay. I got my own plans for the Mulligans over in Erath County."

"You gotta be careful over there, Bill. Sheriff Chisholm over in Stephensville isn't as friendly as Joe Olsen."

"I know that, but Stephensville isn't exactly close to the Mulligan place."

"Just be careful, okay. I'll tell the boys in a couple of days that we'll be visiting the Adlers."

Bill Wheeler nodded and said, "We're gettin' close, Charlie. Real close."

"That we are," Charlie Lynch agreed as they turned back toward the house.

Bill watched him leave and was glad that Charlie hadn't asked him to join in the raid. The Adlers were a bigger ranch than the ones they had been raiding and had more men and more guns. Let him take the risk.

———

Rhonda had to feel useful again and even though she would have preferred to just lay down, she told Doc that she'd make lunch.

"I bought some sausages that would be pretty easy, Rhonda," he said as they walked to the kitchen.

"I never had any sausages. Are they good?"

"I like 'em, and I bought some mustard sauce and some sauerkraut at Miller's, too. All you do is fry 'em up, then spread some of that mustard sauce on top, toss on the sauerkraut and it's a real tasty lunch."

Rhonda smiled and said, "Then that's what we'll have."

Thirty minutes later, Rhonda had her first taste of sausage with mustard sauce and sauerkraut and her tongue was shocked by the explosion of flavor. She'd never had anything so outrageously tangy before.

"This is amazing, Doc! And it was so easy to make!" she exclaimed before taking her second bite.

"Take your time again, Rhonda. You're doin' better'n I expected this soon, but don't go temptin' your stomach to rebel again."

Rhonda looked up at Doc, smiled and said, "I don't care if it wants to declare its independence and run off with my liver. I'm eating this entire sausage and every bit of the sauerkraut."

For the first time in a while, Doc Holt laughed.

Rhonda, for her part, saw his face transform as his hard look disappeared revealing a much nicer visage.

"Why, Mister Holt, you are actually quite handsome when you aren't so grumpy," she said as she smiled.

Doc blushed as he said, "Now, Mrs. Byrne, I know I ain't close to bein' good-lookin'. I'm just a cowpoke."

His reddened face added to Rhonda's perception that the gruff ranch hand was just about the most innocent man she'd ever met, despite all that he must have witnessed in that war and in the years since.

"You let me be the judge of that, Doc. If I think you're handsome, then just accept it."

Doc just sighed, bit into his sausage and nodded.

Rhonda was still smiling at his discomfort as she finished her sausage and didn't want to drink anything to spoil the lingering taste.

"I'll clean up here and then go into my bedroom and begin converting one of my old dresses to a riding skirt. What are you going to do, Doc?"

"I don't rightly know, Rhonda. What do you need done?"

"The wood pile is getting pretty low. Do you know where we could get some more wood for the cookstove?"

"Yes, ma'am. I'll take care of that. I'll be using the wagon, and I'll be takin' it up north, about two miles north of the ranch. Do you think you'll be okay?"

"I think so. How long will you be gone?"

"Oh, I'd guess about four hours or so. You have the shotgun, but I'm sure you're not gonna get any human visitors and those coyotes sure ain't gonna be stoppin' by neither."

"Okay, if you think it'll be all right. Just come back before it gets dark, okay?"

"Yes, ma'am. I'll handle this as fast as I can."

"Thank you, Doc."

Doc stood and smiled at Rhonda before leaving the kitchen and heading out to the barn to harness the mules. Before he did, he swung by the bunkhouse and picked up his Winchester

'73 and the Sharps along with a box of cartridges for each. He may not have expected any visitors to arrive at the ranch, at least not anyone from the Double L, but it never hurt to be prepared.

He walked back out to the barn, set the two carbines in the wagon's footwell, then pulled an axe from the wall, checked its edge and found it acceptable, although it would need sharpening when he returned. He set it on the wagon's bed then began harnessing the mules.

After the mules were in harness, he stepped up, released the wagon's hand brake and drove the team out of the barn and headed northeast to the stand of cottonwoods that he had seen near the creek. What made his job easier was that two of the trees were already down and were devoid of leaves meaning that they had been down for a while, and if they'd been down long enough, the wood would already be seasoned.

———

Rhonda finished cleaning up after lunch, still savoring the lingering taste of Doc's choice in food. She entered her bedroom, took out her sewing kit, then pulled out the yellow dress and thought it was too thin to convert into a riding skirt. Knowing her other dresses were worse, she looked at one of the new dresses that Doc had bought for her. She hated to do it, but selected one, took out her shears, and cut it four inches above the waist, so she'd be able to fold it over to make a belt of sorts.

Once she had made that first cut, there was no going back. She decided that she'd turn her yellow dress and the other two old dresses into blouses to go along with the new riding skirt.

So, with her designs set in her mind, she began to work quickly, first making a long cut in the new skirt to allow her to sit astride Bride, then smiled when she thought of the new filly and that thoughtful, self-deprecating cow hand who had bought it for her.

Rhonda was hard at work by the time Doc left the Circle B and headed for the downed cottonwoods.

————

But Doc had been wrong in believing that no riders from the Double L would be visiting the Byrne ranch.

Lou Robinson had decided that he'd spend his free time visiting the Circle B while the other hands were in Comanche spending their money at The Shotgun Saloon. He'd gone along with the boys, but while they were all drinking, the conversation had swung to the common dream they each shared of owning his own place, even though that dream was out of all their reach because, unlike Doc, they squandered most of their pay in Comanche.

But Lou had begun to think that maybe he could just claim the Circle B because it was empty and if he just squatted on the place, it would be his. He'd be able to move some of the Circle B cattle onto the ranch one or two at a time until he had a decent-sized herd and then he'd be fixed for life.

When the other boys had all gone upstairs to visit with the ladies, he'd walked out of the saloon, mounted his horse and ridden north to check out the ranch. He was already pretty happy from the whiskey he'd imbibed, and the thought of being a ranch owner without having to spend a dime made him giddy.

So, it was a happy Lou Robinson who left Comanche preparing to make the twenty-five-mile ride to the Byrne spread just as Doc Holt was stepping down from the wagon and picking up the axe to begin to chop some wood for Rhonda's cookstove.

———

Doc was actually enjoying himself as he swung the axe and felt the blade bite into the wood. He was at the far end of the tree, cutting the branches off the six-inch thick end of the trunk. The eighteen-inch diameter end of the tree's trunk would have to wait until he bought a good saw in Comanche.

He'd trimmed about sixteen feet off the tree until he reached a point where the trunk had widened to twelve inches. He stretched his back and wiped the sweat that poured from his brow, knowing there was nothing he could do about the perspiration flowing down his neck and back, but he knew that he needed to replace some of the lost moisture.

He pulled off his work gloves and walked back to the wagon, pulled out one of the two canteens and almost emptied it before returning to start cutting the stripped trunk into four-foot-long logs. The branches would be cut up for kindling and firewood, too. That should provide enough wood for the rest of the summer at least.

———

Rhonda had tried on her riding skirt and was pleased with the result. She'd made a cloth belt that wasn't very elegant, but it suited the purpose.

Then she sat down, cut the three old dresses in half and started hemming the bottoms to convert them into blouses.

———

Lou Robinson had passed the Double L ranch house, grinned at the place and passed a short salute, thinking that he might not have to work there much longer, then continued riding north at a medium trot. He began to sing loudly and poorly as he rode along, making up his own bawdy lyrics to "Dream of Jeanie With the Light Brown Hair".

———

Doc had the four logs in the wagon bed and had just dragged the last of the branches to load in back. He had to use the axe to cut it down to a manageable size as he'd done with the other six branches, but it only took a couple of minutes.

Once the last branch was loaded, a tired Doc Holt pulled off his work gloves, tossed them on the seat and finished off the last of the water in the canteens. He was thinking about going down into the creek and refilling the canteens but remembered that Rhonda had asked him to return as soon as he could, so he climbed into the wagon, released the brake and snapped the reins, getting the mules moving.

He may have been only two miles away from the ranch house, but the mules weren't moving very quickly with the heavily loaded wagon over the uneven ground, so he knew he wouldn't make it back before seven o'clock.

———

Lou Robinson was three miles out when he spotted the ranch house and saw it for the first time in the light of day and liked what he saw.

"Yes, sir," he said out loud, "this is gonna be the new Robinson spread."

He ticked his horse up to a fast trot in his anxiety to explore his new ranch but didn't see Doc's wagon coming from his two o'clock because he was still looking at his new house and imagining himself sitting on the porch with his new wife.

But Doc didn't see Lou approaching either as he was concentrating on driving the mules along his previous tracks. Luckily the ground was still hard after almost two weeks since the last good rain, so they were making better time than he expected.

———

Rhonda had finished her blouses and was satisfied with her work, but glad it was done. She'd only stuck herself twice with the needles and vowed to get a good thimble before her next sewing job.

She folded her new riding skirt and blouses, placed them in her drawer, closed it and returned her sewing kit to its proper place before walking from her bedroom and heading for the kitchen.

She tossed some kindling into the cookstove, started the fire and after putting some wood on top, closed the firebox door and slid the coffeepot back on top of the hot plate before walking out the back door and onto the porch to see if she could spot Doc returning.

———

Lou was still looking at his new house when he was stunned to see Rhonda walk out onto the porch, and his motivation suddenly changed as he recalled that night and how exciting it had been. Why she was still alive, or why she was looking to the north didn't even register as he kicked his horse into a gallop to get to the house as quickly as possible before she had a chance to run.

———

Rhonda had just spotted Doc less than a half a mile away and was preparing to wave when she heard the pounding hooves from Lou Robinson's charging horse coming from the south. She whirled around and was horrified to see him just four hundred yards away and coming hard.

She thought about the shotgun, but knew she wouldn't have a chance to reach it and wasn't sure she'd be able to use it, so she raced down the steps and began running toward Doc.

––––––––

Doc saw both Rhonda and Lou Robinson at the same time and instead of trying to get the mules to move any faster, he quickly grabbed the loaded Sharps, leapt from the wagon and started to run toward Rhonda, who was now less than five hundred yards away, cocking the carbine's hammer as he moved.

Lou still hadn't seen Doc Holt as he was watching Rhonda run in panic, getting more excited by the chase. This was going to be better than the first time.

Rhonda had exhausted her small reserve of energy that she had built up since Doc had arrived and felt her legs grow rubbery and then fail as she fell to the ground, knowing that Doc would never reach her in time.

Lou was almost there when Rhonda had fallen and slowed his horse rapidly, so he could dismount.

When Rhonda had collapsed, Doc had stopped running to calm his breathing and took a knee. He set his sights on Lou even as he was preparing to dismount near Rhonda. He hadn't had time to adjust the rear sight, but knew it was set for four hundred yards and had to work off that. He'd only get one shot. If he missed, he'd have to run back to get the Winchester and

Lou would have time to run him down and shoot him with his own repeater.

He held his breath and squeezed the Sharps' trigger. The carbine rammed against his right shoulder and the Sharps muzzle exploded in a big cloud of gunsmoke and a long flame in the failing light of the evening sun.

The .50 caliber bullet followed its shallow arcing path across the three-hundred and thirty-one yards between the muzzle and Lou Robinson's right shoulder in a little over a second, slamming into his clavicle and shattering it into dozens of pieces before decimating his right upper lung and leaving his chest after destroying a rib.

Lou screamed and was thrown from his horse as he was halfway through dismounting anyway. If he hadn't been moving, the round would have struck him almost the center of his chest and killed him instantly, but that motion extended his life for a few minutes as he tumbled onto the ground with blood pouring from the wound.

Doc stood quickly and resumed his race toward Rhonda, who had heard the loud report of the Sharps followed almost immediately by the rider's scream and the sound of him hitting the dirt, not knowing if he was still alive. She kept her eyes closed tightly as she tried to breathe.

It took Doc more than a minute and a half to run the distance to Rhonda, and he was gasping for air by the time he arrived.

"Rhonda," he asked as he huffed, taking a knee beside her, "are you okay?"

"Doc," she asked breathlessly, "is it safe now? Is he gone?"

Doc looked over at the squirming Lou Robinson and replied, "He's not dead yet, but I don't think he's gonna last long. You stay right there and just know you're safe. Okay?"

"Okay," she replied as she kept her eyes closed.

Doc patted her on her back then stood and walked over to Lou Robinson, who had his eyes closed as well as his life's blood spilled onto the dirt.

He took a knee near Lou's head and asked, "Lou? What the hell do you think you were doin'? Didn't you do enough to hurt this lady before?"

Lou opened his right eye and asked, "Doc? What are you doin' here? Did you shoot me? Tell me it wasn't you who done it. You gotta help me, Doc. I didn't even know she was still alive. I just wanted the ranch for my own. That's all."

"I was the one who shot you, Lou. You may have come here lookin' for a ranch, but you were gonna hurt Rhonda again, and I couldn't let that happen. I ain't gonna let any of you hurt folks anymore. I was wrong to let you do it in the first place, but no more."

"Can't you save me, Doc? It hurts so much."

"No, Lou, I can't save you. You're gonna die in a few minutes. Now maybe you know how much you hurt them other folks. All you can do now is ask God to forgive you for what you done."

"I didn't mean it, Doc. I was just doin' what everybody else was doin'."

"Yeah, that seems to be the case, doesn't it? It doesn't make it right though, Lou."

"No, I guess not. Can you bury me proper, Doc?"

"I'll do that Lou. They plannin' on goin' after anybody else soon?"

"Joe said that the Adlers were Jews and I think they're gonna go there next. Doc, do you think I'm gonna go to hell for what I done?"

"It's not my call, Lou. I know I'm gonna be headin' that way for not stoppin' the boys for goin' out on those rides."

Lou laughed lightly, closed his eyes and said, "No, you ain't, Doc. You were the only…"

Then he simply stopped talking and breathing. Doc just sighed and looked at Lou with jumbled feelings then stood.

He turned and walked slowly back to where Rhonda still lay on her stomach with her eyes closed.

He took a knee again and touched her on the back lightly, saying, "Rhonda, he's gone now. If you'd rather not look, I'll walk with you back to the house. You can keep your eyes closed, so you don't have to see him."

Rhonda opened her eyes and rolled slightly to her left, causing Doc to quickly pull his hand back.

"No, Doc. I'll help if I can. I need to be stronger in my heart, too."

Doc smiled at her and took her hand to help her to her feet.

"You're gonna be all right, Rhonda," he said when she was standing, letting go of her hand as soon as she was on her feet.

"I hope so. Why did he come, Doc? I thought they believed I was dead."

"He did think you were dead. He said he came here to try and move into the ranch and have it for himself. Finding you here must have been kind of a bonus."

Rhonda hugged herself, closed her eyes again and shuddered as she thought of just how close she had been to another attack and found it hard to breathe.

"Doc, please don't leave me again. Please? I know I've got to be stronger, but I need time."

"I know. I'll be here, Rhonda. Nobody is gonna hurt you ever again. I promise."

She opened her eyes, looked up at Doc and said, "Thank you, Doc. I feel better now."

"I'm gonna have to bury him now, Rhonda. I'll walk with you back to the house and you can relax for a while. You're probably pretty tired by now. You aren't that strong yet."

"Okay. But I'll make dinner when I've recovered."

"That's fine. I've got to go and get the wagon, too. It's full of wood and the mules probably aren't too happy about bein' forgotten."

Rhonda suddenly latched herself onto Doc's arm, which startled him for a moment then they walked back to the house, passing Lou Robinson's body and his horse.

He walked with her into the house and angled to the kitchen table where he sat her down.

"Are you okay, Rhonda?" he asked as he looked into her dark blue eyes.

"I'll be fine," then she added, "you saved me again, Doc."

Doc didn't want to get into the 'if I had stopped them in the first place' argument with himself again, so he just nodded and left the kitchen.

After leaving Rhonda and the Sharps in the kitchen, Doc trotted back out to where Lou's horse was still standing, took its reins and mounted the tired animal. The stirrups were so high that Doc felt like a jockey as he walked the horse back to the wagon, stepped down and tied the horse to the back. Then he climbed back into the wagon's driver seat and drove it back to the barn, past Lou's body.

He untied the horse, led him into the barn, and stripped him quickly before letting him drink in one of the mule's stalls.

Then he took the pickaxe and spade from the barn and walked back outside to the wagon and tossed them onto the bed with the wood before driving the wagon back to the house where he quickly unloaded the wood near the back porch. He climbed aboard the wagon again, drove the mules to the trough to let them drink, then turned it back to Lou's body.

After loading Lou's carcass onto the bed, he went through his pockets and found $21.76, the leftover of his month's pay, and after stuffing the money into his pocket, removed Lou's gunbelt with its Colt that fired the same .45 Long Colt ammunition as his model.

He then drove the wagon out into the pastures and found a spot behind some rocks that would shield it from any casual observer from the Double L that might come looking for Lou, donned his work gloves again, pulled on the hand brake and stepped down, leaving his Stetson on the seat where it had been since he'd started to cut the wood.

It took forty minutes of hard work to dig the grave for Lou Robinson and when he was done, he just dropped him into the hole and began to shovel dirt on top of him. He didn't leave a mound when he was done, though. He left it slightly higher to allow for settling, but scattered the rest of the dirt, knowing that tomorrow's hot sun would dry it out leaving little evidence of the gravesite.

It was an exhausted Doc Holt who climbed back into the wagon, pulled off his work gloves, released the hand brake and started the mules back to the barn, not bothering to put his hat back on as the sweat continued to pour from his head. His shirt was plastered to his back and his chest as the wagon rolled along.

He had to figure out what to do with Lou's horse, though. The tack would be easy enough to hide, but Lou's horse was as distinctive as his pinto, maybe more so. He was almost all white with a black mane and tail, and it was that distinctive coloring that had let him know that he was shooting Lou long before he could identify him. If he left the horse in the barn, so no one could spot him then he wouldn't even be a horse anymore, just a pet and that wasn't right. Horses needed to run.

He was still thinking about it when he reached the barn and stepped down, then unharnessed the mules and decided to leave them in the corral, at least overnight until he had time to decide what to do with Lou's horse. He was a nice horse, but he was so obviously Lou Robinson's horse that it meant he had to go somewhere off of the Circle B.

With the mules in the corral, the wagon stowed, and the tools returned, Doc walked to the bunkhouse with the two Winchester

'73s and Lou's Colt in its gunbelt hung over his left shoulder and Lou's saddlebags over his right.

After leaving them in the bunkhouse with his hat, Doc walked slowly back to the house. He was used to hard work, but today was a killer with the added excitement of a gunfight, such as it was, thrown into the middle. He was exhausted and wanted to return to the bunkhouse soon to collapse, but he had promised Rhonda he would look after her and knew that she expected him to return to the house.

Rhonda heard him coming and set the table with the baked potatoes and the second steak that he had bought yesterday. She had been resting for the first half hour until she felt she could cook and wanted to make sure that Doc understood that she was grateful for what he had done.

Doc knocked on the door and waited for Rhonda to open it, but instead, he heard her say loudly, "Come in, Doc."

He opened the door and smelled the steak and his salivary glands came to attention as his stomach growled.

"It smells really good, Rhonda," he said as he walked to the table.

"I thought you'd be hungry, and we had to use the steak soon anyway," she said as she stuck a fork in the steak and dropped it onto his plate.

He sat down, then cut the steak in two and set the smaller piece on her plate.

"Doc, you need all of it. You did a lot of work today," she said as poured the coffee before sitting down.

"I'll be fine with this much, Rhonda. You still need to build up your strength. You've only been really eatin' for a day now."

She looked at the steak and it came almost as a shock to think that Doc had only found her on the dirt just the day before. *How was that even possible?* She was already so comfortable having him around, maybe because he made her feel so safe.

She began eating her steak as Doc cut open his baked potato, chopped it up and dropped a large dollop of butter on top, before cutting into his steak.

Rhonda asked, "What was his name? The man who just died?"

Doc swallowed his first bite then replied, "Lou Robinson."

"Was he one of the...one of them?" she asked quietly as she stared at the piece of steak on her fork.

"Yes, ma'am. He was. Before he died, he asked me if he was gonna go to hell for what he did, and I told him it wasn't me who was doin' the judgin', but I think he finally knew what he did was wrong. It was too late maybe, but that's not for me to say, either."

"Did you know him long, Doc?"

"For six years. I even sewed him up twice. Once from a knife cut that he did to himself and once from a piece of glass that caught him in the face down at The Shotgun Saloon."

"Did you think of him as your friend?"

"Yes, ma'am. I did and still do, but it doesn't matter."

"Did you know who he was before you shot him?"

"I knew who he was as soon as I saw his horse. It didn't matter who he was. He was gonna get that .50 caliber piece of lead to stop him from hurtin' you."

Rhonda finally looked up, put her steak into her mouth and began to chew slowly.

"Somethin' else he told me before he died was important, too. He said that they were gonna visit the Adler spread. Do you know the Adlers?"

"Not well. I know that they have a ranch about fifteen miles southwest of us."

"I can't figure out why they'd bother with the Adlers, but I gotta go and warn 'em tomorrow. If you feel up to it, you can ride along."

"Yes, I'd rather come along. Will it hurt to ride so far?"

"I can drive the wagon if you'd like, but it will take a lot longer."

"No, I'll ride."

"Okay, then we'll take breaks more often. If you start feelin' bad, you gotta let me know."

"I promise."

Doc took a big bite of his potato then after swallowing, asked, "Rhonda, why were you walkin' all the way to Comanche instead of headin' to the Adlers? It's a good ten miles closer."

"I wasn't sure where it was, and I was afraid of getting lost."

Doc just nodded then said, "I've gotta do somethin' about Lou's horse, too. He's just too easy to spot as belongin' to Lou. If you got an idea, I'd appreciate it."

Rhonda asked, "Could you just leave his saddle on him and let him wander back to the Double L?"

"I could do that, but they might start lookin' around and trail him back to your place. That would be a problem."

"Yes, I can see that. Can't they track him here now, though?"

"Not likely. They ain't trackers and there's a good amount of traffic on that road, so I figure they won't even start lookin' for a couple of days."

Rhonda suddenly looked up at Doc and said, "Doc, could you turn that horse into a pinto like yours?"

Doc snapped his head up, stared at Rhonda and broke into a big smile before he said, "You are one smart lady, Rhonda Byrne. That's perfect. All I'd need to do is rub in some soot from the fireplace on some places and he'd look like Trapper's brother."

Rhonda smiled at his enthusiasm then added, "I think I can do better than that, Doc. I have some black dye that I was going to use to dye some of my old dresses, so they didn't look so faded. It would be a lot better and wouldn't run if he got sweaty or caught in the rain."

"Now you're makin' me look bad, Rhonda, but I don't mind one bit. I'll do that in the mornin' 'cause I'm just plain tuckered out."

"I'm tired myself, but not as much as I should be. I still can't believe it was only yesterday that I thought I would die from starvation."

"I gotta admit, you're recoverin' a lot faster'n I thought you would. You still gotta put on some weight, though."

"I know. I'm probably down to around a hundred pounds. That's twenty pounds less than I normally weigh."

"Well, we got plenty of food, so startin' tomorrow, I think you can eat whenever you're hungry."

Rhonda smiled and then took a big bite of her potatoes.

They finished their dinner and Doc helped clear the table and told Rhonda that he'd take care of the cleanup, so she could rest.

"Thank you, Doc," she said before she turned and walked down the hallway to her bedroom.

Doc may have been dog-tired, but he knew it was because of all the labor he had put in that day, but Rhonda's exhaustion was because she had no reserves to draw upon and she'd been through another bad experience.

As he cleaned, Doc wondered just what was wrong with the men he counted as friends and good guys. He'd watched Lou chasing after Rhonda with evil intent, but when he talked to him before he died, he seemed like good ol' Lou Robinson again. *What turned good men into monsters?*

When he finished the cleaning, he picked up the Sharps then walked over to the lamp, blew it out and walked out into the night, closing the door behind him.

After he reached the bunkhouse, as tired as he was, he lit the lamp, then spent twenty minutes cleaning the Sharps carbine then loaded it. With the necessary gun maintenance done, he set it down on the opposite bunk, then blew out his lamp, took off his filthy shirt, his boots and then just collapsed onto his bunk.

He stayed awake as long as he could because he suspected he'd be awakened again soon. It was almost forty minutes later before he heard Rhonda's screams from the house then walked to the bunkhouse door to be sure that no one had ridden in somehow. He didn't find any new horses, so he turned back to the bunkhouse and returned to his bunk where he finally let himself drift off to his much needed night's rest.

CHAPTER 3

Despite his bone weariness, Doc still awakened with the coming of the sun. It was helped by the fact that the open door to the bunkhouse faced northeast, so the light flooded his face as soon as the sun cleared the horizon.

He swung his stiff legs across the bed, feeling every day of his thirty-two years, then went to his saddlebags, threw them over his shoulder and walked to the creek.

Twenty minutes later, he was naked in the creek, washing every part of him that he could reach. He had never used shampoo and knew that he never would. Soap was soap as far as he was concerned.

He shaved once he was done and after he was dry, he washed his dirty clothes on the bank of the creek using one of the large nearby rocks to pound the cloth clean.

Doc returned to the bunkhouse and stretched some cord across the bunkhouse then hung his two recently washed shirts, his pair of denims, and two pairs of socks and two pairs of skivvies on the line.

Feeling much better, he pulled on his gunbelt and took some time examining Lou's weapons in detail in the bright sun. The Winchester needed cleaning, but the Colt was in good condition, so he decided to clean both weapons while he waited for Rhonda to wake up.

As he sat on the bunk cleaning the Winchester, he wondered if she would ever stop having those nightmares and couldn't imagine how difficult that made her nights, knowing that as soon as she drifted into sleep, the terrors of that night would return to haunt her.

After finishing with the Colt, Doc set the two cleaned guns on the bunk with the Sharps and walked out of the bunkhouse, checking the cookstove pipe for smoke, not surprised when he didn't find any.

He was going to chop some of the wood but didn't want to get all dirty again before they went to visit the Adlers. He wasn't that familiar with the family and only knew that there was the father and mother, both in their upper forties, three sons and one daughter and that two of the sons and their daughter were married. Some had children, but who had produced the new Adlers was irrelevant, at least to him.

With five adult males on the ranch, they didn't have to hire any permanent ranch hands and had three houses on the spread, the main ranch house, a smaller house and then one more house that was smaller still.

But the biggest mystery was why Charlie Lynch would even bother with the Adlers. Doc simply couldn't figure out why Charlie Lynch would consider them to be outsiders who needed to be eradicated. Then there was the question of the number of men on the Slash A. There were five adult males on the Adler spread. Up until now, the ranches and farms that had been raided had all been smaller. This one could present a problem for the Double L riders.

Finally, he just gave up trying to figure out why or how they were planning on going after the Adlers, only that they were going to do it and the Adlers needed to be warned.

———

"Where's Lou," Rex asked as the men filed into the chow house.

"Beats me," replied Joe Sheraton, "he was with us in The Shotgun, then he just kinda disappeared. I figure he's with Leona or Sally, sleepin' it off."

The others all snickered at the idea, so Rex blew his absence off and said, "The boss wants to meet us all in the eastern pastures in an hour. I think he wants us to visit the Adlers."

Joe smiled at the idea. He didn't care about anything more than seeing that smarmy Lenny Adler getting his comeuppance.

———

Rhonda slept late again but tried to make up for lost time by hurrying out to the privy, almost running down Doc who had decided to start cutting firewood anyway.

She smiled at him as she trotted quickly to the privy. Doc tried not to watch her as she left as it was improper, but it was hard not to. She may have a few pounds to regain, but she was still a very handsome young woman.

Once she was inside the small house, he was able to regain his focus and began to cut the branches into foot long pieces of wood for the cookstove. He was so successful at putting aside the sight of Rhonda trotting past in her nightdress that he was startled when she suddenly walked past going in the opposite direction, waved and then bounced up the steps, crossed the small porch and re-entered the house.

Doc shook his head then returned to chopping the branches as that last bounce she took onto the porch echoed in his mind.

Rhonda washed in the kitchen sink quickly before returning to her bedroom to dress in her new riding skirt and one of her modified blouses. She had to hunt to find the black dye for the horse but eventually found it in the bottom of one of her drawers.

Then she returned to the kitchen, fired up the cookstove and began to prepare breakfast. She felt surprisingly energetic as she fried the bacon and set the table while she waited to turn the slices.

When everything was ready, she walked to the back door which she had left open and spotted Doc still swinging the axe. She waited until he finished his swing and shouted, "Doc, breakfast is ready!"

Doc waved and set the axe down, wiped the sweat from his brow and walked to the house.

Once he had taken his seat, Rhonda set the two plates on the table then the two cups of coffee before sitting down herself.

"Doc, here's that dye I told you about last night," she said as she slid the bottle across the table.

"Thanks, Rhonda. I'll get that done before we leave for the Adlers just in case anyone comes wandering over here. I'll still close the barn doors, though."

She nodded and began to eat her eggs, feeling so very normal having Doc sitting across from her as she ate a regular breakfast. As strange as it sounded to her, and it did sound very strange, she'd never felt so much at home before. Maybe it was because she never felt that this was her home, but Jamie's, even though it had been bought with her money. Or maybe it was because she had never been very comfortable with Jamie at all, especially not after what had happened last year.

Whatever the reason, sharing breakfast with Doc Holt was just a pleasant experience for her.

"When are we leaving, Doc?"

"In about an hour, I think. It's gonna be a bit queer to just ride up and tell Mister Adler that night riders are comin' to cause mayhem, but I've gotta do it."

"Do you think he'll believe you?"

"I don't know why he wouldn't. He could at least keep someone on watch."

"I'd keep everyone on watch if someone had warned me six weeks ago."

"You'd kinda think most folks would."

Rhonda nodded wondering who would be arrogant or stupid enough to not pay attention to a warning that men were coming to kill his entire family.

———

"This one is gonna be hard," Charlie Lynch was saying to his boys, as they stood with the east herd nearby, "They have five grown men at that ranch, and we have to get in there nice and quiet."

Whitey Smith snickered and said, "Jews ain't gonna do nothin' but squeal like pigs."

Before anyone else could laugh, Charlie snapped, "Shut up, Whitey. Ben Adler may be Jewish, but he isn't yellow."

Whitey lost his grin and mumbled, "Sorry, boss."

Charlie glared at Whitey for another few seconds before he turned back to his three sons, his son-in-law and the four ranch hands and said, "Alright. We'll go in a little later than usual after they've been sleeping for a while. Now there are three houses, so me and my boys will take the main house, Rex you and Whitey take the house closest to the access road and Joe, you and Carl take the last house."

Then he looked around and asked, "Where's Lou?"

"He musta had too much last night at The Shotgun and stayed with one of the girls, boss," replied Rex.

Charlie grunted then said, "Rex, when he gets back you tell him how this is going to work, and he'll be with you."

"Okay, boss," Rex replied.

"I'll see you all around ten o'clock tonight."

They all nodded as the boss turned, mounted his black gelding and rode back to the ranch house followed by his three sons and his son-in-law, Ned Smith.

———

"Can you put the saddle on for me, Doc. I still don't seem to have the arm strength," Rhonda asked.

"I didn't think you would, but you're doin' better'n I expected," he replied as he swung her saddle onto Bride.

Without thinking, he automatically dropped to tighten the cinch and almost head-butted Rhonda who had expected to be doing that part by herself.

"Oh, excuse me, Rhonda," he said as he stepped back.

She smiled at him and replied, "No, that's alright, Doc."

After tightening the cinch, Doc watched her mount unsteadily, as he kept his hand poised behind her back to catch her if she fell backwards. But she mounted successfully and was soon astride Bride beaming down at him.

Doc smiled up at her before leading Trapper out of the barn, leaving the newly redesigned pinto in its stall. He had been amazed how much like a real pinto the white gelding appeared to be. It would take a close eye to notice the difference or to spot Lou's horse under the dye. He knew it wasn't permanent, but by the time the dye all grew out, this issue should be settled.

Once outside, he mounted Trapper and started him walking. He had his Sharps in the left scabbard and his Winchester '73 in the right. Even though she had never fired it before, Rhonda had Lou's Winchester '73 in her scabbard as well. The plan was for her to learn on the way back from the Adlers.

Doc kept the speed to a slow trot out of deference to Rhonda's lack of riding experience, but she seemed exhilarated to be riding her own horse as they rode southwest. Doc was pleased to note the filly's smooth gait, so Rhonda would be more comfortable in the saddle.

They had packed some cooked sausages and the bottle of mustard sauce for the journey and each horse had two canteens.

"Doc, Bride is such a wonderful horse!" Rhonda exclaimed as she looked over at him, "She's so smooth that I don't even feel any bumps at all."

"That's good, Rhonda. Now, make sure that you tell me if you start to feel uncomfortable or tired. Okay?"

"I will," she replied, but doubted if she'd have a problem.

––––––

The fifteen-mile trip took them over two hours at the speed Doc had chosen, knowing he and Trapper could have made it in less time, but he and Rhonda had talked along the way about things. She seemed not to want to talk about her past at all, and he hadn't delved into his family either, but for a different reason. He simply didn't think about them much at all, but she did ask him about his time in the army and then about his life at the Double L.

Initially, Doc thought it was because she was still attempting to find out if he had some sort of ulterior motive for helping her, but after the first hour, he knew that wasn't the case because she wasn't acting as if she was suspicious at all. If anything, she seemed to believe he was some sort of angel sent by God, which he believed bordered on blasphemy or some other religious offense.

He finally came to believe that she hadn't talked about her life because she was ashamed or embarrassed by her past or her marriage for whatever reasons. He had wondered why even after two months she wasn't grieving as much as some of the women he'd met over the years who had lost their husbands.

He had thought at first it was because of the horrible events that had surrounded her husband's death, but she had been willing to talk about that night as it related to her easily enough. Then there was that early comment about how her family in New York wouldn't welcome her with open arms. He finally assumed that she had reasons for not wanting to talk about her past, and that really wasn't his business.

They finally picked up the Adler ranch on the horizon and Doc wasn't surprised to see the number of buildings. He'd spotted their main herd of some eight hundred cattle forty minutes ago as it was being tended by four riders. He assumed that the riders were his three sons and his son-in-law. Even with the father around, he thought they were spread too thin to keep an eye on a herd that large. They should have hired at least four more permanent hands rather than the seasonal help they had been hiring, but it wasn't his spread, so it wasn't for him to say.

Doc and Rhonda rode across the front of the ranch as the access road headed south and soon arrived at the front of the house.

Rhonda began to dismount when Doc stopped her and shouted, "Hello, the house!"

A few seconds later, Nellie Adler arrived at the open front door and asked, "Good morning, what do you need?"

"Mrs. Adler, my name is Doc Holt, and this is Mrs. Byrne from the Circle B. I used to ride for the Double L until a couple of days ago and I was wonderin' if I could speak to you and your husband for a few minutes."

"Of course, step down and come in. My husband is in his office."

Doc glanced over at Rhonda and they both dismounted then tied the horses at the hitchrail before stepping onto the porch and entering the house. Doc removed his Stetson and waited for Mrs. Adler to show them where to go.

"Just have a seat and I'll get my husband," she said as she gestured toward the large main room with eight chairs and a sofa.

"Thank you, ma'am," Doc said as he and Rhonda took adjacent seats.

"Ben," Mrs. Adler said as she walked to a nearby open door, "there's a Mister Holt and Mrs. Burns outside to see you."

Doc didn't see any reason to correct Mrs. Adler as she returned and took a seat waiting for her husband to join them.

Ben Adler strode from his office a minute later and Doc stood to shake his hand when it was offered.

Mister Adler sat with his wife on the couch then asked, "What can I do for you, Mister Holt?"

"Mister Adler, as I told your wife a minute ago, I was a longtime ranch hand for the Double L until a couple of days ago when I quit."

"If you're looking for a job, Mister Holt, I'm afraid that I'm not hiring."

"No, sir. I'm not lookin' for a job. But the reason I quit is important. Six weeks ago, Mrs. Byrne here had her husband and two ranch hands murdered at night in her home. She was beaten, assaulted and left for dead. Now, it's to my eternal shame that I knew that it had been done by Double L ranch hands and the family of Charlie Lynch, who I think you know. But I didn't say anything about it 'cause I told myself it wasn't my business.

"I didn't go on any of what they call their nighttime visits over the past few months, but that doesn't make me any less guilty. A couple of days ago, I came across Mrs. Byrne almost dyin' in the open 'cause she was starvin'. Yesterday, one of the ranch hands came back to her ranch to lay claim to it 'cause he thought she was dead, and it was unoccupied.

"He saw her runnin' and he tried to run her down on his horse and I shot and killed him. Before he died, he told me that the next place that they'd be comin' to visit is yours. Now, I don't have a clue why they'd come after you at all, but I came to warn you about it, so you could be ready."

Ben Adler had listened to Doc in disbelieving astonishment. He'd known Charlie Lynch for years. Granted, they hadn't spent much time together, but they'd returned each other's wandering cattle and hadn't had any problems at all.

"Mister Holt, with all due respect, I find your tale hard to believe. I know Charlie Lynch well enough to throw serious doubts as to the truth of your accusations."

"Mister Adler," Doc replied, not as surprised as Rhonda had been over his disbelief, "I can understand that. Charlie was a good boss until a few months ago when him and Bill Wheeler and a couple of the other ranchers kinda got together to get rid of all the folks they thought didn't belong in Texas. They attacked Mrs. Byrne's place because she's from New York and Irish Catholic. Why they want to attack you makes no sense to me at all, but that's what Lou told me when he was dyin'. A man ain't got no cause to lie when he's about to meet his maker."

Nellie Adler had a worried look on her face as she looked at her husband who shook his head and replied, "I'm sorry, Mister Holt. I've heard of the raids and disagreed with their methods, but I agree with their desire to keep Texas for Texans. I have no reason to fear Charlie Lynch and his men."

Doc didn't see any reason to try to convince Ben Adler, so he just rose and said, "Mister Adler, I've got no reason to come here but to try to warn you about what I was told. What you do now is up to you, but if I were in your shoes, just to protect the womenfolk and young'uns, I'd at least keep a night watch for the next week or so."

Ben Adler stood and shook his head, "I'm sorry, Mister Holt, but I can't have one of my sons or my son-in-law stay awake half the night just on your say-so. I need every hand out in the pastures."

Doc shrugged and said, "It's your ranch, Mister Adler, and it's your family. If it's okay with you, we'll water our horses and head back."

"Go ahead. I appreciate your concern, Mister Holt."

Rhonda stood and as she walked past, Doc turned to Nellie Adler and said, "I hope you appreciate my warning a lot more, Mrs. Adler," then he followed Rhonda out the door, across the porch and down the steps to their waiting horses.

After watching them walk their horses away from the front of the house to the trough on the side of the house, Nellie said, "Ben, this frightens me. Don't you think you should take Mister Holt's advice and keep someone awake. It doesn't have to be one of the men. One of the women can keep watch."

"No, dear, that wouldn't be right. We have the windows all open now anyway, so we'd hear if anyone came riding in. I know Charlie Lynch, but I don't know Mister Holt. He could be a disgruntled ranch hand that was fired and wished to cause trouble. I'll ride over there tomorrow and talk to Charlie about it. Don't fret, dear."

Nellie nodded, but she most certainly did fret.

After watering their horses, Rhonda and Doc began to trot back to the Circle B.

"Doc, I can't believe what I just heard. He isn't going to do anything, is he?"

"Nope. I reckon not."

Rhonda didn't want to ask the question but felt she must, so she asked, "Doc, what are you going to do?"

"I'm gonna come back here tonight and then the next night until I'm sure that Lou was wrong. Mister Adler may not trust me, but I can't let it happen again, Rhonda."

"I know. Can I come with you, Doc?"

"Yes, ma'am. But I want to show you how to shoot that Winchester before we leave. We've got to let the horses rest when we get back, too. They're gonna be mighty tired later tonight."

"We have the spare pinto now," she said.

Doc smiled as he turned to her and said, "Yup. We've got a spare pinto."

———

An hour later, they had dismounted to let the horses rest and Rhonda began to feel the effects of sitting in the saddle for so long, but tried to hide it from Doc.

After ground hitching the horses, he took out two of the sausages, and they took turns dipping them into the mustard sauce and sharing a canteen of water. After they finished their casual lunch, he pulled her Winchester from its scabbard and walked over to stand next to her and asked, "Sore, aren't you, Rhonda?"

She gave up, rubbed her behind and said, "Yes, I'm sore, but not as bad as I expected to be."

He smiled at her as he began to explain how the Winchester worked and the basic rules of shooting.

Luckily, Rhonda was smart and a good student, so she understood what she needed to do and after a few dryfire exercises, Doc reloaded the Winchester, handed it to her and let her pick out a target.

She aimed at a small cactus sixty yards away, and with very good technique, squeezed off her first round that was wide right by three feet, but had the range correct.

Doc didn't say anything as she levered in a second round and fired. The second shot was closer but still off by a foot to the right.

Her third was off to the left just by six inches, but her fourth shot obliterated the cactus. She turned to Doc with a big grin, then picked out a second target at eighty yards. This time, she only missed her first shot, and that was only by six or eight inches.

By the time she had emptied the Winchester, she was hitting her target often enough to satisfy Doc, so he nodded as he took the smoking Winchester back and refilled the magazine tube with cartridges.

"I'll clean this when we get back, Mrs. Byrne. You did a very good job."

"Thank you, Mister Holt," she said feeling proud of herself.

Rhonda felt she was no longer useless. Now all she needed to do was to regain her weight.

They remounted and continued their journey back to the Circle B, arriving less than an hour later.

———

"Where the hell is Lou?" asked Rex.

"Want me to ride into Comanche and see if I can find him?" asked Whitey.

Rex thought about it then shook his head and replied, "No. If that bastard is still sleepin' it off, he can sleep it off somewhere else. Let's all get some sleep time now before we head out tonight. We're not gonna be sleepin' much after that."

"Ain't that the truth," said Joe Sheraton with a touch of glee in his voice.

———

Their horses were stripped, brushed down then put away and getting their rest while Rhonda sat at the kitchen table watching Doc clean what she now considered her Winchester.

"Why do you have to clean them so soon, Doc?" she asked.

"The gunsmoke residue will eat at the metal, makin' it all corroded. Then the gun starts losin' accuracy, and any gun that isn't accurate ain't worth shootin'."

He had oiled the Winchester earlier that morning, so after it was cleaned and reloaded, he handed it back to Rhonda.

"There you go, ma'am. Your carbine is ready."

Rhonda took the Winchester, laid it on the table and began to run her fingers softly across the wood and blued metal.

"It is really almost like a piece of sculpture. Isn't it?" she asked as she continued to slide her fingertips over her carbine.

"I think so, but I can't recall any woman sayin' somethin' nice about a gun."

She looked up at him, smiled and asked, "Had a lot of experience with women, Mister Holt?"

"No, ma'am. I hate to admit it, but women just plain scare me."

"Do I scare you, Doc?"

"No, ma'am. You don't scare me, at least not too much after that first day. Just enough to keep me confused."

She looked at him and said, "You don't scare me at all, Doc. Not having you nearby scares me, though."

"Now, Rhonda, that doesn't make much sense to me at all. I always heard that Irishwomen had tempers to scare the Almighty and only feared their Irish mothers."

"That's a myth, at least as far as it applies to me. I am stubborn though, which is another trait usually attributed to Irishwomen."

"I imagine so," he said then asked, "did you want to take a nap, so you don't fall asleep tonight?"

"I think so. Are you going to take a nap, too?"

"No, I think I'll go and cut up some of them branches."

"Thank you for the rifle...I mean, the carbine, Doc," she said with a smile.

Doc stood, said, "You're welcome, Rhonda," then headed out of the kitchen to go to the barn and put an edge on the axe before he attacked the branches.

Rhonda watched him leave then sighed, picked up her Winchester and returned to the bedroom to take her siesta.

———

Back at the Adler spread, Nellie debated about telling her daughter about Doc's warning, but didn't want to alarm her. She was more worried about her five young grandchildren than the men. The children were just so innocent, but in the end, she deferred to her husband's judgement that Mister Holt was just a disgruntled ranch hand and that he'd talk to Charlie Lynch tomorrow to clarify the issue.

———

Rhonda slept for three hours while Doc finished off the branches and had them all stacked near the back porch, but not touching the house. No sense in giving the termites two free lunches.

He finally carried the axe back to the barn before walking down to the creek. He looked around to make sure that no one, especially Rhonda, was anywhere in sight, then quickly stripped and dove into the creek and let the cooling water flow over him. He only stayed in the creek for ten minutes to cool off before leaving the creek and quickly dressing.

He walked back to the bunkhouse and set his Winchester and the Sharps out along with enough ammunition to do the job that he hoped wasn't even going to be necessary.

After Rhonda awakened, she cooked dinner then called Doc into the house to eat while he was saddling Trapper and Bride.

He had thought about riding Lou's horse instead but didn't want to have to depend on an unknown animal if it came to shooting.

"Doc," Rhonda asked as they were eating, "should I be afraid?"

"No, I don't think it helps any. There's only a small chance that they're comin' tonight anyway. I just want to be there just in case."

"What do I do if they show up and shooting starts?"

"It'll be nighttime, so I want you to hightail it back toward the ranch. I want you at least a half a mile away. Okay?"

"Why? I can shoot now."

"Yes, ma'am. You can shoot, but when you shoot at night the rules are different. As soon as you pull that trigger, you let everyone else know where you are. During the day, there's the gunsmoke, but it's not a small target like a muzzle flash. I know how it works, and I'll be okay. I just want you further away, so you don't get hit. You gotta promise me that you'll do what I say."

Rhonda exhaled sharply then said, "I promise. I'll do what you tell me to do."

Doc nodded before saying, "I said you were a smart lady."

Rhonda smiled weakly back, not really comfortable with the promise.

The sun was setting when Doc carried his Winchester and Sharps to the barn with his ammunition laden saddlebags over his shoulder.

He soon led a saddled Trapper and Bride out of the barn and hitched them to the hitchrail before stepping up onto the back porch and waiting for Rhonda who had returned to her bedroom to retrieve her Winchester.

He watched as the last lamp dimmed then she popped out of the back door and closed it behind her.

"I'm ready," she said as she stepped onto the porch.

"Okay, ma'am. Let's go for a nice quiet ride in the night."

The ride took even longer than the one they had made earlier because of the lack of light. There were high clouds that blocked most of the moonlight but didn't promise any relief from the short drought.

Doc stopped a mile away from the Adler ranch house where he and Rhonda dismounted and led their horses to a tiny stream that miraculously still had some water running along its bottom. It was only about a foot wide and an inch and a half deep, but it provided the animals with their much-needed moisture.

After they had been watered, he led the animals to some rough grass and hobbled them before he laid out his bedroll and doubled it over so he and Rhonda could just sit and wait, hopefully for nothing more than a boring ride back.

"Do they always come right after sunset?" Rhonda asked.

"They usually left about an hour after sunset, so if they're comin', they should be here in less than an hour."

"How will we see them?"

"We won't see them at all with these clouds until they're really close, but we should hear 'em. There are nine of 'em and nine

117

horses even walkin' will make enough noise for us pick up from this distance in the dead of night."

Rhonda sat hugging her knees as she stared into the blackness. It wasn't totally silent as coyote calls, the screeching of owls, and scurrying night creatures broke the stillness of the night. Just a few nights ago, those same sounds terrified her, but now they were nothing more than interesting.

"Doc, how long will we wait?"

"About two hours, but no more than that."

"Doc, what was it like for you when you were growing up?"

"Oh, I suppose just like most boys, all that I cared about was doin' the fun things like huntin' frogs and fishin'. My two older brothers kinda hung together, and I was the odd kid out, but that was okay. I had some friends that I liked better anyway.

"Like I said before, my father was a country doctor, so it wasn't like he had a diploma or anything. He learned from his mother, who was a midwife. He read some too, but the local folks didn't expect him to do any surgery or stuff like that. We had a ranch too, which is where I learned about cattle. It wasn't a big spread. It was even smaller than yours, but to a boy, it was heaven on earth.

"Then everything kinda changed in a hurry. My father began drinkin' real heavy, but I never knew why and died from some bad liquor when I was sixteen, just after the war started. I joined up when I was seventeen and when I got out, I was twenty but felt a lot older. My brothers both died in that war, and the ranch was gone when I got back."

"What about your mother? You didn't say anything about your mother."

"I never knew my mother. She died when I was born. Even my brothers never really knew her that well 'cause they were so young when she passed."

It was such a peaceful night that Rhonda thought that maybe it was time.

"Doc, how come you've never asked me about my life or my family?"

"Well, I figured if you wanted to tell me, you would, but it seemed that you were ashamed or embarrassed by somethin', so I didn't think it was my place to ask."

She sighed and said, "Yes, I'm ashamed of my past and with good reason. Remember when you first found me, and I told you that I wanted to die and how God hated me?"

"Yes."

"There were reasons for my thinking that way. My family was very large. I had three older brothers, two older sisters, two younger brothers and two younger sisters. My father was a very important man in New York politics. He was with Tammany Hall as an alderman and had a lot of power. He was grooming his two oldest sons, Peter and Matthew, for career in politics as well. The next son, John, was going to become a priest. My two older sisters, Mary and Cecilia, were both promised to two young Irishmen that my father and mother approved, and I was supposed to become a nun."

That caught Doc's attention and he turned to look at Rhonda.

"I know, it's kind of a shock, isn't it?" she asked with a wry smile.

"Yes, ma'am," he admitted.

"Anyway, I was twelve years old when I was told that I was going to the convent when I turned seventeen, but when you're young, you don't know anything about the world. I didn't even know how babies were conceived because no one talked about it. I used to think that as soon as people got married God just made the woman pregnant.

"So, I was happy with the prospect of becoming a nun. They taught at our schools and even though they scared every one of us, we respected them. But everything changed when I began to change from a girl and my mother had to explain how women became mothers when my first monthly arrived and it shocked me at first and made being a nun even more attractive, just so I could not have to perform such a disgusting thing.

"Looking back, I'm sure my mother made it out to be as vile as possible to ensure that I didn't want to go anywhere near boys. Of course, there were no boys in my school, either, so it wasn't difficult to shield me.

"But then my oldest sister, Mary, married when I was fifteen. I got along well with Mary, and after she was married, she quickly became pregnant and seemed ecstatic about it. Even my parents seemed happy and that confused me. How could they be happy knowing that Mary was doing such a dirty, distasteful act with her husband?

"So, I finally got the nerve to talk to Mary about the unspeakable and she shocked me. She told me how wonderful it was and how much she enjoyed it. I was stunned and asked her to tell me more. Then over the next few months, I began to wonder what I might be missing after I entered the convent.

"I had just turned sixteen when Jamie Byrne and his family arrived from Ireland. They were friends of our extended family still living back in Ireland, so my father set them up in an apartment near ours.

"Jamie was eighteen when I first met him, and he was a handsome boy, but like most of the young Irish that arrived in New York during the war, they were handed a rifle and a uniform and sworn in as soldiers. The war was already nearing its end by then, and Jamie was given a week to prepare before being sent to the west."

Rhonda then paused as she neared the confession of her sins.

"When I heard that Jamie was going to leave, I thought that it was a good opportunity to see what I might be missing, so I essentially seduced him although, to be honest, it didn't take much other than a smile and a kiss to go there. I'll admit to being disappointed because it wasn't as exciting as Mary had made it out to be, but I had at least tried.

"Jamie was sent off to war and I thought that was the end of it, but I was so very wrong. I missed my next monthly and then I knew I had a serious problem. I could have just run away, but I had nowhere to go and had no idea what to do, so I told my mother.

"Remember when you commented about an Irishwomen's temper? Well, if you had seen her reaction to my news, you would have seen it in all its spectacular glory. She didn't slap me, but she came close. After calling me every name you could think of for a loose woman, she banished me to the privy until my father returned home and he did slap me, several times. He was so outraged that he said he never wanted to see me again. As you might expect, I was crying and thought my world was over, but they both calmed down in a few hours and asked who the father was, and I told them.

"My father contacted Jamie's regimental commander and told him that he was sending Private Byrne's wife to join him in Texas, where his unit was camped. They put me on a train with my clothes, gave me the five-hundred-dollar dowry that was supposed to go to the convent when I was accepted as a novice and told me not to return."

Doc then asked quietly, "So, did you ever really get married?"

Rhonda shook her head and replied, "No. I was what they called a common law wife. I'm not even sure if my last name is Byrne instead of Brady."

Then she continued her story, saying, "The trip to Texas took me three weeks, most of it by overland coach. The war was mostly over by the time I reached the camp and Jamie was mustered out because of my father's political power. He was really angry to see me because he was being taken away from his friends, but he was happy with my dowry.

"Because land was so cheap right at the end of the war if you had Yankee dollars, we bought the ranch and it even had thirty head of cattle on it. But it was hard to make it go and my baby died when it was born, which made Jamie even angrier because he was trapped and the reason he was trapped wasn't even there anymore. That was ten years ago. We worked the ranch alone for a year, until the Clancy brothers were mustered out and joined Jamie. They were the best of friends and things were all right for a while.

"I became pregnant twice more over the next few years but lost both babies. Jamie said it was because God was punishing me for not becoming a nun and what I had done to him. I even agreed with him. He was angry at me almost all of the time and preferred to spend his time with the Clancy brothers. Money was very tight because he and the brothers would go to Comanche and drink and visit the brothel, but I had nothing to complain about because it was all my fault, you see."

Rhonda lowered her head slightly as tears began to gently roll down her face. There was just enough light for Doc to see them glistening as they traced their way over her cheeks.

"Then a little over a year ago, I…I sinned again. I was so very lonely that I allowed Will Clancy to have his way with me while Jamie and James Clancy were out with the herd. I was so ashamed of myself, but Will bragged to Jamie about it over the next time they went to the saloon and when they returned Jamie beat me. But I deserved it and I knew he had every right to kill me if he wished, but he didn't kill me, or even beat me again after that. What he did…"

Rhonda began breathing very quickly in short, halting breaths before continuing.

"…what he did, he…he gave me to James Clancy while he and Will Clancy watched. It was all my fault. Do you understand now, Doc? I deserved everything that they did to me, even what happened that night at the ranch. I'm a terrible sinner and God was punishing me for rejecting him when I turned away from the convent.

"I don't understand why Jamie and the brothers had to die for my sins, and I suppose the only way I'll know is when I ask God Himself. I never even went to Mass or confession after leaving New York because I was beyond forgiveness."

Rhonda then calmed down somewhat and said more clearly, "But then you came, Doc. I blamed you for all the bad things of that night, knowing I was to blame and then I thought you had gone, and I was terrified, so I finally dropped to my knees and prayed for the first time since I left New York. I prayed so hard for God and Jamie's forgiveness and to have you return to protect me. Then I heard you knock, and I knew I had been forgiven. That's why I was so happy to see you, Doc. Do you understand?"

Doc said quietly, "I understand, Rhonda, but you don't. You were just a girl who didn't understand anything about life at all. You were bein' told that you were gonna be a nun whether you wanted it or not. Now, I'll admit that it's not much different than folks tellin' their daughters who they're gonna marry but still, they were decidin' for you and that just isn't right.

"They shoulda never told you that you'd never get the chance to be a mother. You were just a girl who wanted to find out what she was gonna be missin'. It wasn't such a terrible thing. It's like when I was a boy and I was told not to reach into a hole because there might be a rattler inside. I had to do it, and I got bit, too. You can't tell a youngster not to do somethin' 'cause they're gonna do it.

"Now Jamie, he was wrong, too. If he'd been a man, knowin' he was getting' ready to leave, he shoulda told you 'no', but he didn't. He took something he had no right takin'. Then your parents shoulda been good Christian folks and forgave you for what you did and taken care of you and your baby.

"Folks who love their kids do things like that. They don't send 'em away. What happened when you got to the ranch wasn't your fault either, Rhonda. Remember I told you that you can't be blamin' or thankin' God for things that happened to you? You aren't even close to bein' a sinner. Now, you listen to me, Rhonda Byrne. You are the nicest, sweetest lady I ever met, and if God doesn't let you in heaven just for all the sufferin' you been through, then I don't want to go there myself."

Rhonda stared at Doc in the low light as she replied, "But the babies, Doc. I lost all my babies and never even got to hold any of them. If God wasn't angry at me for not being a nun and then giving myself away, then why did I lose my babies?"

"Rhonda, there are lots of reasons why women lose their babies. You've had a hard time since you left New York and that didn't help. You've never been happy since you were just a girl, have you?"

"No. I can't remember the last time I laughed."

"Do you really think that God punishes innocent children? 'Cause that's what you were when you were sixteen, Rhonda. You were just an innocent child that made a mistake 'cause you didn't know any better."

Rhonda wiped the tears from her face and asked quietly, "Do you really mean it, Doc? Do you really, truly believe that I'm not a sinner?"

"Yes, ma'am. As sure as I believe the sun's gonna come up tomorrow and it's gonna be hotter than Hades by noon."

Rhonda laughed lightly and said, "Thank you for not hating me, Doc."

Doc shook his head and replied, "Rhonda, you have got to be the most guilty-feelin' innocent person I've ever come across. Why in tarnation would I hate you?"

"Maybe because I've hated myself for so long."

"Well, stop doin' it right now. Okay?"

She nodded, began to tear up again and said softly, "Okay."

"Good. Now that we've got all that behind us, how are you?"

"I'm much better, Doc, so very much better."

"You're a good person, Rhonda, and you gotta start thinkin' of yourself that way."

Rhonda smiled and nodded, very pleased that she had talked to Doc and began to see him as a real doctor who could heal souls as well as bodies.

Doc exhaled then began to stare in the direction of the Adler ranch house. There were no lamps lit and he was pretty sure that there was no one on watch.

"They don't have anybody out there, Rhonda. Ben Adler must really trust Charlie Lynch, but he's got too much in that pot to gamble. He's gambling his family's lives that I was lyin'."

"That's a foolish thing to do, Doc," Rhonda said as she stared at the ranch as well.

————

Charlie Lynch and his sons, son-in-law and his four ranch hands had departed the Double L at eleven o'clock, knowing it would take them about ninety minutes to make the ride to the Adlers.

————

Rhonda yawned and asked, "Doc, has it been two hours yet?"

"Probably closer to three by now," he replied as he stood, "I don't think they're comin'."

"I think the horses are asleep," she said as she stood and glanced over at them.

"They're smarter'n us humans, I guess. Let's get headin' home, Rhonda."

"Okay."

Doc returned his bedroll to its tightly bound condition, tied it off on Trapper's back and then removed the hobbles from both horses and let them know it was time to head for the barn.

Rhonda mounted Bride as Doc climbed atop Trapper and they began heading northeast at a walk.

————

A half a mile south, the riders from the Double L were walking their horses almost due west and were just a mile out from the Adler ranch as Doc and Rhonda were increasing the distance from the ranch house.

Despite his claim that someone would hear the horses as they walked onto the ranch, Ben Adler didn't hear a thing, nor did anyone else in the entire family, even with the windows open because the riders had all dismounted at the end of the access road and hitched their horses to the fencing marking the entryway to the ranch. They walked with their Winchesters in their hands for the remaining two hundred and fifty yards to the ranch houses.

Charlie had them split up into their assigned groups, two ranch hands taking each of the smaller houses and the Lynch men taking the main house with the idea of peppering the houses with gunfire, which should drive out the menfolk with their guns to defend the women and children. After the men were all dead, then the women would be fair game. None of them gave any thought to the children because they didn't want to face the idea.

They were all in position ten minutes later, and each waited for Charlie to begin the shooting.

————

Doc and Rhonda were just past a mile out when the first Winchester report broke the silence and startled both of them and their horses.

Doc shouted, "Stay here, Rhonda! And don't argue!"

He didn't wait for a response as he whipped Trapper around and set him off at a dangerous gallop across the dark ground, knowing that he was risking his and his horse's life by doing so, but knew he had no choice.

————

Charlie's first shot was aimed just under the window of one of the bedrooms as he had instructed each of the others to do. Suddenly, the night was ablaze in Winchester fire as each of the three houses began to get peppered with .44 caliber holes.

Inside the houses, men were scrambling to get their wives on the floor as they ran to the children's rooms to get them on the floor too. Although all of them knew that blind firing into a building was usually a waste of bullets, it didn't matter as panic soon dominated the interiors of the three Adler houses.

The first casualty was Ben Adler who had popped to his feet then run from the bedroom to get to his office and the stored weapons, when he was hit in the left side of his chest as he crossed into the main room. The hit was fatal as he screamed and went down, bleeding heavily. His death shriek added to the terror of the night.

With Ben out of action, the next adult male in the main house to move was Lenny Adler, the one who had inadvertently caused the attack by offending Joe Sheraton. He ran past his father's body and made it to the office as bullets continued to rip through the house and was pulling a Winchester from its rack when a .44 caught him in the right buttock, sending him to the floor.

The second oldest son, Harold, had raced out of their bedroom with his wife Agnes behind him as they ran into their children's room and pulled their three children, including their one-year-old daughter from their beds and crib to the floor, all them crying as their parents covered them with their bodies.

The oldest Adler son, Richard was in the middle-sized house with his wife, Prudence and their three children and were doing the same thing, as they did all they could to protect their precious children from the bullets that pounded into the rooms. There was no chance that they would survive, and they knew it.

The smallest ranch house was the home of Ben Adler's only married daughter, Linda, and her husband Robert, but Robert wasn't trying to protect anyone. As soon as he was awakened by the first shots, he raced to the window, threw it open and was trying to escape as his wife lay on the floor screaming in terror.

It was a bad choice as Whitey Smith was able to spot him as he began climbing out of the window and shot him at point blank range, knocking him back inside, where he fell atop his still-screaming wife making her night of terror so much worse, and it wasn't over.

When he knew that he had shot the only male occupant of the house, Whitey began to run around to the entrance of the small house and shouted to Rex on the other side that it was safe to go inside.

Rex didn't need a second shout as he kicked open the door and ran into the house where he found Linda still in complete panic with her dead husband lying next to her.

Rex tossed the body aside as Whitey ran into the house.

———

Then things changed dramatically when suddenly, Winchester fire began hitting Lynch men. The shooters didn't realize that one of the firing Winchesters was directed at them, as the muzzle flashes lit up the night all around the ranch buildings.

Doc was walking along the walls of the buildings waiting for muzzle flares to identify shooters, hoping that none of the Adlers had made it out of the house yet. As soon as he saw one, he whipped his Winchester to the spot and squeezed off a round before walking to a different spot in case they fired at his flash.

One by one, Doc began picking them off. The first to take a hit was Joe Sheraton, who was firing into the ranch house occupied by Richard Adler's family. He caught the .44 square in the middle of his back, smashing two of his thoracic vertebrae before punching into his heart. He dropped like a sack of potatoes.

The next was the other ranch hand who was firing into the same house, Carl Henson. Doc's shot hit him on his left side, just above the hip, but was a lateral shot at only twenty yards, so the .44 entered his left side and drilled through most of his gut before barely exiting on the right side and dropping to the ground, its energy expended after having done its killing.

Doc then walked to the smallest house, having seen two of them enter the house and hearing the screams of a woman. With the diminished light, this would be difficult as he entered the shattered door and barely was able to see Whitey standing over the foreman as Rex prepared to rape Linda.

"C'mon, Rex, get movin'" Whitey said in an excited voice, "I ain't never had no Jew before."

Doc took two steps forward and didn't care about niceties as he squeezed the trigger with the muzzle two feet behind Whitey's back, sending the .44 blowing through his spine and then exploding through his sternum a tiny fraction of a second later. Whitey actually lived for three seconds after feeling the thump of the bullet pound into his back and half-turned to see what had happened before he almost gracefully pirouetted to the floor beside Rex who had stopped and swiveled his head, wondering what had just happened.

Doc couldn't risk firing down as the woman was underneath Rex Crenshaw, so he whipped the butt of the Winchester into Rex's upturned jaw, fracturing in two places as teeth went flying before Rex followed them to the floor. Once he was off Linda and by himself, Doc levered in a new round and fired from three feet into the foreman's gut but didn't have the time to see if he was alive, but he did notice a third body that he hadn't created lying on the floor nearby.

He finally spoke when he said, "Ma'am, I'd like to help you, but I gotta go."

Linda had been terrified just moments before, but her sudden release from what was about to happen made her giddy and she began to laugh and cry at the same time.

Doc turned quickly and trotted out of the house, trying to remember how many should be left and came up with five, but he wasn't really sure. He had only been able to identify Whitey and Rex of the four he'd shot, but it didn't matter which ones were left. He had to stop them all.

He levered in a fresh cartridge as he cleared the porch and stalked toward the big house.

———

A mile away, Rhonda was close to panic herself but not for herself but for what might have already happened to Doc. She knew she had promised to do what he had told her, but she had to know, so she turned Bride back toward the ranch house, still seeing the almost firefly-like flashes in the distance followed by the pops of the rifle fire.

———

One of those pops was when Doc fired at a shooter who seemed to be concentrating his fire at one of the front bedrooms. The .44 slammed into Ned Smith, Beth's husband, just above his left shoulder, but ripped through the back of his neck, shattering his spine and spinal cord, dropping him straight to the ground.

Doc then spotted another shooter near the back of the house as he fired into what must be the kitchen area and as soon as the flash appeared from his Winchester, Doc squeezed his trigger.

But the shooter, Joe Lynch, was somewhat fortunate, although he might have argued the point, when Doc's bullet drilled through his Winchester's stock, exploded the wood, then ripped his right bicep to shreds as splinters flew into his face.

He screamed, dropped his destroyed repeater and grabbed his face with this left hand, his right arm now useless. But even using that one hand was a mistake as his palm, instead of helping him, banged the splinters further into his face. But he was still alive, although Joe might be wishing otherwise as he went to his knees, sobbing.

It was then that the remaining three Lynch shooters realized that there was someone shooting back. Each of them assumed it was one of the Adlers, so they mistakenly increased their fire into the main ranch house.

Doc walked around the front of the house and spotted another shooter who had just fired his last round from his Winchester and was reaching into his pocket for more ammunition, but he was outlined by another shooter's muzzle flash, giving Doc a target that he didn't waste.

When he squeezed the trigger, his Winchester popped back against his shoulder sending its deadly missile where it had been aimed. In one of those oddities of chance, Doc's bullet slammed into Charlie Lynch's jacket pocket containing a dozen rounds of .44 caliber Winchester cartridges and set off one of them, beginning an almost instantaneous chain reaction as more cartridges were touched off.

The original .44 fired by Doc had ricocheted off the pocketed cartridges and took an upward angle into Charlie's right lung, where it lodged after having lost almost all of its energy in the ricochet.

The subsequent discharged .44s created an almost firework-like display as the flames erupted from Charlie's pocket and the bullets blasted in one direction and the empty brass went flying in the other. Some of the bullets wound up punching into Charlie with devastating results. Two blasted straight into the ground and the others went God only knew where.

Doc quickly stepped over Charlie's body and looked for the one who had created the flare that had made Charlie a target. There were only two left who still posed a threat.

By now, the other two, Johnny and Eddy Lynch, both finally realized that the shooter was outside with them and had stopped turning themselves into targets. It was now a chess match after the checkers game that Doc had won easily.

Johnny and Eddy's problem was that they didn't know which one of those moving around was the new shooter, or if one of the shadows was a Lynch or one of their ranch hands. Doc didn't have that problem. If he spotted movement, it was a target. His only concern now was that his muzzle flash would give him away.

So, for three silent minutes, the three men circled in the darkness, looking for an advantage. Even Joe Lynch seemed to understand the need for silence, and despite his injuries, he stayed on his knees with blood still leaking heavily from his upper arm.

———

Rhonda had stopped about a hundred yards from the ranch houses, believing that it was a safe distance and had satisfied her promise to Doc. But after two whole minutes without gunfire, she mistakenly believed that it was over and her anxiety for his welfare overrode her concern for her personal safety, so she started Bride forward again.

———

Doc had one other hole card. He knew who they were, but they didn't know him, so he could call out one of their names as if he needed help. He would only use it if he had to, but it was there and if he used that trick, he'd only be able to get one, but leave himself vulnerable to the last Lynch shooter.

But as it happened that ruse didn't have to be used, as Johnny made a nervous mistake when he spotted a shadow moving near the ground, and thought the shooter was taking aim at him. He quickly ripped his Winchester to the shadow and squeezed off his shot, sending his .44 smashing into his brother, Joe, who took the shot just below the throat and fell over backwards.

The flash and report were witnessed by Eddy who hesitated, but finally shouted, "Papa?"

Johnny then responded, asking loudly, "Eddy? Is that you?"

Before Eddy could reply, Doc's Winchester answered with a .44 that punched through Eddy's left side, fracturing two ribs whose jagged ends then rammed into his lung causing it to collapse. He fell to the ground and as he fell, his Winchester's butt slammed into the ground and his head smacked into the barrel, ramming the muzzle into his left eye and crashing through the orbit into his brain.

That left Doc and Johnny as the only two combatants in the yard, and now Johnny knew where Doc was and fired before Eddy even hit the ground.

But Doc wasn't there anymore, having stepped away and levered in new cartridge into his hot carbine. Johnny's shot was still close enough for Doc to hear the hissing sound of the passing bullet, but he didn't take time to thank his lucky stars as he fired just above Johnny's rifle flash, the .44 almost creasing Johnny's front sight before it hit his right cheek, entered his skull and slid along the inside of his left parietal bone and actually rode the inside of the skull's curve like a rolling ball being spun down the inside of a wooden barrel, destroying brain tissue as it spun past before it bounced off a bone fissure and exited the right side of the skull.

Johnny screamed and whirled clockwise screwing himself into the ground.

Doc wasn't sure if that was all of them, so he kept moving and searching for another shooter.

He was still walking when he heard a horse approaching and turned his Winchester in that direction. He couldn't see the rider but obeyed the first rule of using guns in a gunfight: always know your target. He waited and then angered when he recognized Rhonda's curly hair in the subdued light.

He didn't call out to her but released his Winchester's hammer and began to run toward her, but even then used a zigzag just in case he was in someone's sights.

If he was angry with Rhonda before, he was beside himself when she suddenly asked loudly, "Doc?"

He didn't reply, but as soon as he was close enough, he dropped his repeater, jumped and grabbed her by her hand-made blouse and yanked her from the saddle and held onto her as she fell on top of him onto the ground.

Rhonda hadn't seen him coming in the dark, but only heard his footsteps at the last second and was stunned when she suddenly found herself being pulled off her horse.

She screamed as she fell, but then stopped when her breath was blown out and suddenly realized that it was Doc who had pulled her down.

"Rhonda," he loud whispered, "what the hell are you doin'? I told you to stay back!"

She was lying on top of him with her face inches from his when she replied quietly, "I stayed back until the shooting stopped and then I had to make sure you weren't hurt. I'm sorry, Doc."

Doc exhaled and then said softly, "Alright, I suppose it's okay, and I don't think there are any left, but I gotta be sure. See that small house just above your head?"

Rhonda looked up and said, "Yes."

"I want you to walk quickly into the house. There are three dead bodies in there and a woman who was under one of 'em before I killed him. She probably could use your help. Move her to a room away from the bodies and wait for me to yell 'all clear', then you can come to the main house. Got all that?"

"Yes, sir," she said, then added, "I suppose I should get off you now."

"Yes, ma'am."

Rhonda rolled off Doc who then quickly stood, took her hand and helped her up. He kept her hand in his as he reached down, picked up his Winchester and walked with her quickly to the small house.

When they stepped onto the porch, Doc said in a normal voice, "Ma'am, all those bad men are dead, but I gotta be sure. I'm sendin' in Rhonda Byrne to help you while I go and check on the others."

A female voice came from inside the darkness, saying, "Alright," and Doc let go of Rhonda's hand as she stepped past the broken door.

Doc then jogged quickly to the middle-sized house and walked near one of the windows but didn't show himself in the frame in case someone was armed inside.

He shouted, "My name's Doc Holt and I think all the shooters are dead, I'm gonna make sure they're gone, so don't start throwin' shots willy-nilly. I'll call out when I'm sure none of them are alive."

Again, he got a response, only this time a man's voice shouted, "Okay."

After not receiving any gunfire from making the loud announcement, he was positive that there were no more shooters, so he walked with a much more relaxed step toward the main house, but still was leery of any armed defenders in the house.

Just as he had done with the last house, he stopped out front and shouted, "All clear! The shooters are all dead. This is Doc Holt and it's safe to light some lamps. I need to know if there are any wounded and I'll need a lantern to check on all the bodies. Let me know when I can come into the house."

He had to wait a minute before lamps began to spread their light in the house and the reactions to the devastation caused by the attack began.

"My God! They've killed my Ben!" wailed Mrs. Adler as she discovered her husband's body.

Doc didn't wait for an invitation as he trotted up the porch steps and into the house, seeing Nellie Adler over her husband's body on the floor of the main room.

He walked over to her and took a knee before he said, "Mrs. Adler, there's nothin' I can do for your husband. We need to check on the others that might be hurt."

Nellie was still crying as she stood, then backed away from her husband's body and before she could say anything, Doc heard groans coming from the office and told her to stay put while he entered the room then found Lenny on his stomach on the floor, his pants covered in blood.

Doc set his Winchester against the desk then knelt next to Lenny and asked, "Where were you hit?"

"In the butt. The bullet's still in there."

Doc reached over and ripped Lenny's trousers apart then his skivvies as he examined the wound. The bullet must have been a ricochet because it hadn't behaved as a .44 from close range, even after going through a wall would have. It would have gone right through him.

"Okay, it's not too bad. As soon as I make sure nobody else is hurt worse, I'll come back and fix you up. Okay?"

"Okay," Lenny replied as Doc stood, grabbed his Winchester and returned to Mrs. Adler who was weeping as she stood over her husband's body.

When she heard Doc approach, she asked, "Why? Why did they do this?"

"Ma'am, we can talk later, but we need to see if anybody else needs help."

Nellie nodded and slowly turned away and walked out of the main room into the hallway.

They began their search through the bullet-riddled house, first finding Harold and Agnes sitting with their three children, holding onto them and comforting them.

Harold looked at his mother and asked, "Papa?"

Nellie just shook her head and Harold nodded, having heard his father's scream and expecting the worst.

"Is anybody hurt?" asked Doc.

Agnes replied, "No, nobody was hit. Are they all dead?"

"Yes, ma'am. I believe so, but I gotta go out there in a little while to be sure."

Nellie then asked, "What about the rest of our family? Do you know about them?"

"I found two of 'em in the little house tryin' to take advantage of the lady inside, but I don't think they did anythin' before I killed 'em both. There already was a body in there before I made two more. The other house I didn't go into yet, but a man answered when I told him that I thought all the shooters were dead. You got a young man in the office who took a ricochet in the butt, so I gotta take the bullet out and sew that up when I get a chance, but he'll be okay."

Agnes looked up at him and asked, "Who are you? Why did you kill them all?"

Doc replied, "I don't have the time to answer all that right now, ma'am. But Mrs. Adler can answer some of your questions. I need a lantern when I go outside and check on the Lynches."

"*The Lynches did this?*" asked a shocked Harold.

Doc just said, "Talk to Mrs. Adler. I need to go."

He then turned and headed out of the house and as he was leaving, almost banged into a crowd as Richard and Prudence were escorting their three children into the house and Rhonda was entering with Linda.

Doc said loudly, "Everybody inside is okay, except Mister Adler didn't make it and one of the boys took a ricochet in the buttocks. I've gotta go and check on the Lynches to make sure they're not gonna pop back up and start shootin' again."

Richard and Prudence both just nodded and nudged their children into the house, but as soon as they were past, and Doc took a step forward, Linda shot into Doc and latched onto him and began to kiss him all over his face as she cried.

Then she began to say, "Thank you...thank you..." repeatedly.

Doc looked over at Rhonda and just gave her a non-verbal request, so Rhonda pried Linda off Doc, with just a surprising bit of jealousy fueling the strength she didn't really have.

Once free of Linda, Doc nodded to Rhonda then trotted down the porch steps and headed for the barn. Once inside, he lit a match, found the lantern then had to light a second match to set it ablaze.

Then came the grisly discovery of the death that he had delivered to the Lynches and their four ranch hands. He was positive that the two in the smallest house, Whitey and Rex were dead, so he first walked around the big house, where all the Adlers were now huddled and began to examine bodies. Some weren't so bad, but others like Johnny's were hideous, but it was Charlie Lynch's body that was the most unusual due to the exploded ordnance that had been in his right jacket pocket.

After he counted the five Lynches, that left the two other ranch hands, Carl Hanson and Joe Sheraton, who he found outside the middle house.

His last stop was at the small house where he was finally able to find the third body belonging to Linda's husband. He assumed that he had died trying to protect his wife.

With all the bodies accounted for, Doc slowly left the small house and headed back to the barn. He picked up Bride on the way and led her to where he had tied off Trapper, then led them both to the barn. Once inside, he let them both drink from the trough while he searched through the tools and found a pair of needle-nosed pliers and slid them into his pants pocket. It was the best he could do.

He left Bride and Trapper in the barn as he walked with the lantern and his Winchester back to the house, wishing he had availed himself of that nap earlier as his adrenalin began to leave him, and overwhelming exhaustion took its place. But he had more work to do tonight and later this morning as he remembered that it was past midnight and it was a new day.

When he re-entered the house, everyone was in the main room except for Lenny who was waiting for him in the office.

Luckily, Rhonda was explaining to everyone what had happened, so he was able to just pass by and enter the office. Then when he looked at Lenny, he remembered he didn't have a sewing kit, so he gestured with his index finger to tell Lenny he'd be right back, then stuck his head out into the main room.

"Rhonda, I'm gonna need a sewing kit. If somebody could bring me one, I'd appreciate it."

Rhonda stopped in mid-sentence and Linda hopped up, saying, "I'll get one," then trotted out of the main room and disappeared into the hall as Doc returned to the office.

He spotted a nice glass cabinet with some bottles of whiskey inside, so he walked over and pulled one from the shelf and headed for Lenny.

"What's your name?" Doc asked as he pulled a chair next to Lenny and took a seat.

"Lenny. Lenny Adler."

"Lenny, I'm gonna take that bullet out and it's gonna hurt some. Did you want to take a few swigs before I do?"

"No, I'll be okay."

"Good man. Now, this is gonna sting like crazy, so get ready for it."

Lenny nodded and watched as Doc opened the bottle and poured some whiskey onto the open wound that despite the warning, caused Lenny to cry out.

"Sorry," he said with a grimace.

"No, it's okay. Most men cry streams of tears when I do that. You're doin' good, Lenny. Now, let's dig out that .44."

Just as Doc pulled the pliers out of his pocket, Linda entered the room with the sewing kit.

Doc looked up at her and said, "Sorry about your husband, ma'am."

Linda handed him the sewing kit and snapped, "Well, I'm not! That coward was trying to escape through the window leaving me alone in the house when he was shot," then she added for good measure, "and he wasn't good in bed, either."

Doc just replied, "Thanks for the sewing kit, ma'am. If you could, I'll need a needle threaded with some heavy thread while I dig out the bullet."

Lenny was embarrassed to have his naked butt and his privates displayed while Linda was there, even if she wasn't paying much attention to him as she pulled out a needle and some black thread.

While she threaded the needle, Doc poured more whiskey over the pliers, hoping it would be enough.

"Okay, Lenny, here's where it's really gonna hurt while I dig out that bullet, but if you're lucky, it won't take me long."

Lenny forgot about his embarrassment and looked away.

Normally, Doc would have cut away some of the surrounding muscle tissue to make removal of the bullet easier, but he didn't know how much longer he could stay focused, so he just spread the tissue apart with the tips of the pliers and dug them into the muscle until he found the bullet's base and pushed the tips around the bullet as Lenny made noises that didn't quite make it to screams but were well beyond moans.

Doc had a good grip on the bullet but instead of working it out slowly, he gave it a quick yank as if he was pulling a tooth and popped the projectile free then dropped it on the floor.

"You're doing good, Lenny. The bullet's out, now I've gotta get the cloth from your pants outta there. This won't be so bad."

Doc slid the plier's nose back into the wound until it reached the bottom then pulled the jaws back slightly, opened them and pushed them down a bit before closing them and pulling them back out and saw the bloody cloth on the tips. He set the pliers down and without warning Lenny again, poured some more whiskey onto the wound, which did generate a scream from Lenny.

"Okay, Lenny, it's all clean now, so all I gotta do is throw on a couple of stitches and you'll be done."

Linda held out the threaded needle to Doc, who accepted it without comment and quickly sutured the wound closed and tied it off.

"Lenny, now you gotta be careful, for a while. You can walk real slow, but it'll be okay in a week or so, but the sutures gotta come out in a couple of weeks. Okay?"

"Okay," Lenny said as he felt relief that it was over, then asked, "Why did they do this?"

Before he could answer, Linda replied, "One of them thought I was a Jewess. Why would he think that?"

Doc had no idea what the cause of the suspicion was, so all he could say was, "I have no idea, ma'am. All I know is that Charlie Lynch and some others around here don't like anybody who ain't like them. When I warned Mister Adler about them earlier today, I couldn't figure out why they said they were gonna come here either."

"You knew they were coming?" Linda asked in shock.

"Yes, ma'am. One of the Double L ranch hands rode out to Mrs. Byrne's ranch today to take over the place after they killed her husband and the ranch hands six weeks ago and I had to shoot him to keep him from hurtin' her. He told me before he died that they were gonna attack this ranch, but he didn't say when. So, me and Mrs. Byrne came over here this mornin' and told him and Mrs. Adler about it, but Mister Adler must've thought I was lyin' or somethin', 'cause he didn't even set up a night watch like I told him he should. He said he needed the men out in the field."

Doc's statement stunned Lenny and Linda both, and they were both still silently digesting that revelation as Doc stood, picked up his Winchester, then blew out the lantern, leaving it and the pliers on the desk before returning to the main room.

Rhonda looked at him and said, "Doc, everyone else is okay. They're just shaken."

Doc nodded and said, "I left a real mess out there that needs cleanin' up. Now, the second problem I just made was that I left the Double L without a single man to help Mrs. Lynch or Beth. I don't think either of them knew what was goin' on, but I need to borrow a wagon and get those bodies all loaded onto it and covered with a tarp.

"I'll drive it to the Double L when the sun comes up in four or five hours and tell Mrs. Lynch what happened. I'm not gonna like doin' it either. She and Beth are two fine, soft-hearted women and it's gonna hurt 'em really bad."

"I'll help with the bodies, Mister Holt," Harold said as he stood.

"Me, too," said Richard, "I'll go and harness the wagon."

"I appreciate it," he said then looked at Rhonda and said, "Rhonda, I left Bride and Trapper in the barn. You don't have to come to the Double L. I'll come back with the empty wagon when I'm finished."

"No, Doc, I'll come," Rhonda replied.

Doc nodded and said, "Okay. We should have 'em all loaded in an hour or so."

"I'll make some coffee," said Prudence as she stood.

Doc walked to the office, lit the lantern again, then carried it and his Winchester back out of the house following Richard and Harold Adler to the barn.

Even though Rhonda had told everyone what had happened, they both had a lot questions for Doc, which he answered as they prepared to move the bodies.

146

It took them over an hour to gather the nine corpses and fill the bed of the wagon then cover them with a tarp.

"We need to bury papa and Robert," Harold said to Richard.

"As far as I'm concerned," Richard replied, "Robert can rot out in the open. You heard what Linda said. The bastard left her to die to save his own skin."

Harold said, "We don't have to bury him in the family cemetery, Richard, but I sure don't want to let him stink up the place."

"Okay, we'll dig a hole for him after we bury papa."

Then Doc said, "I wonder where they put their horses. They've gotta be around here somewhere, and it wasn't east, so I'm guessin' that they're out near the access road somewhere. I'm gonna drive the wagon out that way and if I find 'em, I'll trail hitch 'em to the back of the wagon."

"You go ahead, Doc. We're going to go back to the house to talk to our wives before we dig those graves," said Richard.

"Alright," Doc replied as he stepped into the wagon seat and had it moving as the brothers returned to the house.

Thirty minutes later, with the sky lightening with the pre-dawn, Doc drove the wagon to the house trailing nine horses and stopped before the front porch.

He stepped down, leaving his Winchester on the seat as he wearily walked toward the house, stepped up onto the porch and headed to the open door where he stuck his head inside and found only Rhonda waiting, but even she was asleep on the couch. He didn't know where everyone else had gone, and he didn't smell any coffee, so he guessed everyone had just returned to bed after their own adrenalin levels dropped back to normal.

Doc wanted to sleep himself so badly that he ached, but instead, walked slowly to the sleeping Rhonda and took a knee where her head lay atop her bent arm.

"Rhonda," he whispered, "are you still coming to the Double L?"

She didn't stir, so Doc stood looked down at her peaceful face then backstepped quietly, turned and left the room.

He climbed back into the seat of the wagon, released the handbrake and flicked the reins. The two draft horses strained to overcome the wagon's inertia, then began to pull the body-loaded wagon back down the access road. It would add a mile or so to the trip, but he decided it would be easier on the team if they stuck to the road rather than cut cross country. The last thing he wanted was to be stranded in a field with a bunch of dead bodies.

He had to keep from nodding off as the wagon trundled eastward toward the Double L, wondering just how bad it was going to be for Martha and Beth. He knew it would come as complete shock but hoped that they had at least some inkling that that the men of the family were up to no good.

Then there were the other issues involving the sheriff and the other ranches that participated in the raids. He knew about Bill Wheeler but was vague on any others. Bill Wheeler owned the Bar W southeast of the Double L and was almost as big as the Lynch spread, and Doc was sure that he was the main cog in the hate machine.

When he thought of what he had just done in the past twenty-four hours, he found it amazingly foggy. He had killed a man he had respected for years, his three sons, made his wife and daughter both widows and killed five men he thought of as friends, yet he felt no guilt whatsoever, despite having shot some of them in the back and one at very short range.

His biggest concern now was for Martha and Beth. *How could they cope with the Double L without a single man around to help?* It was like Rhonda's problem only much worse except, of course, that neither of them had been raped multiple times and beaten nearly to death.

They would be alone with a large herd and a very nice house which would open them to all sorts of miscreants trying to take advantage of the situation, though. He needed to come up with a solution to prevent that from happening and began to think about asking Rhonda to move into the Double L ranch house, so he could keep watch on all three of the women until he could come up with a better plan.

It was the aspect of range wars or gun battles like this that no one talks about; the aftermath when all the widows and orphans are left to cope with the dangers of life without protection. Doc knew it was up to him now to provide that protection. At least the Adler family was mostly intact. He knew that if the patriarch had just listened to him and stationed a lookout, everything would have been far different. A single warning shot fired by a lookout would probably have sent the Lynches scurrying back to the Double L and everyone would still be alive when the sun rose.

The other angle about the attack that really bothered him was the Jewish accusation. Someone had thrown that at Charlie Lynch, and he'd believed it without question, risking his entire family without so much as asking Ben Adler if it was true, not that it should have made any difference if it was or not.

But the fact that Charlie hadn't even verified the accuracy of the rumor bothered him a lot. *So, all it would take to go out and murder an entire family was just some loose gossip? Then after they ran out of Jews, coloreds, Irish, Catholics and Indians, who was next? Did they progress to Episcopalians or those with green eyes? When did it end?*

The constant whirring of Doc's mind ate up the time while the sun flooded into his eyes as he drove the wagon east.

―――――

Rhonda's eyes flickered open as the sun blazed through the open window into her face. It was day and Doc was nowhere in sight. *Where was he?*

Everyone else was still sleeping as she popped up from the couch and trotted out of the still open front door into the clear morning. She scanned the area and didn't see a wagon or any of the bodies. She hurriedly jogged down to the front yard and headed for the barn, neglecting the privy for more urgent business.

She spotted Bride and Trapper inside and then made her rapid trip to the privy, returning three minutes later.

She quickly mounted Bride, leaving Trapper in the barn, walked her out of the barn and toward the access road where she spotted the fresh wagon tracks going east on the road with a large number of hoofprints. Doc had gone without bringing her along for some reason.

She urged Bride into a fast trot and followed the roadway to the Double L.

―――――

Doc reached the Double L, pulled out his pocket watch and found it was 7:25, so he assumed that someone was awake, then he remembered Fred Richards, the cook was still there and was probably already up cooking and wondering where everyone was. Doc wasn't sure how much Fred knew about the raids, but he was pretty sure that Fred knew as much as he had. He had never even been invited along as he was just the cook, and Doc had never gotten his opinion of the nighttime visits.

Sure enough, Doc picked up smoke from the cookhouse stack, but he needed to see Martha and Beth before he even talked to Fred, so he kept the wagon heading for the large ranch house.

It seemed as if it had been years since he'd exited the house with his three twenty-dollar-bills to ride back to the Circle B, but it had only been four days now. Less than ninety-six-hours ago, he'd found Rhonda Byrne face down on the ground, and now everything had changed.

He pulled the wagon to a halt in front of the house, set the hand brake and stepped down, again leaving his Winchester on the seat. The other Winchesters, including the one with the shattered stock were in the bed with the bodies. Each man still had his gunbelt and revolver, and whatever had been in his pockets when they rode out of the Double L the night before was still there. Even their hats were in the back.

He stepped up onto the porch, removed his own Stetson, checked to make sure he didn't have any blood on his clothes, then knocked loudly on the door.

Inside the ranch house, Martha and Beth were having coffee, both very concerned about the absence of their men, yet neither knew that the ranch hands were gone as well.

When they heard the knock on the door, they both set their coffee cups on the table and walked quickly down the hall and crossed the huge main room. It was Beth who opened the door and saw Doc Holt standing before her.

She smiled widely and said, "Doc, what a pleasant surprise to see you again. What brings you here? I hope you don't need to see my father. We don't know where he, my brothers or my husband are."

"May I come in, please, Beth?" Doc asked.

"Of course," she replied as she stepped back to let him pass, noticing that he had called her Beth again and wondered why he had dropped the formal Mrs. Smith.

Once he was inside, Beth closed the door and followed Doc to the sitting area, where she and her mother took a seat.

Doc had been running through different ways to tell them since he'd left the Adler ranch, and none had sounded right, so he just began with a question.

"Beth, Mrs. Lynch, do you know why I quit the Double L?"

"No, Doc. We were wondering what could have made you leave. You seemed happy here and we all liked you," Martha replied.

Doc paused and asked, "Ma'am, do you know what Charlie and the others were doin' when they left the ranch some of those nights over the past few months?"

"No, we assumed they were out having one of those boy shindigs that men seem to enjoy."

"Well, Mrs. Lynch, they were sorta shindigs, but they weren't much fun for some of your neighbors. A few days ago, I was ridin' north lookin' for strays and came across a starvin' young woman on the ground. She and her husband had two hands on the Circle B, just up north. You probably never met the Byrnes."

"No, but I knew of their ranch."

"Well, it seems that six weeks ago, some men descended on that ranch after dark and shot and killed her husband and the two ranch hands and then they all raped her and then beat her almost to death, leavin' her for dead."

Both women could already see where Doc was going but didn't say anything as their minds and stomachs churned.

"Now, you both know that I didn't go with the boys on those night visits, but that doesn't make me innocent of what they were doin'. They'd come back and brag about it, but I didn't say a damned word, and that made me just as guilty as all of 'em. But when I found Mrs. Byrne out there in that open ground almost dyin', it kinda woke me up. I knew I had to do somethin', so I quit this job and took care of Mrs. Byrne, feeding her to get her strength up."

Martha asked quietly, "Doc, where is my husband and our sons?"

"Mrs. Lynch, two days ago, Lou Robinson came to the Circle B to try and claim it 'cause he thought it was empty, but when he saw Mrs. Byrne, he chased her down like she was a stray calf, and I shot him. He told me that Charlie and the boys were gonna visit the Adlers soon. So, I went and told Mister Adler that they'd be comin', but he didn't believe me. So, I hung around the ranch after dark, and was headin' back to the Circle B around midnight when your husband and the others showed up at the Slash A and they all started shootin' up the ranch houses

153

with their Winchesters. I had to stop 'em, Mrs. Lynch. They were shootin' at women and children. I had no choice."

Martha nodded slowly and whispered, "Is my husband dead, Doc?"

"They're all dead, Mrs. Lynch. I've got their bodies all outside in the back of the wagon under that tarp. I wish Mister Adler had done what I told him and put out a night watch. Just a single warning shot woulda sent them back to the Double L, but once they started shootin', I had to stop 'em."

Neither woman shed a single tear as they both stared at Doc.

"Did they kill anyone, Doc?" Martha asked.

"Ben Adler and his son-in-law were killed, and one of his boys was wounded, but no one else was hurt."

Martha looked up at the ceiling for a few seconds, then looked back at Doc and said, "I don't blame you, Doc. I'm just so shaken that this could have gone on without me suspecting anything. I guess they went out of their way to hide it," then she turned to Beth and asked, "Did you have any idea, Beth?"

Beth nodded and said, "More than you, Mama. Ned would come back sometimes, and he was all excited and I asked him why he was acting this way and he just laughed and said it was better when they fought. After that, I began paying more attention to what was going on and I began to suspect what they were doing, but even I didn't think it had gone this far. Doc, how many families have they murdered?"

"I'm not sure, Beth. It only started about three months ago, and I only know what Charlie did. Bill Wheeler is the one who started him down this road along with Sheriff Olsen. There are others involved, but I think Bill Wheeler is the center of it."

"What can we do, Doc? What about the bodies?" asked Martha.

"Well, there are nine of 'em, and the best thing would be to take them to Comanche, but that would alert the sheriff, which I suppose is only a matter of time anyway. I'm most worried about you and Beth. I put you in a bad spot with no men around to protect you, other than Fred, and I don't think Fred knows what end of a gun the bullet comes out. With a big herd like you have and the big house and with you both bein' pretty ladies, I'm really worried about what kind of men would come out here when they know you're alone."

"We'll worry about that when we have to, Doc. I'll tell you what we'll do. Beth and I will come with you when you drive the wagon to Comanche. You can drive it straight to the mortician's and we'll arrange for the burials. Then we'll walk with you to the sheriff's office and back whatever you tell him."

Doc nodded and was about to ask a question when Beth interrupted, surprising Doc as she said, "I should have married you and not Ned, Doc."

Doc looked over at Beth and smiled before saying, "No, Beth, you need a good man who will treat you like the princess you are, not some ignorant cow hand."

Martha didn't comment but said, "Doc, you look exhausted. Are you sure you're up to doing this right now?"

"It's gotta be done, ma'am. Now's as good a time as any."

"We've already eaten. Have you had anything yet, Doc?"

"No, ma'am, but I'm fine. I'd just as soon get this done, but I can grab somethin' when I go over and talk to Fred. I'll be ready to roll in ten minutes if that's okay."

"Beth and I will get ready," Martha said as she stood.

Doc and Beth both rose, and he smiled weakly at them before he turned and left the room.

After he was gone, Martha looked at her daughter and said, "We should have seen this coming, Beth."

Beth replied, "I almost hoped it would, Mama. I'm sad that it had to happen this way, but I was so worried about what Ned was doing that I prayed that he'd die. Is that a horrible thing to say?"

"No, Beth. When men do something as evil as they did, all we can hope for is that there is an avenging angel out there to stop it. In this case, He sent Doc Holt."

Beth looked out the open door, sighed and followed her mother into their rooms to change for the ride into Comanche.

———

Doc walked into the chow house and spotted Fred Richards sitting at the table drinking coffee. He looked up when he heard Doc enter and grinned.

"Doc! Are you back now?" he asked.

"I don't know where I am, Fred. Can I grab somethin'? I'm hungry enough to eat a mule."

"Go ahead, none of the fellers showed up this mornin'. I guess they're still out havin' a good time."

Doc tossed some bacon and a pile of scrambled eggs on a plate and filled a large mug with hot coffee before taking a seat across from Fred.

"Fred, do you know what the boys and the Lynches were doin' when they went out on those rides?"

While Fred made a face, Doc began shoveling eggs into his mouth.

"Kinda. Some of the boys bragged about stuff and I wasn't sure if they was serious or not."

Doc swallowed his eggs, took a sip of the scalding coffee, then replied, "They were very serious. Fred, they were out murderin' and rapin' those nights tryin' to rid Texas of anybody they didn't like. Last night, they went over to the Adler ranch thinkin' they were Jews somehow and nine of 'em began shootin' up the ranch houses that had women and children inside."

Then after taking a deep breath, he exclaimed, "They were shootin' kids, Fred! I caught up with 'em with my Winchester while they were firin' and they didn't even know I was shootin' at 'em because so many Winchesters were goin' off. I killed every mother's son of 'em, Fred. The only two men on the Double L now are sittin' right here."

He took a big bite of bacon watching for Fred's reaction.

Fred exhaled, slowly shook his head and said, "I shoulda known, Doc. I shoulda said somethin', but I didn't. I was too afraid."

"Well, don't feel bad, Fred. I knew a lot more and I didn't do a damned thing either, because I told myself it wasn't my business. But when I found Mrs. Byrne north of here almost dyin', I knew it was my business. Now, me, Mrs. Lynch and Beth are gonna drive that wagon load of bodies down to Comanche. Sheriff Olsen was in on it with 'em and so is Ed Wheeler. In fact, he's the big boss in all this, I reckon.

"Fred, it's up to you and me to set this right. I ain't askin' you to get involved in the shootin', and I hope I can get this cleaned up without pullin' one more trigger, but Mrs. Lynch is gonna need our help."

Fred nodded and said, "I'll do anything you need, Doc. I'm glad you stopped 'em."

Then Doc asked, "Fred, do you know why they thought the Adlers were Jews?"

He shrugged and said, "Joe Sheraton told Rex that he'd seen Lenny out swimmin' and he was fixed the way Jews do."

"Oh, that kinda explains it, but I'm here to tell you that it isn't true. I had to pull a bullet out of Lenny's behind and he wasn't trimmed at all."

"I wonder why Joe lied about it."

"He musta had somethin' against Lenny and figured it would be a way to pay him back, but it kinda backfired on him."

"Yeah, it did."

"Fred, after we're gone, can you unsaddle the nine horses they rode in on and leave 'em with the remuda?"

"I'll do 'er, Doc," Fred answered.

Doc then smiled at Fred, quickly finished his breakfast, stood and lightly tapped Fred on the back before leaving the chow house and walking quickly back to the house.

———

Fifteen minutes later, after leaving the horses with Fred, Doc was driving the wagon back down the access road with Martha on his left and Beth on his right.

Just before the wagon reached the end of the road, Doc spotted a rider coming from the west and knew who it was the moment he spotted the red hair positively exploding in the morning sun.

"There comes Rhonda," Doc said as he pulled the horses to a stop and waited for her to arrive.

Beth was very interested in Rhonda as she slowed Bride to a stop near the wagon, and Rhonda was very interested in Beth as well.

"Doc, you didn't wake me. I thought you said I'd be coming along?"

"I asked you, Rhonda, but you were asleep and didn't answer me, and you looked so peaceful, I couldn't wake you up."

"Well, I'm here now. What do you need me to do?"

Doc then said, "Rhonda, this is Mrs. Lynch on my left and her daughter Beth on my right. Ladies, the red-headed lady ridin' the pretty filly is Mrs. Rhonda Byrne of the Circle B. Now, we're going to drive down to Comanche to leave the bodies at the mortician. Do you want to come along, or do you want to get somethin' to eat? I'm guessin' that you kinda rushed outta the house to hunt me down and didn't get any food into that shrunken stomach of yours. Is that right?"

"Yes, that's right, but I can get something in Comanche. I'll just ride alongside."

"It'll take a few hours, Rhonda, are you sure? I don't want to see you fall from Bride."

'I won't fall. You look as if you're ready to fall over, though."

"Well, if I fall over into those horses' behinds, it'll be 'cause I earned it."

He flicked the reins and the wagon set off south on the long journey to Comanche.

As Rhonda walked Bride on the right side of the wagon, she couldn't help but notice Beth Lynch sitting right up against Doc and didn't like it one bit. She had been irritated enough with Linda's display earlier in the day back at the Adler ranch, but this was much worse. Not only was Beth sitting close to him, she was probably six or seven years younger than she was and probably even prettier. Not only that, Beth hadn't lost any weight like she had, and it was noticeable. But Doc didn't seem to be paying her any attention, so she'd live with it, but she did wish she'd thought to bring Trapper along so he could ride rather than drive and sit next to Beth.

After driving for an hour, Doc began to nod off and found himself blinking to stay awake in the rising heat and the boredom of the clopping hooves and the creaking wheels. He seriously began thinking of just crawling onto the tarp and catching some sleep.

"Doc," Rhonda asked loudly, "Are you going to be able to stay awake much longer?"

Doc snapped out of his haze, turned to Rhonda and replied, "Just another two hours, Rhonda. How were the Adlers when you left?"

"They were all still sleeping. Richard and Harold buried their father in the family cemetery and just dug a hole for Linda's husband, Robert. I guess they weren't too happy with him for leaving her on the floor and trying to escape out the back window."

"I found out why Charlie attacked the Adlers. It sounds like Joe Sheraton had a grudge against Lenny Adler and told the foreman that he was Jewish, and they bought into it. Just one lie and it cost eleven men their lives."

Martha snapped her head to look at him and said, "Doc, tell me that they didn't do this because they thought the Adlers were Jewish! Please!"

"That's what I was told, ma'am. They attacked Rhonda's ranch 'cause she was a Yankee, Irish and a Catholic. They aim to get rid of anybody they don't think belongs here."

"If he was that upset about it, why didn't he just go and talk to Ben Adler?"

"I got no idea, Mrs. Lynch. This whole thing is just crazy beyond any kinda explainin'."

————

It was nearly noon when the wagon lumbered into the streets of Comanche. No one knew what was under the tarp, so there was no clump of spectators as it rolled down the main street and then turned behind Farley Brothers Mortuary.

Beth stepped down then Doc followed while Martha climbed down from the other side. Rhonda had stopped out front, slowly dismounted from Bride after the very long ride and walked to the back after tying her off at the front hitchrail. She desperately wanted to rub her sore backside, but didn't want to bring that kind of attention to herself in front of Doc, not with Beth standing so close.

Doc held the door while the three women entered then followed them inside where they were met by Henry Farley, the older of the two brothers.

"How can I be of service," he asked Doc.

"Last night, nine men attacked the Adler ranch. I arrived and wound up shooting all nine of 'em. I got their bodies out in a wagon outside. I need to arrange for their burials. Mrs. Lynch is the widow of one of them and the mother of three of the others. She'll tell you what she needs."

Henry blinked twice when Doc finished then slowly turned to face Mrs. Lynch and said, "I'm sorry for your loss, Mrs. Lynch. What would you have us do for your husband and sons?"

"I'd like to have them buried in the family cemetery on the Double L. The other four, and Mister Holt will point out which ones, can be buried in the town cemetery."

Then she turned to Beth and simply asked, "Ned?"

"He can be buried with the ranch hands," she said without a hint of emotion.

Doc waited while Henry wrote some things down then asked, "Mrs. Lynch, how would you like the memorial stones to read?"

Martha sighed, and for the first time, as he handed her a pencil and paper, tears began to roll down her face as she began to write. It took her ten minutes to finish writing then she stepped back and looked at Doc.

"Doc, I'd rather not look at them. Could you do that for me, please?"

"Yes, ma'am. Why don't you ladies all go over to the café and get somethin' to eat? I'll be along when this is done."

"Thank you, Doc," Martha said, which was echoed by Beth.

Henry Farley then told Martha that they'd be able to bring her husband's and sons' bodies back to the Double L for burial around one o'clock the day after tomorrow. Martha nodded, took Beth's arm, then the two women turned and left the mortuary.

Rhonda looked at Doc, smiled slightly then followed Martha and Beth out the door.

When they were gone, Henry accompanied Doc out the back door to the wagon with his brother Edwin following.

Doc pulled back the tarp and almost lost his breakfast, seeing them stacked up like cordwood in the bright noonday sun.

The Farley brothers were nonplussed and asked Doc to identify each man which he did as Edwin wrote a short note and put it in each man's pocket.

"What about the guns, Mister Holt?" Henry asked.

"Leave 'em on the bed. Can you give me a cost for the burials?"

Edwin looked at the bodies and then said, "Three hundred and twenty dollars."

"Okay, I'll go over to the bank and get the money and I'll be back after I go and see Sheriff Olsen."

"We'll begin moving the bodies to our shop," Henry said as Edwin finished putting his identifying notes on the bodies.

"I'll be back as soon as I can," Doc said before he turned, walked out onto the main street and then headed for the sheriff's office.

Doc was so dog-tired that he almost didn't care what the sheriff said. He might be able to say something about the one who had bullet holes in the back, but Doc knew that there would be no way to admit that one man had killed nine men in a gunfight and not say it was self-defense and yet, stranger things had happened.

He decided to visit the sheriff before he went to the bank, just in case he didn't get to leave the jail.

Doc walked into the sheriff's office three minutes later and found Deputy Sheriff Malcolm Lionel behind the desk reading a dime novel.

"Deputy, I just dropped off nine bodies at the Farley Brothers and need to talk to Sheriff Olsen.'

Deputy Lionel set his book down, looked at Doc and started to laugh.

"That's a good one. Did you shoot 'em all or make 'em laugh to death?"

"I shot 'em. I was sleepin' in the barn at the Adler ranch last night 'cause I was gonna ask Ben Adler for a job when right around midnight, a regular drumroll of Winchester fire woke me up and I saw a bunch of fellers in the dark shootin' into the houses they got out there. Now, I didn't know who they were, so I grabbed my Winchester '73 and ran out there and started pickin' 'em off. I mean, there wasn't even any gunfire comin' back at 'em.

"So, I commenced to just shootin' the bastards figurin' they were some kind of gang or somethin'. It wasn't till I got 'em all that I found it was Charlie Lynch and his boys that was doin' the shootin'. They killed Ben Adler and wounded his son, Lenny, but everybody else come out okay. I felt really bad for shootin' 'em, but they didn't have any right to be shootin' away at the houses like that, not with all the women and children inside."

Deputy Lionel's eyes were wide open when Doc finished when he realized that this was no joke.

"Hang on, let me get the sheriff. He's in his office."

Doc stood there waiting for Joe Olsen to come out, knowing his story would be hard to disprove, although he'd like to get back to the Adler place and fill them in on what he had said officially.

Sheriff Joe Olsen walked out quickly behind Deputy Lionel, almost completely hidden by his much larger deputy. Joe Olsen may have been the smallest lawman in Texas at only five feet and an inch and no more than a hundred and twenty pounds and tried to make up for his lack of stature by wearing the tallest heels he could put on a pair of boots and combing his hair high. He also tended to be overbearing to compensate.

"What's this you're sayin, Holt?" he asked when Deputy Lionel turned and sat behind his desk.

Doc repeated the story to the sheriff and Doc could see the wheels spinning in his head. Doc could tell that Charlie Lynch hadn't told the sheriff about this raid just by the look of surprise on his face.

"They were just shootin' into the house?" he asked.

"Yes, sir. Except I did find two of 'em in the smallest house gettin' ready to rape Mister Adler's daughter."

"And they're all dead? Every single one of them?" he asked in disbelief.

"Yes, sir. See, when I got there, they were so busy shootin' into the houses, they didn't notice that somebody was shootin' back until there was only a couple left. I felt really bad about it, Sheriff. Why would a good man like Charlie Lynch and the boys all start shootin' up another fine feller like Ben Adler?"

The sheriff shook his head and said, "I got no idea. Does Mrs. Lynch know?"

"Yes, sir. I stopped by and told her and Beth this mornin' before comin' here. They came along in case you wanted to talk to 'em. They're over at the diner right now."

"She lost her husband and all her sons in one night. That's downright terrible. Terrible! How are she and Beth takin' it?"

"Better'n I figured they would. They seemed to kinda expect it for some reason, and that don't make a lot of sense to me. Why would they think somethin' like this would happen?"

"I don't know. Tell you what, Holt, you go ahead and write up what happened. Don't make it too long. I'll call it justifiable homicide and let 'er go, but don't go runnin' around talkin' about it."

"No, sir. The less I think about what happened, the better I like it."

"Good. Malcolm, get Mister Holt here some paper and pencil so he can write his report."

"Yes, sir," Deputy Lionel said as he opened the drawer, pulled out two sheets of paper and a pencil and handed them to Doc.

———

Twenty minutes later, Doc left the sheriff's office, stopped at the bank and withdrew three hundred dollars, then went to the Farley Brothers and paid the bill, which turned out to be $248.22 after subtracting all the money that had been recovered from the bodies.

The guns were all in the bed of the wagon as Doc pulled out from behind the mortuary and drove to the diner, hopped down and walked inside.

Rhonda waved him over to their table, so he headed that way and took a seat.

"What happened?" asked Martha.

"I told the sheriff what happened, but I acted like I didn't know why they went to the Adlers and told him I was sleepin' in the barn when they showed up. I was kinda surprised 'cause I kinda figured your husband woulda told him that I didn't go with the other fellers but knew what was happenin'. Anyway, he didn't seem to care much but he was kinda surprised that they attacked the Adlers. I reckon he hadn't been told about that one. Other than that, it was a straight story. He asked how you and Beth were doin' and called it justifiable homicide, then I wrote my statement and came back."

He gave his order to the waitress before Rhonda asked, "What do we do now?"

"That's a good question. I reckon that the sheriff is gonna be out of here like a shot and run over to the Bar W to tell Bill Wheeler what happened. Maybe they'll call it off after all this, but I don't think so. I think they're too crazy to do somethin' that smart."

"They're going to look for you, aren't they?" Rhonda asked.

"I'm not sure. It all depends on how much of my story the sheriff swallowed. But I know one thing for sure, they're not gonna go out on any night visits anymore. They're gonna try somethin' different. I just don't know what it will be."

Then he looked at Martha and said, "Ma'am, I want to let you know that I don't think that Charlie was his normal self. I think that Bill Wheeler kinda got him all twisted up. He was a good man 'til all this started happenin'."

"I know, Doc, but that's no excuse for what he did."

Doc nodded before Beth said, "Don't try to make Ned into anything more than he was, Doc. I know he was a weak, shallow man. Everything that Ned was could be seen on the outside and I found that out much too late."

Doc couldn't respond to what Beth had said because he knew it was true.

Then Martha said, "I forgot to ask Henry Farley about the bill."

Doc replied, "It's taken care of, ma'am."

Martha shook her head and said, "That's not right, Doc. That's my responsibility."

Doc replied, "I put 'em there, ma'am, and I should pay for 'em."

———

An hour later, the wagon was rolling north again, trailing Bride as the three women sat in the driver's seat with Martha driving. Doc was stretched out on the bed with eight working Winchesters and nine gunbelts with assorted revolvers chambered for three different cartridges and two percussion revolvers. He had his Stetson pulled over his eyes and Bride's bedroll under his head.

———

As soon as he watched the wagon taking the north road out of Comanche, Sheriff Olsen walked out of his office, mounted his horse and rode east to the Bar W to tell Bill Wheeler what had happened.

Deputy Lionel had watched him leave and was more than mildly irritated by the sheriff's sudden disappearances without a word of explanation. One of these days, he'd trail the sheriff and find out what he was up to. He knew that the sheriff played favorites, and that wasn't exactly unique to Joe Olsen, but sometimes it was beyond just playing favorites.

———

With Doc asleep, Beth said, "Mama, Doc was right when he said we had a problem with no men around except for Fred. I think we should hire him back and make him the ranch manager, so he could hire some ranch hands and run the ranch for us. He could live in the house, too. We have the room."

Martha suspected that Beth had another reason for the suggestion, but knew it was a good one nonetheless, "I agree, Beth. When he's awake, I'll ask him."

Rhonda was knocked off-kilter by Beth's comment. She hadn't even thought that Doc would leave the Circle B but should have recognized the possibility. He'd worked at the Double L for six years and the only reason he'd gone was because of his disagreement over the men's nighttime activities, and that was over. *How could he turn down an opportunity to not only take control of the ranch, make more money, and live in a big house with Beth so obviously angling for his attention? What incentive did he have to stay at her small ranch with a miniscule herd and nothing but hard work?*

So, Rhonda said nothing as the wagon bounced along the crude roadway back to the Double L.

The wagon pulled back into the Double L just before five-thirty, and just as it came to a stop, Rhonda took it on herself to wake up Doc before Beth could.

"Doc, we've arrived at the Double L," she said loudly as she rocked his shoulder.

Doc shook his head and then slowly sat up and pulled on his hat before standing on the wagon's bed, then taking two steps and hopped to the ground and walked around Bride, patting her on her flank as he did.

"Mrs. Lynch, I've gotta take this wagon back to the Adlers and get Trapper. Where did you want me to leave the guns?"

"You take care of that, Doc. I don't care what you do with them."

"I'll go and leave 'em in the bunkhouse for now. The Winchesters all need a good cleanin'."

Then he turned to Rhonda and asked, "Rhonda, why don't you head for the ranch house and I'll be along in a couple of hours."

"Okay, Doc," she replied as she stepped down from the wagon, walked back to Bride then stepped into the saddle and rode off without so much as a wave, believing that by the time he returned, if he returned, he'd be telling her that he was moving into the Double L ranch house with the new young widow.

Doc was surprised she hadn't asked to come with him when he rode to the Adlers and had no idea of the reason for her abrupt departure.

After Martha and Beth stepped to the ground, Martha said, "Doc, I need to talk to you about the Double L when you have a chance. I know you still have things to do, but could you stop by tomorrow morning?"

"Yes, ma'am. I'll do that."

Beth smiled at him and said, "I'll see you tomorrow then, Doc."

Doc smiled back before replying, "I'll see you then, Beth," before climbing aboard the wagon and turning it toward the bunkhouse as the two women returned to the big house.

After unloading all the weapons, Doc turned the empty wagon down the access road then westward toward the Slash A ranch.

As he drove the wagon, he concentrated on what he could expect from Bill Wheeler and the sheriff. He was pretty sure that the sheriff viewed him as just another cowhand who happened to be in the right spot at the wrong time and nothing more. But men like Bill Wheeler, who seemed to suspect the worst of every man might not. He had to operate on the assumption that Bill Wheeler would see him as the enemy and take steps to eliminate him.

That meant he'd have to do the impossible. He'd have to protect Rhonda and now the two women at the Double L without actually staying in either location unless he could convince Rhonda to move to the big Double L ranch house and stay with Martha and Beth. He may not have understood the reason, but even he could detect the coldness between Beth and Rhonda and wished he understood women better.

———

"All of them?" exclaimed Bill Wheeler, *"He shot all of them?"*

"Yes, sir," replied Sheriff Olsen, "Just bad luck. He was sleeping in the barn when he heard the Winchesters. With the dark night, and with them not suspecting that there would be anyone outside shooting at them, he was able to just start picking them off."

"That's impossible, Joe. I don't care how damned lucky he was. One ignorant cow hand doesn't shoot and kill nine men by himself. I'll bet he found out somehow about Charlie's raid, warned Adler and they opened up on Charlie and his boys as soon as they arrived."

"I don't think so, Mister Wheeler. He told me what happened, and I think he was telling the truth. How come you and Mister Lynch set this up without even warning me?"

"I didn't think he'd go so soon. Did you know that Adler is a Jew?"

The sheriff's eyebrows shot up as he said, "Ben Adler, a Jew? No, sir! I can't believe it. I've known him for eight years."

"Well, he was. One of Charlie's ranch hands saw one of the Adler boys at the swimming hole and he'd been circumcised."

"Well, I'll be. A Jew right under our very noses. How come Charlie's ranch hand never said anything about it before? Why did he hold back that little tidbit?"

"I've got no idea. They're all dead now, so we'll never know. Let's get back to talking about Doc Holt. Despite your belief that he was telling the truth, that makes no sense. Charlie told me that he wouldn't go on any of the raids and was even thinking of firing him, so that part of his story checks out.

"But if he got wind of the night visit before they left the Double L, then he'd go running to the Adlers and warn the Sons of Abraham. Hell, I wouldn't be surprised if he wasn't a Jew himself. What kind of a name is Holt, anyway? Maybe it's short for Holtenstein or something. What I need you to do is to go out to the Double L and then the Adler place and talk to Martha Lynch and Nellie Adler and get their stories. Women don't lie as well as men."

"I wouldn't say that. Some of them can pull it off better than we can. They can distract us, too."

"Just ask those questions tomorrow and come back and tell me what you find. Check the Adler place and see if the buildings were all shot up, too. If Holt warned them, there won't be any bullet holes. I'm going to have Will Hatfield and Mike Green come to the house tomorrow and we're going to have to come up with a change in strategy, including dealing with Mister Holt."

"I don't think he's a problem, Mister Wheeler, but I'll go and talk to Martha Lynch and Nellie Adler tomorrow."

"You do that, Joe."

Sheriff Olsen nodded, then turned and left the house, believing that Bill Wheeler was placing too much importance on Doc Holt. The man was just an ignorant cowhand.

———

Rhonda reached her empty ranch house as the sun was dropping low in the sky and preparing to perform its closing act. She wasn't in a good mood as she entered the kitchen and leaned her Winchester against the wall near the shotgun.

She regretted telling Doc about her past now. At the time, it seemed like the right thing to do but now she believed that it had put a barrier between them despite Doc's arguments that she wasn't a sinner at all. Her admission of her poor decisions and almost perverse behavior would offend any man with a solid moral base, and Doc was certainly that.

Doc Holt may not be a polished man, but he was more of a gentleman than any man she had ever met, and she'd met quite a few well-heeled men in New York before she left.

But she knew that he'd have to take the offer from Martha Lynch. *How could he afford not to?* Beth had known him for more than six years now and without saying so, had already told Rhonda that she had first claim. Rhonda had only known Doc for a few days and hadn't exactly dazzled him with her behavior and then there was the lost weight, too.

She walked into the bedroom, took off her homemade blouse and riding skirt and put on a camisole and one of her new dresses. She bunched up the cloth in the back of the dress to pull it taut across the front and wished she could gain back those lost twenty pounds more quickly.

Rhonda sighed, released the cloth from her grip and returned to the kitchen. She started a fire in the stove and put on the coffeepot before taking a seat.

She asked herself what she would do if Doc left and the very thought almost made her sick. It had only been a few days but life without Doc Holt was simply not worth contemplating. Her options were simple: either surrender or fight.

Rhonda took in a deep breath, walked to the cold room and took out some potatoes and smoked brisket then returned and placed them on the counter, took out the butcher knife and began to prepare dinner for herself and Doc, who she hoped would be back in a couple of hours.

She had made up her mind. If she had to go toe-to-toe with Beth then she'd do it. She was no longer going to wallow in self-pity or guilt over what she had done. She'd push away the Irish guilt and draw on her Gaelic stubbornness to get her way.

Rhonda cut up some of the smoked brisket and set it aside as she began to chop the potatoes taking pieces of the meat and tossing them into her mouth as she worked. She wanted her twenty pounds back.

————

Doc Holt pulled the wagon onto the Adler ranch's access road and was glad to have the day over with or at least he believed it was done.

As he drove it close to the house, Linda Travers who had been sitting on the porch, stood and waved at him wearing a big smile.

Doc pulled the wagon to a stop, waved back then dropped to the ground and headed for the house.

"Doc, how did it go?" she asked as he reached the bottom of the porch steps.

"Okay. I dropped off all the bodies in Comanche and talked to the sheriff. I gotta talk to everyone, if I could."

"Come in, please," she said as she took his arm when he reached the porch.

Doc walked with her into the main room and she guided him to a chair and said, "I'll get them, Doc. You just have a seat. You look tired. Can I get you something to eat?"

"No, ma'am. I'm fine," he replied as he removed his hat and sat down.

"Call me Linda, Doc. You surely earned the privilege. I never thanked you for stopping those men from hurting me. I was so afraid and thought I was going to die and then you appeared in the dark and saved me. I can never thank you enough."

Doc just nodded, not knowing how to respond.

Linda smiled at him again then turned and walked down the hallway to get as many adults as she could find.

Doc may have said he was fine, but he was surprisingly hungry. He'd had a good lunch just hours ago and didn't know why his stomach was being so demanding, but it was.

After three minutes, Nellie Adler, her two walking sons, their wives, and Linda were all in the main room while Doc explained what had transpired since he left the ranch.

"So, if the sheriff comes visitin', and I'd be kinda surprised if he didn't, it's important that you tell him I was in the barn sleepin' when they started firin'."

Richard asked, "Do you think they'll leave us alone now, Doc?"

"I'm not sure. I don't think they'll be comin' at night again if they do come back. Havin' a whole bunch of 'em killed in a night raid will make 'em think different, but you still need to keep your eyes open."

"What are you going to do now, Doc?" asked Linda.

"I'll head back to the Circle B, then tomorrow, Mrs. Lynch wants to talk to me, so I'll head down that way. I kinda left her in a bad way with no menfolk on the ranch except for the cook."

"That was hardly your fault, Doc," said Nellie.

"Yes, it was, ma'am. Everything about this mess is my fault. I shoulda stopped 'em months ago, but I didn't," then after a short pause he said, "well, I'd best be getting back before it gets dark again. Do you mind if I leave the wagon as is? Those two horses did a lotta work today and need some lovin'."

"I'll take care of the horses, Doc," said Harold.

"I appreciate it," he said as he stood.

Nellie also stood and took two steps over to Doc, kissed him softly on the cheek and said, "You're a good man, Doc. Don't beat yourself up for what happened."

Doc half-smiled then turned and walked out of the front door, crossed the porch and hopped down to the ground before walking briskly to the barn to saddle Trapper.

Harold followed to take care of the team while Linda walked outside to stand on the porch and watch Doc leave.

She was still watching fifteen minutes later as a mounted Doc left the barn and waved before turning northeast to go cross-country to the Circle B.

After she had waved in return, Linda entered the house deep in thought.

————

Doc felt good riding Trapper again after spending the day in a slow-moving wagon. Not surprisingly, he hadn't a clue about the secondary problems he'd created over the past few days. He'd created two young widows who had both shifted their attention to him and there was the young widow he hadn't created but taken care of for the past few days and who was now waiting anxiously for his return.

As he rode, his thoughts centered on how he could end the complicated dilemma he did understand. He believed the focus had to be on Bill Wheeler. Unlike Charlie Lynch, Bill wasn't a man who had been swayed by rhetoric. He was a true believer from the start and had been the convincer, and unlike Charlie Lynch, he had ranch hands that were all proficient with their firearms.

Part of Bill Wheeler's problem was that he had no wife in the house to settle him down. In fact, there was no female presence on the Bar W at all. His wife had given him four sons before running off with a Yankee army sergeant ten years ago. Maybe that was what had started him down the path he had chosen, but Doc didn't think so. He was probably already walking that trail before she left and maybe it was the reason that she flew the coop.

His four sons all worked the large ranch with the six hired hands, and Doc knew that each of them supported the boss's ideas. But Bill Wheeler wasn't stupid either. He'd kept his sons and hands mostly on the ranch for the night rides, only sending them out for easy targets. He'd accepted the horses from the raids but let the others keep the cattle, which gave him a huge remuda of over eighty animals.

Bill Wheeler would be a hard nut to crack, and unless he missed his guess, Wheeler had already identified Doc as an enemy. He arrived at that guess through very simple reasoning. Charlie Lynch had most assuredly told Bill about Doc's refusal to go on the raids, yet Doc's presence in the bunkhouse with the men who did participate would mean that Doc would know about what they were going to do.

So, despite his assurance to Mrs. Lynch that he didn't think that Bill Wheeler or the sheriff would see him as a problem, he was convinced that Bill Wheeler would try to kill him and kill him quickly. His only advantage was that he was just as sure that Bill Wheeler and the sheriff didn't know where he was.

———

Doc walked Trapper into the barn in the dark, stepped down and began to strip him down in the moonlight that crept in through the barn doors.

He was still working on some kind of strategy to overcome the almost insurmountable odds that he faced and wished it had been Bill Wheeler's crowd that had attacked the Adler ranch last night because he believed that he'd be able to talk some sense into Charlie Lynch and the boys once Wheeler was out of the picture. But it hadn't worked out that way, leaving the situation maybe even worse than it was before.

He finally left the barn carrying his filthy Winchester with his saddlebags over his shoulder as he walked toward the back of the ranch house.

Doc stepped onto the porch and was about to knock on the open door's jamb when Rhonda popped into view wearing a big smile.

"Doc, you don't have to knock," she said when she saw his knuckles poised near the side of the doorway.

"Just habit, I guess, Rhonda," he said as he walked inside.

"Whatever you're cookin' sure smells good," he said as he set his Winchester beside hers and dropped his saddlebags to the floor before taking off his hat and hanging it on a peg.

"Oh, it's just something I whipped together quickly. Have a seat, Doc, you still look tired."

"I'll confess to that," he replied as he sat down at the table.

An unhungry Rhonda set two plates on the table with equally sized servings of hash browns and sliced brisket with gravy, then poured two cups of coffee and sat down.

The tines on Doc's fork had barely entered the hash browns when Rhonda asked, "Doc, what are you going to do now?"

"I've been thinkin' about that most of the day, and I'm not quite sure," he replied, thinking that she was asking about his strategy for dealing with Bill Wheeler and the sheriff.

Rhonda took a bite of meat and gravy as she expected more explanation from Doc, but by the time she swallowed, she realized that nothing more was forthcoming.

"What will happen to me?" she finally asked softly.

Doc looked up and replied, "I was gonna ask about that. I was thinkin' that it might be a good idea for you to move down to the Double L and stay with Mrs. Lynch and Beth until I can figure out how to deal with Bill Wheeler."

"You want me to leave my ranch?" she asked in surprise.

"Just for a little while. I feel kinda responsible for leavin' Martha and Beth alone with only Fred on that big place. They'll need to hire some new ranch hands and that'll put 'em in a bad spot, too. I can't protect them and you if you're livin' in two different places. That's why I asked."

Rhonda set her fork down and said, "They're going to ask you to be the ranch manager of the Double L tomorrow. Will you take the job?"

"They said that?" he asked, then said, "I suppose I shoulda seen it comin'. It makes sense, but I'm not sure that I'd be all that comfortable livin' there anymore. I killed every man who lived there except for Fred, and I'm not sure I'd ever rest easy livin' in that bunkhouse again. I'd be seein' the faces of all the boys every night and that would make me crazy."

"You could move into this house, Doc, if you'd like." she said quietly.

Doc was surprised and replied, "I think that's a bad idea, too," not understanding her real question.

He honestly thought she was just asking him to move into the house and sleep in a different room, and there were both moral and physical reasons why he thought that wasn't a wise thing to do, and with Rhonda's horrible memories, he surely didn't want to make them worse.

Rhonda flared and asked, "Why is that a bad idea?"

"It just wouldn't be right," Doc replied, not believing he had to explain.

Rhonda totally misinterpreted what he said, thinking he was simply rejecting her in favor of Beth, so her jealousy ignited her temper as she shouted, "So, it comes to this, doesn't it? I confess my past to you and now you think I'm some dirty harlot because of what I did and I'm not good enough for you.

"I thought that you were better than that, Mister Holt. I thought you meant what you told me last night and you thought I wasn't guilty of anything wrong, but obviously that's not true. You may as well return to the bunkhouse where you feel better and leave the whore to live alone in her house alone."

She stood and stomped off down the hallway and slammed the door leaving a stunned Doc Holt sitting at the table wondering what had just happened.

He looked down at his food then back down the empty hallway in utter confusion. He thought he'd given her an honest answer, but spent a few minutes recalling and rethinking what he had said. He had said what any man who respected a woman should have said, but she acted as if he had insulted her. She had even called herself a whore. *How could anyone like Rhonda even think such a thing?*

He stayed there for another couple of minutes picking at the food, but not taking another bite. He did sip some coffee to try to understand, but it didn't help. He simply didn't have a clue why Rhonda was so angry with him.

Finally, he pushed the plate aside and fell back on something he did understand. He stood, walked three steps, picked up his saddlebags and his Winchester and returned to the table. He took his cleaning kit out of the saddlebags and began to rid the Winchester of its dirt and corroding powder residue.

———

Rhonda was sitting on the edge of her bed with her head down, letting tears fall straight to the floor. She had hoped that she at least would have an opportunity to put the weight back on so she'd at be able to compete with Beth as far as figures were concerned, but she knew that Beth was younger, prettier and had known him for much longer, so she wasn't surprised by his rejection.

She began to sink even lower when she knew that she had essentially offered herself to Doc Holt as she had done to Jamie all those years ago, but there was one huge difference. With Jamie, it had been to see what she was missing, but with Doc, she wanted to be with him because she knew that she loved him.

She had never known love before, especially not like this. At first, she thought it was gratitude for all he had done for her, but the more they talked and the more she realized what an incredibly thoughtful, caring man he was, the deeper she had come to care for him.

Then last night, when she had bared her soul to him, he had reacted as she had hoped he would when he absolved her of her sins as no priest ever could. He didn't tell her that her sins were forgiven, he had told her that she had never sinned at all, and she knew he meant it.

Now he was going to leave her and unlike when Jamie and the Clancy brothers had died, this would break her heart. She was no longer concerned about what would happen to her if she was left alone. All she thought about was loving Doc Holt and the likelihood that he would marry Beth and take over the big ranch.

After sitting for ten minutes, she lifted her feet onto the bed and put her head on the pillow.

————

After the Winchester was clean, oiled and reloaded again, Doc cleaned up the food and washed the dishes before putting his saddlebags over his shoulder, picking up his repeater then snatching his hat from the wall. He blew out the lamp then left the kitchen, closing the door behind him before heading for the peace of the bunkhouse.

CHAPTER 4

Doc was up early as usual and took a quick bath in the creek before shaving and getting dressed. He returned to the bunkhouse, tossed his saddlebags over his shoulder then grabbed his Winchester and the Sharps then walked to the barn, glancing at the cookstove pipe to see if Rhonda was awake and wasn't surprised that she wasn't.

He was still flummoxed by her sudden hostile response to his answer about not moving into the house. *Did she really expect him to?*

Life without women around was a lot simpler, he thought as he saddled Trapper, but he did admit to himself that even with the complexities, he did enjoy being with Rhonda. When she wasn't in one of her foul moods, she was a very pleasant person. He just couldn't get a handle on why she would suddenly turn into a snarling puma. Men were much less confusing, but maybe that was the way it was supposed to be. Women may be a puzzle, but it made them much more interesting.

He finished saddling Trapper and led him from the barn, looking at the cookstove pipe once more. It was only around seven o'clock but by the time he got to the Double L, it would be about the right time. He'd be able to get some breakfast from Fred, too. Then he had all those Winchesters to clean and really wanted to look at that one with the shattered stock.

He climbed into the saddle, gave one last look at the house then set Trapper southbound at a slow trot.

———

Doc was halfway to the Double L when Rhonda slid out of bed and trotted down the hallway and out of the house to use the privy. After she left the little house, she walked in her nightdress to the bunkhouse and peered inside to talk to Doc, only to find it empty. Even his Sharps was gone.

She trotted back to the barn then looked inside only finding Bride, the fake pinto and the two mules. She slowly turned to the house and shuffled across the back yard then into the kitchen where she took a seat at the table.

She didn't blame Doc for leaving. She had driven him away with her outburst and knew that no amount of praying would bring him back this time. Beth would win without having to throw a punch.

Rhonda drank a glass of water, returned to her bedroom and laid back down. *What was the point of trying to put the weight back on now?*

Rhonda Byrne was slipping into a deep funk and one that was compounded by intense jealousy and not a small amount of Irish temper. The temper may not have been new to her, but the jealousy arrived as a completely new sensation, at least in this context. Rhonda had simply never loved any man before and had to cope with the useless yet powerful emotion for the first time. but instead of recognizing the danger of unrestricted jealousy, she welcomed the green monster with open arms.

———

Doc arrived at the Double L and rode straight to the bunkhouse with all the Winchesters, spotted Fred as he was walking out of the chow house and waved.

Fred waved back and stopped to wait for Doc to get close.

When he did, Doc stepped down and said, "Fred, I've gotta clean all those Winchesters. Did you make any coffee this mornin'?"

"I got more'n coffee, Doc. I made some bacon and flapjacks for Mrs. Lynch, Beth and Juanita 'cause I figured none of 'em would wanna cook. They already had some, but I got some left."

"That'll work, Fred," Doc said as he led Trapper back to the chow house.

As he ate his bacon, cold flapjacks and drank some coffee, Fred said, "I hear you're comin' back to take over the ranch, Doc?"

Doc shook his head, swallowed the butter and molasses covered flapjack and said, "Nope. I aim to help as much as I can, but I got a bigger problem with Bill Wheeler and his crowd. I can't stay here and turn this place into another shootin' gallery like the Adler place any more than I could stay at the Circle B or the Adlers. I'll keep an eye on the places, but I can't stay in any of 'em."

"How will you manage that, Doc?" Fred asked.

"I'm gonna set up a pack horse and stay out in the open country. If I position myself right, I can see all three places, or at least close enough that nobody can get to 'em without me knowin'. I gotta get a set of field glasses, but I already got my spot picked out."

"What can I do to help, Doc?"

"Just keep an eye on Mrs. Lynch and Beth in case they get me. I gotta tell you, Fred, this ain't gonna be a picnic."

"I figgered as much."

Doc finished his food, washed his dishes, despite Fred's protest that it was his job then led Trapper down to the bunkhouse to clean the eight intact Winchesters and to see if the one with the broken stock was salvageable.

He set up what appeared to be a production line as he had the Winchesters lined up and he'd clean them part by part rather than gun by gun. He finished the last Winchester, having determined that the one with the shattered stock was useless, then examined the pistols and took the nicest Colt that shot the same .45 Long Colt cartridge as his and put the second gunbelt around his waist with the pistol's butt facing forward.

He then walked out of the bunkhouse carrying two of the best Winchesters and headed for the house. He knew that Charlie Lynch had kept his weapons in the office but wasn't sure if they'd been used on the raid and wanted to leave the Winchesters in the house.

As Doc stepped up onto the porch, he was sure he looked like a Mexican bandito with this two rifles and cross mounted pistols, and then wondered if a bandolero filled with extra .44 caliber rounds wouldn't be a bad idea. He knocked on the door and didn't have to wait long when Beth opened the door and greeted him with a big smile, whether he was overloaded with weaponry or not.

"Good morning, Doc. I see you're well-armed. Come in, please."

Doc stepped inside and waited for Beth to close the door before he said, "I'm gonna leave these two Winchester in the house. I wasn't sure if you had any guns left."

"We do, but you can leave them in the office anyway. You need to know where everything is now."

Doc didn't comment as he walked to the office and was going to put the two rifles on the racks, but found that they were already full, so he leaned them on the wall then removed his hat.

Martha heard him enter, left the kitchen and arrived in the main room just as Doc was leaving the office.

"Good morning, Doc. Beth saw you arrive and head for the chow house and thought you'd be having breakfast. Would you like some coffee?"

Doc replied, "Yes, ma'am. I had to clean all the Winchesters, too. That's what took most of the time," then followed Martha and Beth down the hallway.

They reached the kitchen and Doc angled over to the table and held a chair for Beth who took a seat while Martha poured the coffee into the three cups, and after setting the pot back onto the cookstove, took a seat while Doc held it for her.

After he sat down, Martha said, "Doc, as you are well aware, we are in a bad situation, and before I go any further, don't you dare try to say it was your fault. Not a word! Do you understand?"

Properly chastised, Doc replied, "Yes, ma'am."

"And, Mister Holt, you will address me as Martha now. Is that understood?"

"Yes, ma…, I mean, yes, Martha."

Martha smiled, feeling that she had just issued a tongue-lashing to a little boy rather than a six-foot plus, two-hundred-pound rugged man, but continued.

"As I was saying, we're in a bit of trouble without any men around and I'd like to make you the ranch manager, so you can hire the men we'll need and take over the operation of the ranch. You can name your own salary and I'd expect you to live in the house. Will you do that for me, Doc?"

Doc was ready to turn her down, but she had to end her proposal with that question that really made it much more difficult, because despite her firm declaration and his agreement not to blame himself for what had happened, he still felt an overwhelming sense of guilt for his lack of action much more than for his actions.

He took a sip of coffee and looked at Martha, whose brown eyes were boring into him.

"Mrs., I mean, Martha, you kinda put me in a tough spot here. I have a feelin' that Bill Wheeler is gonna want my hide hangin' on his wall, and he's got the men to do it, too. I keep thinkin' that if I was here, the bullets would be flyin' and that'd put you and Beth in danger, and I can't have that. I told Fred what I was gonna do was to stay out in the open and keep an eye on the place and see what I could do to stop any more killin'. I still think that's the best way. Now, if it's all right, I'd rather not think that far ahead, not till I get this problem put to bed. You can understand why I've gotta do it this way, can't you, Martha?"

Martha nodded and replied, "Yes, Doc, I do. How can I help?"

"Just go about your business and I'll set up. I've got a spot already picked out. Do you know that big pile of boulders and rocks that we all kinda stacked up on the northern edge of the ranch?"

"Oh, yes. You and the others turned it into a bit of a fort, like little boys, if I recall."

"That's it. Well, I'm gonna set up my camp in there. Did Charlie have a pair of field glasses?"

"Yes, they're in his office in the cabinet under the gun racks."

"If you don't mind, Martha, I'll use them to keep an eye on the place."

"Doc, whatever is in the house is at your disposal."

Doc smiled and said, "Thank you, Martha."

Then Beth smiled at him and added, "Anything in the house, Doc."

Martha shot a glance at Beth but didn't say anything.

Doc, of course, didn't catch her meaning and said, "I appreciate that, Beth."

Beth then asked, "What about Rhonda, Doc?"

Doc scratched the side of his neck and said, "She got kinda mad at me for sayin' somethin', but I've got no idea what it was, but then I can't figure out ladies anyway."

"Is she still mad at you?" Beth asked.

"I don't know, I kinda left while she was still in the house asleep. Well, I've gotta get goin'. I'll pick up those field glasses on my way out."

"Let me know if you need anything, Doc," Martha said as Doc stood.

"I'll do that, Martha," he replied before he turned and walked quickly down the hall.

He stopped in the office, found the field glasses and was about to leave when he noticed that one of the Winchesters on the gun racks had a brass plate on its stock's butt. He took the Winchester '76 down from its perch, then levered the chambered cartridge onto the floor and picked it up. It was a much bigger .45-75 Winchester center fire cartridge and wondered how Charlie had managed to get one so soon. He'd never seen one before. It was the rifle version with the longer barrel for increased range and accuracy, too.

He reinserted the cartridge into the loading gate, put one of the '73s into its spot on the gun rack and then sat on his heels and pulled open the ammunition drawer finding two boxes of the new Winchester cartridges among the more popular .44s.

After setting the two boxes aside, Doc closed the drawer, hung the field glasses around his neck then left the house with the new Winchester '76 and felt better about his chances of coming out of this alive.

————

Rhonda hadn't eaten and hadn't even left the bed as she let her mind drift aimlessly which she believed would be her fate. She remembered those early years when she was just a young girl, and everything was so simple. She had her fairytale dreams as they all had and never believed that they wouldn't come true.

But ever since she learned the facts of life from her mother, those fairytales had turned into one nightmare after another. First, the fear of becoming a mother and then the fear of not being one. Her decision to dally with Jamie, then her banishment and failed pregnancy, her horrible common law marriage, more failed pregnancies, and then the second dalliance with Will Clancy.

After that it had been one continuous nightmare culminating in that horrible night. But then Doc had come, those long-forgotten fairytales had resurfaced, and she thought that there might be a chance after all.

But that was all gone now and again, it was because of her own failings. At least now she could saddle a horse, fire a Winchester and had those five cattle that Doc had returned to the ranch. She began to rise out of her depression as her other, more combative moods expanded to push it out of the way.

"To hell with him," Rhonda said aloud, "let him go and marry Beth. She's a nice, sweet little girl. He wouldn't know what to do with a real woman, anyway."

She slid from the bed and stomped out to the kitchen to fix herself something to eat. She needed the strength if she was going to run her ranch by herself.

———

As Doc rode north at a medium trot with his new Winchester '76 in the right scabbard replacing his trusted '73, which now rode behind him in the bedroll, he decided he'd at least find out why Rhonda was so mad at him. He felt he owed her that at least, despite her vacillations. Maybe there was a reason for them that would make sense and they could be avoided in the future.

Regardless of her mood, he knew that he couldn't leave her alone in the ranch house. If she didn't want to move into the Double L, then he'd have to do the best he could. If they tried to reach her ranch then they'd be most likely to be coming from the south anyway.

He'd passed the odd-looking pile of boulders and big rocks twenty minutes ago which would be his defensive location. It had been almost a game with the ranch hands when they discovered five large boulders in a tight semicircle on the northern edge of the ranch. They began toting big rocks, some requiring two horses to drag to the spot, adding length and height to the construction. There was no real reason for it to exist other than to give them something to focus on during the rare quiet times, but now it had a purpose. One of the features that he had added was to create gun ports along the top of the boulders, like the drawings of the old castles he'd seen in the history books that he loved. It even had a nice firepit in the corner.

He spotted Rhonda's ranch house in the distance and noticed the smoke coming out of the cookstove pipe. He didn't see any strange horses nearby, so he knew no one had come to visit, good or bad.

Doc approached the house keeping Trapper at a walk as he glanced into the barn, spotting Bride, his fake pinto, and the two mules inside. That meant she was in the house, so he just turned his real pinto to the back of the house, stepped down and tied off the reins to the back hitchrail before stepping up onto the porch.

Without knocking on the open door, Doc entered the house, and saw Rhonda at the cookstove, cooking some bacon.

Rhonda had heard the hoofbeats and knew he was coming but didn't even look in his direction as she flipped her bacon.

"All set up in your new place?" she asked, her question heavy with sarcasm that Doc apparently missed.

"Not yet. I gotta move the guns and set up next. I just figured I'd stop by and see if I could convince you to move into the Double L ranch house."

Rhonda snapped her head to look at him and said, "Are you sure you don't want to sully that big, fancy house by having me move in? Well, I'm not about to go there, Mister Holt, so don't waste your breath. I can take care of myself now. I don't need you or anybody else to watch over me."

Doc stood up and threw his hands into the air in frustration.

"What the hell is goin' on with you, Rhonda? I've got no idea why you're so mad at me. Now, I don't have time to try to figure it out, 'cause Bill Wheeler isn't gonna be just waitin' around for somethin' to happen."

"Then just leave and go back to the Double L. You don't owe me anything."

Then Doc did probably the worst thing he could have done, even though to him, it was perfectly logical.

"Okay, Rhonda, if that's what you want. But you're gonna need this," he said as he pulled a wad of cash out of his pocket and slapped it onto the counter.

Rhonda stared at the cash, then grabbed it and hurled it at Doc, screaming, "Why pay me, Mister Holt? I didn't spread my legs for you, so you don't owe me a dime!"

Doc was totally lost as the bills floated to the floor and just said, "No, Mrs. Byrne, I don't owe you a dime, but if you're gonna be on your own, you need money to buy supplies."

Her last words were, "My name is Brady, Rhonda Anne Brady, Mister Holt, and I don't want you on my ranch ever again!"

Doc just backed out of the kitchen, turned, then jumped onto the ground and mounted Trapper. He turned the pinto to the barn where he put the pack saddle on Lou Robinson's disguised white gelding, then fashioned a trail rope and led him out of the barn and then south off the now forbidden Circle B, feeling confused and deeply hurt by Rhonda's anger.

Rhonda had watched him leave then after she heard hoofbeats receding to the south, grabbed the hot handle of the frypan, and hurled it against the wall, burning her hand in the process. She looked down at the currency on the floor, some already wet with bacon grease, and began to pick them up. He may have thought of her as a whore, but even whores had to have money to survive.

Her temper was so completely in control, she never even bothered to analyze Doc's replies to her accusations and invectives. She just knew he was gone to the Double L and Beth and she was alone again.

But as she stood in her kitchen, clutching her greasy banknotes, she was even more miserable than angry and was more despondent than she'd ever been in her entire life, which was a truly deep abyss.

————

Bill Wheeler was in his office with Will Hatfield and Mike Green, his other two associates. Neither had a big ranch and were just borderline disciples, unlike Charlie Lynch, who had been a true believer, but he wanted their added manpower after listening to Sheriff Olsen's description of the shootout at the Adler ranch.

"How could one man kill nine, Bill?" asked Mike Green.

"I'm not sold that he acted alone, but I've decided that before we do anything else, we eliminate Doc Holt. I think he knows more than the sheriff thinks he does."

"So," Will Hatfield said, "what do you need us for? You've got a lot more manpower than we do with your four boys and six ranch hands. Me and Mike only got four ranch hands and our two boys between us."

"Look, Will, I've got a much bigger ranch to run and there'll be more in it for you both when we get the cattle from the Double L."

Mike Green put up his hands and said, "Whoa, there Bill. That's rustling, and I want no part of it. Martha Lynch still owns the Double L and besides, Charlie was one of us."

Will nodded vigorously to express his agreement with Mike Green.

Bill then said, "I didn't say I was going to rustle the herds. I said that I'd be able to share them with you. I aim to go and console Martha Lynch and convince her that her future is with me. I want to marry her and then, after I join the two ranches, I'll be willing to cut you both in for some of the cattle."

"Bill, that's not right. Martha's got it hard now because of what happened. We should try to help her out, not try and weasel her out of what's hers. We owe that to Charlie," Will Hatfield said as Mike Green nodded.

"Weasel her out of it? I'll be helping her just like you said. Now, I've been a widower too long and Martha's still a fine-looking woman. I've admired her for some time now."

Mike Green blanched and said, "Tell me that you didn't get Charlie to go after the Adlers to get him killed, Bill."

Bill shook his head, replying, "No, no. Of course not, but I'm not about to let this opportunity slip by. I'll go and convince her that it's best for her to marry me and then she can live with my protection, and I'm sure that Beth would be happy to marry Chuck, too."

Will Hatfield glared at him and said, "You did send him over there on purpose, Bill. Did you warn the Adlers that he was coming, too? Or maybe you sent Holt there to gun them all down after they killed Ben Adler."

Bill Wheeler heard the accusations and snapped, "So, you two think that, do you? Well, to hell with both of you! I'll do what I need to do, and when my herd more than doubles, I'll drive you to lily-livered cowards out of the state next. I'll send you back to Rhode Island where you belong!"

The two ranchers looked at each other then stood before Mike Green pointed at Bill Wheeler and said, "Was this what it was all about, Wheeler? All this other crap was just window dressing to get your hands on the Double L?"

"Both of you just get out! I never want to see your faces again and don't try and double-cross me, either. I know where you both live with your wives and families."

Will Hatfield snarled, "If you or yours set one toe on my land, I'll blow your head off!"

Then he did an about face and he and Mike Green stomped out of the room.

They had barely left the house when Bill Wheeler walked out of his office and into the kitchen where his two oldest sons,

Chuck and Ira were sitting at the table drinking coffee. They both looked at their father when he entered, having heard most of the loud conversation.

"Looks like we're on our own, boys. Those two yellow bastards went running home with their tail between their legs."

"Want us to go and visit 'em, Pa?" asked Ira.

"No, they're not gonna do anything. Chuck, I want you and Ira to take Jack Brown and Fatty over to the Double L and see if you can find Doc Holt. He's got to be close to the ranch. If you find him, kill him. He's the only one in the way now. Chuck, if things work out, you'll get Beth Lynch in your bed soon."

Chuck grinned and said, "Now, that's a right nice bonus, Pa," then added, "I ain't sure I can recognize Holt, Pa."

"He's a little over six feet and rides a pinto. That should be enough."

"He's supposed to be on the Double L?"

"Maybe. He might be over at the Slash A, or I'm beginning to think he might have moved into that abandoned ranch that those Yankees owned just north of the Double L."

"What if we don't find him, Pa?" asked Ira.

Bill glared at his son as he snapped, "You stay out until you do."

"Okay, Pa. We'll go and get Fatty and Jack. We'll draw some chow to take with us, too."

"Get going. Come and see me when you get back."

The boys left the kitchen, going out the back door to hunt down some food and the two ranch hands. They expected to be back in time for supper.

———

After they left the Bar W ranch house, Mike Green and Will Hatfield rode quickly down the access road to escape any possible rifle fire from the ranch house.

"Mike, I'm going to ride to the Double L and tell Martha what we just heard. It's only a little out of my way."

Mike Green shouted back, "She's going to be really mad at us for what happened, Will, and we've got to think of our families."

"I am thinking of our families, Mike. Do you think for an instant that Bill is going to let us live in peace now that his true flag is flying?"

"Alright, you go ahead. I'm heading back to the ranch and let everyone know what might be happening."

Will waved and peeled off heading west toward the Double L not knowing that two of the Wheeler boys along with two of their unpleasant ranch hands would be behind him by forty minutes.

———

Doc had ridden Trapper to the rock fort and decided to start setting up using his supplies before he returned to the Double L for the rest of the things he'd need, including some food.

As he unloaded the extra guns and ammunition, he examined the structure more carefully than when he and the boys were putting it together. It wasn't bad at all, but he knew he'd need someplace to keep some water for the two horses. He couldn't expect to lead them to the creek that was over two hundred yards away without being seen.

So, using some of the smaller rocks, Doc began constructing a well of sorts near the fire pit. Trying to make it watertight without mortar would be impossible, but when he lined it with one of the treated panniers and anchored the pannier with more rocks, he knew that it may lose some water, but not too much. It took him two trips using the two horses and their four canteens and one water bag to fill the new cistern. He watered both horses and then began to harvest some of the nearby grass to bring it into the fort.

———

"*You mean he was just after the ranch?*" asked a startled Martha.

"I'm not sure that was his original purpose, but he surely wants it now, and he wants to marry Beth off to his son, Chuck. He threatened me and Mike Green and our families, too. I'm really sorry, Martha. Charlie was a good man who just got turned in the wrong direction."

"He was a good man but going in that direction was his own decision and the things that he did earned him his fate."

Will nodded and then said, "I've got to get going, Martha. I need to get my son and the hands ready just in case."

"Thank you for stopping by, Will. I'll let Doc know about it, too."

Will paused and said, "I'm ashamed to have been a part of it, Martha, and even more ashamed that it seems like we're letting Doc Holt do all the dirty work."

"I think Doc feels like he's trying to make amends for not stopping them before they did those things, Will."

Will nodded then picked up his hat and strode from the room.

Martha turned to Beth and said, "Go and tell Fred what you just heard. If Doc isn't here in an hour, tell him to ride north to the Circle B and tell him."

"Okay, Mama," Beth said as she left the house, sickened by the thought of Chuck Wheeler being her new husband.

———

Will Hatfield was trotting his horse out of the access road and turned west to go back to his ranch. He was deep in thought and not paying attention as he should have. It had been a long time since he'd had to concern himself with gunfights or being trailed.

"Ain't that Hatfield comin' out of the Lynch spread?" asked Ira as he pointed at Will Hatfield.

"Damned straight it is!" growled Chuck, "let's go and see what he told her."

The four men picked up the pace to a fast trot and were soon just a half a mile behind the unsuspecting rancher.

That's when Will Hatfield heard their hoofbeats, came out of his reverie and knew he was in trouble.

He whipped his horse to the north and set him off at a gallop.

———

Doc had just finished bringing the grass into the fort when he heard racing hoofbeats to the south. He took off his Stetson and tossed it aside as he stuck his head between two of the rocks on the top and saw a rider being pursued by four men. He didn't know the four men, but he identified one of their horses and knew they must be from Bill Wheeler's Bar W.

He quickly unhitched Trapper, swung into the saddle and galloped him out of the fort, heading for the four Bar W men about mile and a half away.

Doc pulled the new Winchester '76, very grateful for the more powerful cartridge and the rifle's added range.

———

Will Hatfield's horse was lathered and winded as it began dramatically slowing while he turned and kept an eye on his pursuers. They were less than four hundred yards behind him now and gaining rapidly. He had made the cardinal mistake of using up his horse's stamina for the tradeoff in speed and now he had neither as they gained on him.

All four of the charging Bar W riders were pulling their Winchesters as they closed the gap.

Will knew he was dead when something unexpected happened as Ira Wheeler pointed to the right and shouted something that Will couldn't hear.

All four suddenly veered in that direction away from Will, so he turned to see what had made them change their minds and saw a rapidly approaching rider on a pinto and knew who he was. It was Doc Holt, who obviously didn't know that he was riding into four Winchesters.

But Doc not only knew it, he wanted it. He had recognized Fatty Tapper just from his horse, if not his size. He rode the biggest black gelding that Doc had ever seen, and it needed every bit of its strength to carry the three-hundred-and-twenty-pound rider.

Doc waited until they were within eight hundred yards and then ripped Trapper to the left and then again to make an exaggerated U-turn, hoping that the four shooters would take that as a sign of flight. He glanced over his shoulder at them and saw that they had indeed continued the chase.

He wasn't going to use the fort as protection because they could trap him inside and ricochet bullets into it, but there was a second spot that he was heading for that was almost the opposite of the fort. It was a shallow gully and it was almost invisible until a rider was almost on top of it. He planned on drawing them in close until they were in no man's land less than two hundred yards away, then he'd jump down to the ground with the '76 and slide into the gully, letting Trapper go. Once he disappeared, they'd know that they'd been had and either have to start firing or break away. Either way, he'd be able to open fire because they'd be in range of the deadlier '76.

Chuck, Ira, Fatty and Jack Brown didn't wait for Doc to reach the small gully when they began firing at two hundred yards, knowing that the .44s could reach him, but probably not kill him. They also had to know that the odds of getting a hit while firing a gun from a moving horse at that distance were very slight, but they must have figured they each had fifteen rounds and one in sixty sounded like pretty good odds to them.

Doc heard the staccato of their Winchester fire and took a quick glance back to make sure that he hadn't missed something and they were a lot closer than he had expected, but they were right where he thought they'd be, so he looked forward again and spotted the three mesquite bushes that heralded the edge of the gully and kicked his feet out of the stirrups and waited until he was almost at the bushes, then swung his right leg over the saddle and leapt from Trapper who veered to his right.

Doc hit the ground then rolled right into the gully, hugging his Winchester to his chest.

He quickly stood in his dust cloud and then lunged back to the edge of the gully, dropped to his chest, cocked the hammer and had to wait for his vision to clear from the dust for a second before he was able to aim.

When he did, he selected the easy target first, Fatty Tapper.

When the four Bar W riders had seen Doc drop from the saddle and then fall, they were momentarily elated thinking that one of those .44s had found their mark after all, but when they spotted him moving quickly, they knew that he had set up a defensive position, and as Doc had anticipated, their only options were to charge or to break away. But they were so close by then, about a hundred yards out, that they still believed they had the advantage.

That perceived advantage was soon exposed as a false sense of security when they all saw the sudden bloom of gunpowder smoke from the gully and Fatty felt the power of the Winchester '76's more powerful round, as it punched into the left side of his chest. If it had been a .44 at that distance, even hitting his chest, he might have survived the hit because his bulk would have prevented the bullet from penetrating into his lung cavity, but the more powerful Winchester '76 round blasted through his fat and muscle, exploded his left ninth rib and then entered the left atrium of his heart.

Fatty fell backwards and dropped off the left side of the horse, crashing into the dirt and adding to the enormous clouds of dust generated by the galloping horses.

His sudden departure startled Jack Brown, who no longer wanted any part of the gunfight, so he turned his horse to the right to leave the shootout.

But his decision came too late as Doc's second shot caught him in the left armpit as he was turning his horse and almost lifted him from the saddle, but it didn't matter as it ripped his left arm almost completely free of his torso, sending him to the ground.

The Wheeler brothers weren't made of sterner stuff, but they really had no choice after watching Jack hit the dirt. They were simply too close to do anything else, so they continued to fire and were now within killing range for their '73s.

Doc knew that they were able to reach him after he fired his second shot that killed Jack Brown and had ducked down into the gully, counting on the obscuring gunpowder clouds to give him a chance to change his firing position by a few feet.

When he popped back up, his old position was being obliterated by concentrated .44 caliber gunfire.

But to have the accuracy to shoot at Doc Holt, the brothers had slowed their horses to a walk, unwittingly making themselves better targets.

Ira found that out the hard way when Doc's third shot drilled into the left side of his chest, at an upward forty-five-degree side angle as Ira was facing towards Doc's old position.

The chunk of aerodynamic lead tracked through his left lung, missing his aortic arch somehow, but leaving lead pieces behind as it ripped through his trachea before exiting his upper right lung. Ira didn't die right away but fell to the ground gasping for oxygen that would never reach his blood system.

Chuck saw his younger brother fall, then turned to fire at Doc and screamed, "You bastard!", before rapidly firing his repeater at him.

Doc had underestimated how quickly Chuck would be able to redirect his fire, and was almost caught flat-footed, but just as that Winchester's sights reached his eyes, he dropped into the gully as his shooting spot disintegrated. He was on his back and levering in a new round when he heard the pounding hooves of Chuck's horse approaching.

It was going too fast to stop, and Doc thought he was going to try and run the horse into the gully and crush him under its steel-clad hooves, but his mind did its automatic math and it told him the horse was moving too fast, so Doc remained motionless on his back, as he aimed his Winchester at the spot where the pounding sound originated.

This would have to be a snapped shot at a rapidly moving target, and he should be using his pistol, but didn't have time to change weapons.

It was a terrifying one and a half seconds and when the big gelding's head suddenly appeared just three feet lower and eight feet above his boots, Doc kept his aim stationary and as Chuck's face appeared, he squeezed the trigger.

The horse completed the jump with Chuck still aboard, so Doc rolled onto his stomach and then scrambled to the other edge of the shallow gully, bringing his Winchester to bear where he expected to see Chuck Wheeler turning his horse, so he could take another shot, but all he saw was the horse. It took him another few seconds to find Chuck Wheeler lying on the ground, mercifully face down.

Doc finally stood and let his heart stop pounding as he walked out of the gully before he turned back when he heard a slow-moving horse, and spotted Will Hatfield walking his horse in his direction. He suspected that Hatfield had been one of Bill Wheeler's followers, but he gave him the benefit of the doubt and just stood with his cocked Winchester waiting for him. Besides, the four men had been chasing Hatfield before they had seen him, and he wondered what that was all about.

Will stopped about thirty feet short of Doc and said, "Are you Doc Holt?"

"I am. You must be Will Hatfield, or am I wrong?

"That's my name, and before you ask, I was one of the fools that was a believer in the garbage that Bill Wheeler was throwing around. He called me and Mike Green over to his place today and told us that we had to kill you, so he could get his hands on the Double L by marrying Martha Lynch."

"Are you tellin' me that all this was just to get the ranch?"

"I'm not sure, but when the Double L was cleared of all its menfolk, he saw an opportunity. Those four were probably going to kill me for telling Martha Lynch what he had said. He threatened our families, Mister Holt."

"Now you know how all the other families felt, Mister Hatfield. I think you'd better get home now. I think things are gonna get bad now."

Will glanced around at the four dead bodies and said, "Worse than this?"

"Yes, sir. I think so."

Will nodded and said, "Good luck, Mister Holt."

As Will Hatfield began turning his horse, Doc suddenly asked, "Mister Hatfield, is there anyone other than Bill Wheeler's crowd and the sheriff that I have to worry about?"

"No, but I believe that is enough."

Doc didn't reply as Will Hatfield finished turning his exhausted horse south and walked him away.

He then began walking east to Trapper and knew he had a lot of work to do before he returned to the Double L. He had to get those four bodies underground to keep the buzzards at bay. He didn't want to give Bill Wheeler a big pointer to where his boys were.

He reached Trapper, mounted the pinto gelding and slipped his Winchester into the scabbard. Then he collected each of the other four horses and made a trail rope before leading them back to the creek near the fort to let them all drink. Once they were satisfied, he hitched them all, including Trapper, outside the fort to keep the grass in the fort from being eaten, then took the spade he had brought along on the pack saddle and walked to where the bodies were. He didn't take the Winchester with him, as there were four Winchesters strewn around on the ground that he could use if he needed them.

Doc cheated a bit in digging the graves, using the same gully that had served him well as an impromptu redoubt.

He dug into the side of the gully with his spade, then rolled the body into the slot and just collapsed the gully's edge over the newly created burial cave. If there had been only one or two, he might have taken more time, but he knew he had to move quickly.

The biggest problem, literally, was Fatty Tapper. His bulk made Doc alter his burial process by having to drag the big man's body into the narrowest part of the gully and shovel dirt on top. When he finished, that part of the gully was back to being almost flat ground, at least until Fatty decomposed and the dirt collapsed onto his remains.

After the last corpse had been covered with dirt, but probably not enough to keep the coyotes from digging them up, a bareheaded Doc Holt took a seat on the gully's edge and inhaled what was left in his last canteen of metallic, warm water before setting the empty canteen on the ground.

He looked at the six horses grazing on the scattered clumps of grass nearby and concentrated on the fake pinto. This disguised horse made him realize just how futile making plans seemed to be. He remembered how word would come down through the ranks during the war about what the generals were planning to do, but then the engagements simply took on a life of their own.

His whole plan about staying at the fort was gone as Bill Wheeler would be alerted and Doc didn't think he'd just sit back and wait. He guessed that he had maybe one day before Wheeler acted, and he had to make the most use of the next twenty-four hours.

At least now, he only had to concern himself with Bill Wheeler. He was discounting the sheriff, who he thought was spineless and if things got dicey for him, would deny any involvement and just try to keep his job.

But all his preparation would amount to nothing unless he was alert, and he was far from that now. He was physically, mentally, and emotionally drained and felt like he'd been in one continuous gunfight for two days. He needed to somehow wind down before he fell apart. He was putting on a strong front, but he had to be honest with himself or he wouldn't be able to survive what he now perceived as the final skirmish in this war.

Doc Holt engaged in self-diagnosis and prescribed a dose of separation from the continuous stress of danger and death. He needed a break in the action where his mind was free of Winchesters, Colts, bullets…and women.

Rhonda's completely unexpected and confusing dismissal bothered him immensely, but he couldn't afford the distractions. John 'Doc' Holt needed to cleanse his mind of all the hectic past few days and those that would soon be here. Doc needed to be a boy again.

He snatched his hat and pulled it on his head, grabbed the canteen then walked back to the fort to Trapper and stepped into the saddle.

Instead of riding south to the Double L, he turned east, heading for his distraction.

———

Sheriff Olsen had ridden to the Slash A to see the Adlers first for two reasons. He wanted to verify Doc Holt's story and check on the bullet holes and somehow get them to admit to being Jewish. He'd never met one before and was a bit nervous after hearing all the stories about them when he was a boy. He knew they didn't have horns or anything, but they were mysterious and he only heard tales about their dark ways.

As he turned down the access road, he stopped and turned to look to the east. He thought he heard distant gunfire, but by the time he listened, it was gone. He shrugged and started his horse back down the access road.

Because he was the sheriff, he just stepped down and walked onto the porch then knocked on the screen door. He could already see the bullet holes that peppered the side of the house and had to admit that it must have been a serious amount of shooting.

Nellie Adler appeared behind the screen door, then swung it open, saying, "Come in, Sheriff Olsen."

"Thank you, ma'am," he replied as he removed his hat and walked into the house.

As he entered the front door, Richard, Harold and Linda all entered the room from the hallway and took seats in the large main room.

Nellie directed him to a chair, took a seat on the couch, then said, "I assume that you need to talk to us about that unprovoked attack on our ranch by Charlie Lynch and his men."

"Yes, ma'am. Mister Holt showed up yesterday morning with a wagonload of bodies and gave his statement, and I wonder if you could tell me what happened."

She exhaled loudly and said, "Very well. This will be difficult for me because I lost my husband in that attack and if it hadn't been for Mister Holt, we would have lost many more, if not the entire family."

"Yes, ma'am. I understand that, and I'm sorry for your loss."

"Mister Holt had stopped by earlier that day and asked my husband about a job, but we didn't have anything available, so he asked if he could sleep in the barn and was given permission. That night, around midnight as we slept, we were all awakened by rifle fire as bullets riddled the walls. My husband ran to his office to retrieve some weapons and was shot and killed. My son, Len, tried and was wounded. He's in his room if you need to speak to him.

"We were all going to die, Sheriff. All us were on the floor as the bullets kept pouring into the house. It went on for what seemed like hours, but it was only a few minutes. Then, the shooting slowed down and stopped. Suddenly we heard Mister Holt's voice announcing that they were all dead and it was safe to come out. We couldn't believe we'd survived.

"He not only saved our lives but came into the house and removed my son's bullet, sutured his wound and then took the bodies back to the Double L to tell Mrs. Lynch. All this by a man that had been turned down for a job just hours before. He risked his life to save us, Sheriff."

"I understand that, Mrs. Adler. Do you know why they attacked your ranch?"

Linda said, "When I was on the floor in my house and one of them had me pinned down on the floor, the other one said that he'd never had a Jew before. Why would he think such a thing? Mister Holt then appeared shot one, knocked the other one off me and shot him. Do you know how much humiliation he saved me by doing that, Sheriff?"

"Yes, ma'am. I understand."

Nellie then said, "Sheriff, why on earth would Charlie Lynch believe we were Jewish?"

He shook his head and said, "I don't know, Mrs. Adler. People sometimes believe rumors."

Nellie snapped, "So, rumors justify coming to our ranch in the middle of the night and trying to murder us all? Even if it were true, would that make it acceptable in your eyes?"

Sheriff Owens shook his head and replied, "No, ma'am. Well, I've got to go and interview Mrs. Lynch now. Again, I'm sorry for your loss."

By the time he reached the access road, Sheriff Owens had already decided not to bother interviewing Mrs. Lynch. He already knew that disaster was in the offing and he didn't think that he could do anything to even slow down the Tragedy Train but hoped it didn't careen into him before it stopped rolling.

———

Martha and Beth were sitting in the main room while Juanita prepared lunch. The subject of their discussion, naturally, was Doc Holt.

"He can't keep on like this much longer," Martha said, "I don't care what he says or how strong he is. He needs to stop."

"What can we do?" asked Beth.

Martha stood, walked to the window and answered, "Not a damned thing," as she looked outside and spotted two hearses and a wagon rolling down the access road. The Farley brothers had arrived with the coffins.

———

Doc knew it was there. It had to be. He put one foot slowly forward his eyes glued to where it had to be, waiting for any sign of motion.

Then there was the expected flash of motion and Doc lunged forward with his hands outstretched and caught the massive bullfrog in midair.

"Gotcha!" he shouted with a big grin on his face.

The frog struggled to regain its freedom, so Doc tossed it gently into the pool of muddy water in the small pond. It was the only still water in the area and it wasn't much, but right now, it was exactly what he needed.

His pants were rolled up to his knees above his bare, muddy feet, and he wasn't wearing a hat or a shirt as his toes squished into the mud.

He'd stalked the master of the pond for twenty minutes before successfully making his snatch. Just as he had when he was a youngster, it was the catch that was important, not the keeping. As he watched the frog's strong legs propel itself through the water in one massive stroke after another, he wondered if the frog knew that he was a frog or what had just happened.

He glanced back at Trapper and asked, "Trapper, do you understand that you are a horse?"

Trapper just looked at him and Doc laughed.

"If you do, then my hat's off to you, 'cause I sure wouldn't put up with havin' some cowhand sittin' on my back all day."

He took a seat on the bank and began tossing rocks into the murky water, watching the ripples fan out from each splash, wondering how that worked. He could see that the water got pushed out of the way by the rock and then had to rush back into fill the hole, but it was the waves that now fascinated him. Sound was waves too, but when he let his mind drift into that realm, he found himself thinking of bullets and guns again.

He'd watched cannon and muskets being fired during the war and knew that if they were close enough, he'd see the smoke and the round would hit before the sound arrived. But if he was more than a couple of hundred yards, he'd see the flash or the gunsmoke, followed by the sound and then the bullet or cannonball. The bullet may have been faster than sound when it left the muzzle, but it started slowing down right away but the sound waves didn't, just like those waves on the pond. They kept the same speed, but as they were further away from the splash, they grew smaller and weaker, just like sound.

He hurled one more rock and didn't even bother watching it make its waves. He'd spoiled a perfectly tranquil few minutes by thinking about guns and bullets. Doc walked away from the pond, knowing he couldn't go return to his life as a boy again. He was a man now and he had to do man things, but those few minutes of chasing the frog had given his mind enough of a break to go on.

After putting on his shirt, socks, boots and pulling on his Stetson, he mounted Trapper then turned him west toward the fort to pick up the five extra horses and then he'd head for the Double L.

———

"You're sure?" asked Bill Wheeler.

"Yes, sir. Every house in that place was covered in bullet holes and Mrs. Adler was really mad about what happened."

"What about Martha Lynch?"

"Her story matched what Holt told me. It sounds like he was telling the truth. He was in the barn and heard them open up. He killed them all by himself."

Bill Wheeler snorted then asked, "Did you see two of my boys and two of my hands when you were on your way over here?"

"Nope. Where were they headed?"

"I sent them out after Holt. He's got to be in the area around the Double L. I'm surprised you didn't see them."

"I thought I might have heard some gunfire when I was arriving at the Adler place, but I'm not sure."

"How much gunfire? Was it a Winchester or a shotgun?"

"I only heard it for a little while and it was far enough away I couldn't tell you how long it went on, but it wasn't a shotgun."

"Son of a bitch!" snapped Bill Wheeler, "If they aren't back by this evening, I don't think that they'll be coming back."

"You think he got all four of 'em?" asked the sheriff with peaked eyebrows.

Then Bill Wheeler calmed down and replied, "You're right, Joe. He couldn't have gotten all of them. They probably got him."

"Shouldn't they be back by now if they did?"

"Maybe. Maybe not. They might have run across Will Hatfield or Mike Green, too. Those two yellow curs backed out on me and if Chuck saw either one of them or both of them heading off to warn Martha Lynch, then they could have been shooting at them, too. Then they'd go and look for Holt."

"Wait a minute. What do you mean, warn Martha Lynch? Why are Hatfield and Green backing out? What the hell is going on, Bill?"

Bill snarled, "It doesn't matter, Sheriff. Just get your butt back to Comanche and let me handle this. You'll still get your donations, and that's all that you should care about."

The sheriff was about to argue, but after his meeting with the Adlers and the stunning news about Mike Green and Will Hatfield backing out, he wanted no part of this anymore, but knew that he'd still do what Bill Wheeler told him to do.

"Okay," he said then quickly turned and left Bill Wheeler's office and house.

Bill then walked out of the office behind the sheriff, watched him ride off and then sent for his other two sons, Mo and Al to talk to them about the situation. He was debating about sending them out to find their brothers or keeping them on the Bar W. He just wasn't sure about what happened with Chuck and Ira but not worrying one bit about the ranch hands.

———

Doc finally rode Trapper leading the four Bar W horses and Lou Robinson's horse into the Double L yard late in the afternoon. As he had ridden south, despite the uselessness of his prior planning, he'd come up with a plan of sorts. He would have to count on the bravery of the women, knowing he'd leave them defenseless and the willingness of Fred to take part in the action.

After stepping down, he spent the next forty-five minutes stripping the six horses then releasing them into the large corral when he was done. He left the unused Sharps and the four gunbelts with the saddles and his saddlebags as he didn't intend to stay long. He carried his '76 and the other four dirty '73s in his arms to the bunkhouse for cleaning before he went and talked to Fred first then Martha and Beth.

When he finished cleaning the repeaters, he walked to the chow house to see Fred, who would be playing a critical role if he agreed to his plan.

Ten minutes later, he was sitting with the cook at the large, empty chow table.

"I don't care if I don't gotta shoot, Doc. I'll do it. I gotta make up for not doin' anything about it before."

"It'll be dangerous, Fred, but I need to get some kind of advantage. The other times, they were kinda taken by surprise but this time, they'll be ready for me."

"You didn't have to ask, Doc. When do you figure they'll show up?"

"I'm guessin' tomorrow mornin'. They might show up later this evenin', but I don't think so. I figure Bill Wheeler needs to be sure that his boys ain't comin' back."

"Okay, Doc. I'll head out right after breakfast tomorrow."

"Thanks, Fred. I hope that it's the last time."

"Me, too, Doc."

Doc then stood and headed to the ranch house to talk to the women.

Bill Wheeler was talking to his remaining two sons, explaining what he'd been told.

"The sheriff thought he heard some gunfire a few hours ago but wasn't sure. Now, it's possible he was mistaken, or Chuck and Ira found Holt and killed him, or they found Hatfield or Green warning Mrs. Lynch. I'm just not sure."

"Pa, you figure that Holt got Chuck and Ira?" asked Mo.

Al said, "Come on, Mo. They had Fatty and Jack with 'em, and they were lookin' for him, so he couldn't ambush 'em like he did to the Lynches."

Mo shrugged and replied, "I guess."

"If they aren't back by tonight, what I'm going to do is send out Ted and Cajun Lou out in the morning to find out what happened and see if they can track down Holt, while I go and console the grieving widow."

"We can go find 'em, Pa," offered Al.

"No, I'm not sending either of you out. Not now. If there's a chance that Chuck and Ira are dead, I don't want to risk losing you, too. That's why we pay these ranch hands. Let them take their chances. I'm just letting you both know what will be happening."

"Where are you gonna send 'em, Pa?" asked Mo.

"While I pay my visit to the Double L and see if I can convince Martha Lynch to either sell the ranch or marry me, they'll be searching for Holt. He's got to be between the Slash A and the Double L, and probably north. I'll bet he's staying at that abandoned ranch just north of the Double L. The one that had those Irish Yankees. I'll send them in that direction first.

"Okay, Pa. Do you want us to send Cajun and Ted over?"

"Yes, I'll be in my office."

The last two of the Wheeler sons stood and left their father's office to find Cajun Lou and Ted.

———

Doc sat in the easy chair staring at Martha as she sat on the couch across from him.

"When Will Hatfield told me that, I couldn't believe it. It was bad enough that he was gettin' everyone all riled up about folks he didn't like, but now it all comes down to plain old greed."

Martha said, "I have no intention of giving up this ranch to the likes of Bill Wheeler and I know Beth surely doesn't want any part of Chuck Wheeler."

Doc said, "No, ma'am. No woman is gonna have to suffer puttin' up with Chuck Wheeler anymore. He was one of the four that I buried in the gully. Another was his younger brother, Ira, and the other two were ranch hands. I figure losin' those four is gonna change the way that Wheeler approaches this problem."

"What should we do, Doc?" asked Beth.

"I just told Fred what I want to do is lure them out to near the fort and get behind them, but that would leave you both in danger, and I can't let that happen either, so I'm gonna have to change my plans again."

"Whatever you need, Doc," Martha said.

"I'm thinkin' that it might be better if you both head over to the Adlers for a couple of days. The Wheeler crowd won't know you're there and you'd still have some protection. What do you think, Martha?"

"We can do that, Doc. When should we leave?"

"Go ahead and pack your things for a few days' stay, and you can leave in the mornin'. I don't think they'll be comin' until later in the day. I'll have Fred drive you over in the wagon and I'll wait here for them."

"Do you think they'll all show up, Doc?" asked Beth.

"If Wheeler's smart they will. Even with just his two sons and four ranch hands, it'll be hard to deal with 'em all."

"Why can't you get Mike Green or Will Hatfield to help?" asked Martha.

"They have families they'll want to protect, and I just plain old don't want their help. I won't know if I can count on them once the bullets start flyin', and that's a bad time to find out."

Martha then asked, "How are you, Doc? You can't keep this up much longer."

Doc smiled and replied, "I'm okay. I spent some time hunting a bullfrog and that helped."

Neither women could see how catching a large amphibian could make him feel better but didn't comment.

Doc then added "I'll be in the chow house with Fred to tell him about the change in plans, then I'll start getting set up for tomorrow."

He stood, smiled at them both then turned and left the house to chat with Fred.

————

After Doc finished explaining the modified plan, Fred nodded and said, "Okay. I gotta tell ya, Doc, I was kinda lookin' forward to runnin' around gettin' shot at. I haven't had any fun like that for a long time, but I'll take Mrs. Lynch and Beth to the Slash A in the mornin'."

"Thanks, Fred. I'll sleep in the bunkhouse tonight after I get everything set up. I'm plannin' on leaving loaded Winchesters around the place so they'll see me unarmed and chase after me. As long as I don't get plugged, I'll have 'em close and take 'em down one at a time."

Fred shook his head and said, "Doc, is that the best you can come up with? Hopin' that you don't get shot?"

"Fred, you gotta understand. All of this, the shootings, the deaths and makin' so many widows, all could've been stopped if I had just done somethin' earlier. I shoulda said somethin' that first night when they went out. Rhonda lost everything she had 'cause I let it go. Mrs. Adler lost her husband and now Martha and Beth are widows and the ranch is empty of men except for you. All of it, every last bit of it didn't have to happen, but I let it go. I told myself it wasn't my business and folks died. If I get shot, then so be it."

"Doc, that's a pile of horse dung. I knew about it and I didn't stop it 'cause I was scared and didn't want to lose my job. Hell, I bet even Mrs. Lynch and Beth had some kinda idea that they were up to no good. They had to have heard about what had happened at the other ranches and put two and two together."

"Beth probably did, but I think Mrs. Lynch didn't want to hear it or believe it, but it doesn't matter, Fred, they're all widows because I waited too long."

"How's Mrs. Byrne doin', Doc? She's all alone up there, ain't she?" he asked.

He nodded then replied, "Yup, she's all alone. She hates me, Fred, and I don't have a clue why. She told me to get off her ranch and never come back. Then when I left her some money to get by, she got even madder. I just don't get it. I can't understand women at all and understand her less than any of 'em. Of course, I've spent more time talkin' to her than any of the others, too. Maybe if I talked to Beth more, I'd be just as confused, but I don't think so.

"Rhonda is a real puzzle to me. I like her a lot, and want to take care of her, but I'm kinda mixed up a bit. I know that this sounds unmanly and everything, Fred, but I've never been with a woman before. It's not that I don't want to, but the opportunity just never showed up. I know I could go and buy a woman down in Comanche, but it's not the same. I gotta love the woman I'm with, but I don't know what that feels like."

"You ain't never been with a woman?" Fred exclaimed loudly.

"No, and thanks for lettin' the whole ranch know," Doc said, regretting his confession.

"Damn, Doc, that's a shocker, that's all. I mean we all knew that Beth always had her eyes on you, even before she married Ned, and even Juanita hinted around that she wouldn't mind if you warmed her bed."

"Now, you're just pullin' my leg, Fred. Beth is Beth, and I'm just a cowhand. And Juanita? You're kiddin' me, Fred. I probably said no more'n ten words to her in the past six years."

"First off, Ned was a cowhand, and Beth married him."

"Yeah, but she didn't see him as a cowhand, and neither did any of the rest of us. He was just a pretty boy in chaps."

"I'm just passin' along what I heard, but I still can't believe you never been with a woman."

"Fred, you gotta understand. I never knew my mama, didn't have any sisters or aunts, and didn't go to school, so I never got to meet any girls. Then I went into the army and the only women were the camp followers, and I couldn't do that with any woman I didn't love, and I didn't even know what that was supposed to be like."

Fred still sat in disbelief as he stared at Doc.

"Doc, you probably got more women hankerin' after you than any other feller I know, and you never noticed?"

Doc shook his head and replied, "No. Like I told you I can't understand women and have a hard time talkin' to 'em about anything serious. Women kind scare me a bit, but Rhonda was different. If she's not mad at me, I really liked talkin' to her and just bein' with her. There's just so much that I don't know about her, it makes it more interestin'. You know what I mean?"

Fred grinned and said, "You, Doc Holt, are smitten by that red-headed lady, and you gotta admit it to yourself."

"I am, huh?"

"You are seriously smitten. How does she feel about you?"

"She hates me and kicked me off he ranch tellin' me not to come back, ever."

"And you got no idea why she told you that?"

"That's one of the things that's makin' me crazy. She asked me if I'd move into the house, and when I told her it was a bad idea, she almost threw a knife at me."

"Why in tarnation did you tell her it was a bad idea?" Fred asked in disbelief.

"Because she didn't understand that it would look bad if I lived in the same house that she was in. I didn't want to embarrass her by bein' so close."

Fred smacked his forehead with the palm of his hand, saying, "Doc, you can't be that ignorant. If she asked you to move into the house, she wanted you to move into her bed."

Doc was aghast and said, "No, Fred. That can't be. She's had a hard life and the last thing she'd want is to have a man sleepin' with her, especially after what happened to her a couple of months ago. She still has nightmares about it, too. I'm sure she was just bein' considerate."

"Believe what you want, Doc, but I'll bet that she's smitten with you, too. When you said 'no', you were tellin' her that you didn't want to be with her, and that's why she's mad."

Doc shook his head in disbelief before he said, "Then explain why this mornin', when I went to ask her why she was mad, she asked me if I'd moved into my new place and when I told her I did, she got even madder. Then when I asked her if she'd move into the Double L ranch house, so I could protect her, she almost exploded and made it sound like I'd insulted her. That's when she told me that she didn't want to ever see me again and to get off her ranch. So, I left her some money to get by, and I swear, if she had her Winchester with me, she woulda pulled the trigger. Explain that, Fred."

"Wow! Sounds like she's really smitten even more than you are."

Doc threw up his hands and exclaimed, *"Now, how the hell did you think that?* I just told you how mad she was."

"If she wasn't smitten, she wouldn't get so mad," then after a brief pause, Fred asked, "Did she and Beth talk at all? You know, alone?"

"Probably. What has that got to do with anything?"

"I'm guessin' that your Rhonda found out that Beth has her cap set for you and she's jealous. Let's face it, Doc, Beth is one amazing filly."

Doc couldn't believe any of this. *Beth and Rhonda?*

"Sorry, Fred. I think you're as crazy as that red-headed Irish lady. I'm just gonna worry about Bill Wheeler and his crowd and maybe I'll get lucky and catch a .44 right between the eyes."

"I ain't wrong, Doc, but you gotta do what you gotta do."

Doc didn't answer but finished his coffee then returned to the bunkhouse to prepare for tomorrow.

———

Cajun Lou Lafontaine and Ted Frank were cleaning their guns in the bunkhouse while Jim Porter and Larry Jones looked on.

"How come the boss sendin' you two to hunt for him?" asked Jim Porter.

"Maybe he figures we're better than you two," Ted replied, following it with a snicker.

"Not hardly," Larry replied, "I think he knows you two are both worthless and he can't afford to lose me and Jim."

Cajun Lou was studying his Colt's rifling as he said, "You think what you want, but me and Ted are gonna find that Holt troublemaker and fill him full of lead."

Jim Porter asked, "You really think he killed all four of 'em, Lou? That'd be kinda hard for one guy to shoot four of 'em."

Cajun Lou set his Colt down on the table then looked at Jim.

"He killed every man on the Double L in fifteen minutes. I figure killin' those four would take him just five."

"Then how are you gonna kill him, Lou?" asked Larry.

"Easy. I'm better than him and any of those others, includin' you."

"Just askin', Lou. No need to get worked up."

Cajun Lou didn't comment as he began loading cartridges into his Colt.

———

Doc was getting ready for tomorrow's showdown. He and Fred had eaten their dinner and Fred had gone into his own quarters in the chow house leaving Doc alone in the bunkhouse on his old bunk that he'd abandoned less than a week ago.

He had taken three of the gunbelts, removed the holsters, trimmed the excess leather and hooked them all together creating the bandolero that he'd imagined earlier. When he was done, it gave him easier access to another twenty-four cartridges for the Winchester '76. After having seen the devastating effect of a bullet hitting a pocketful of cartridges, he had opted for the homemade bandolero.

After filling it with the .45-75 cartridges, he wondered how he could safely carry some of the much larger Sharps cartridges, but finally figured he'd just leave them in the box and pull them out when needed. He didn't want to suffer the same fate as Charlie Lynch. The Sharps would give him maybe two shots at range before he'd have to switch to the '76 anyway.

Then over the next hour, he carried an armload of fully loaded Winchester '73s and hid them in over a dozen locations around the buildings. By the time it was dark, the Double L had been transformed into a giant Winchester store.

He finally pulled a bar of soap and a towel and walked the half a mile to the creek for a bath. No sense in staying filthy for what promised to be a dirty day.

He finally blew out the lamp in the bunkhouse and laid atop the blankets on his old bunk, reviewing what he expected to have happen tomorrow and recalling what Fred had told him about Rhonda. He admitted to himself that he was definitely smitten with the lady but doubted that Fred was right about how she felt. He knew that she was grateful for his help, at least before today, but that was all.

Beth was an entirely different problem. If Fred was right about her, then that would lead to even more problems after this was all done, especially in light of Martha's offer to take over running the ranch. If Beth really expected him to marry her, then he'd just hire the ranch hands in a couple of weeks and then move on, knowing it would be better for all concerned.

———

Rhonda had just jerked up from the pillow, ending the nightmare as the echoes of her screaming still reverberated from the walls and her heart pounded against her ribs and the sweat plastered her nightdress against her skin. Then she lowered herself back to the bed, her eyes now wide open as she relived the terrors from the horrible dream.

This one had seemed worse than the others because in this dream, one of the faces of the brutes that had struck and taken her was Doc Holt's and for the first time, she began to wonder if he hadn't been lying all along. Maybe the dream was really a weak memory that had returned to her consciousness.

As lonely as she was, Rhonda Brady, not Byrne, now felt that she had made the right decision to send Doc Holt away. She rationalized that all his helpful behavior had just been to assuage his guilt for what he had done. He was no better than those monsters he had killed and probably worse. He had killed them, so none could ever expose his participation in that night.

Rhonda stayed awake on her bed staring into the darkness and let her irrational thoughts control her, so she could justify having sent him away, convincing herself that everything he had done was just a sham. He was just another evil bastard but masked it better than the others.

CHAPTER 5

Doc waved to Martha and Beth as the wagon started to roll toward the access road. Fred was driving, but both women waved back to him, unsure if they'd ever see him alive again.

He'd had Fred handle moving their things into the wagon, so he didn't have to talk to Beth, just in case something slipped out one way or the other. He'd only shown up to help them onto the wagon then left a Winchester in the seat well for their protection but didn't think it would be necessary for the two-hour ride.

Once the wagon turned west on the road, Doc walked onto the porch and took a seat in one of the three large rockers. He wasn't wearing his gunbelt but had one of his Colts sitting by his side. The nearest Winchester '73 was leaned against one of the porch support posts and wouldn't be visible until any visitors were so close to the house that they'd be able to dismount onto the porch. The '73 was already cocked. He wanted the Wheeler boys to get close. If they were close enough to start firing without talking, it would be a problem but this whole mess was nothing but a series of problems.

———

Bill Wheeler knew now that somehow Holt had killed his two sons. The two ranch hands didn't matter, but losing his sons mattered to him a lot.

"The sheriff guessed he was north of the Double L. Now, the only place he could be hiding up that way was that Yankee's ranch, the Circle B. You find that bastard and you bring his body back here. Do you understand?"

"I wasn't gonna bring him back alive, boss," Cajun Lou said.

"Then, don't. I want to see so many holes in his body that you can't even count them."

Lou turned to Ted Frank and just jerked his head sideways letting him know it was time to go.

After they were gone, Bill walked out to the barn to saddle his horse for his ride to the Double L.

Twenty minutes later, Bill Wheeler was riding southwest along the road while Cajun Lou and Ted were cutting cross country due west.

————

Rhonda had eaten her breakfast and then began to clean and dust the house. It was a distraction as much as a necessary job.

She was still in a foul mood after last night's dream revelation about Doc Holt. She had to convince herself that it was true, and he was nothing more than another selfish, despicable man to chase away the green monster of jealousy.

She had counted the cash that he had left and was surprised to find almost two hundred dollars. The only time she'd seen that much money was when she had handed over her dowry to Jamie. Since then, she'd never seen more than ten but as much as she needed it, she vowed that she would only use it if she was near starvation again. She'd make her own way somehow.

She had even hated getting dressed in one of the dresses that he had bought for her, wishing she hadn't chopped her old dresses in half to make them into blouses. Maybe she'd reattach the bottoms and make them dresses again. They'd look a fright, but she wouldn't be reminded of that man again, the one who was probably down at the Double L with Beth right now doing… whatever.

With that vision in her mind, Rhonda let her anger take over and began to sweep furiously just making the dust fly to resettle in another part of the room.

———

Doc spotted a rider coming from the east along the road and wondered if he was alone or had backup riding a few hundred yards back or maybe riding cross-country to show up at the ranch house from behind. He may be someone else just riding past the ranch too, so he'd have to wait.

When the rider turned onto the access road, Doc identified Bill Wheeler and was surprised at first, but then recalled that Wheeler was planning on convincing Martha to part with the Double L, so maybe he was alone after all. He guessed that Bill Wheeler was due for a rude surprise.

He just sat rocking slowly as he watched Wheeler approach, waiting for him to spot him in the rocker. It didn't take much longer.

Bill Wheeler had seen Doc in the rocking chair, but hadn't made the connection yet, unsure of who else could be at the ranch. But when he drew within a hundred yards, he was pretty sure it was Doc Holt sitting there staring at him, and he wasn't even armed!

He was going to pull his Winchester and just shoot him, but he desperately wanted information about his boys, so he simply slipped his hammer loop off as he walked his horse closer to the porch.

When he drew within thirty feet, he stopped and asked, "Are you Holt?"

"I am. You don't remember me very well, do you, Wheeler?" Doc asked in return.

"That's Mister Wheeler to you, Holt. You're nothing but a cowhand."

"You're right about that, Wheeler. And you're the bastard that started all the killin' in Comanche County and other places. You're the one that messed up a good man when you poisoned Charlie Lynch. You are just about the poorest excuse for a man I can think of, and here you come ridin' in here to try and steal Martha Lynch's ranch."

"What I do doesn't concern you, Holt. Where are my sons? They've been missing since yesterday morning and I think you ambushed them."

"No, I didn't ambush them, Wheeler. They were chasin' after Will Hatfield and they spotted me and all four of 'em then forgot about him and started chasin' me instead," he said as he dropped his right hand slowly to his side where the Colt was pressed against his thigh, "Then they began firin' those Winchesters from two hundred yards tryin' to get a hit. Kinda stupid, wasn't it, Wheeler?"

"You are a liar, Holt! I know you bushwhacked them."

"How in holy hell am I gonna bushwhack four men, Wheeler. At least now I know where Chuck and Ira got their dose of stupid. I picked them all off one at a time and buried 'em in a gully about three miles north of here. They mighta been dug up by the coyotes already, though. I didn't dig the graves very deep."

234

Bill Wheeler had heard enough and slapped the leather of his holster as his hand gripped his Colt. He was drawing the pistol free when Doc pulled his Colt from the chair, cocked the hammer and fired.

The .45 didn't go where Doc intended, but still smashed into the right side of Bill Wheeler's chest. It didn't punch into his lung but rode along the rib and exited the muscle tissue on his back. The impact threw Bill's right arm backward as he was squeezing his trigger, firing his Colt into the top of the porch before he dropped the pistol.

Doc had a cocked Colt in his hand, but Bill Wheeler was disarmed and wounded, and Doc just couldn't pull the trigger again. Besides, he suspected that Wheeler might have sent his other two sons or ranch hands to cover his back, so he stood, released the pistol's hammer and trotted to the porch stairs.

Bill Wheeler was bleeding, but he could breathe normally, so he wheeled his horse to the west and shot away from the yard then after he was out of range, turned him north at a fast trot to find Cajun Lou and Ted Frank. He couldn't even lift his Winchester, but he wanted to lure that damned Holt into their sights.

Doc watched him race away to the west, then turned and ran to the barn where Trapper was saddled and waiting for him. He quickly donned his gunbelt and secured his Colt before mounting his pinto then chasing after Bill Wheeler.

He spotted him more than a mile away and now heading north at a fast trot which Doc matched.

As Doc chased, he kept his head on a swivel, looking for the other riders he knew had to be there.

———

The other riders, Cajun Lou and Ted Frank, were trotting along and were just six miles from the Circle B ranch house. So far, they had seen nothing interesting, but Cajun Lou was convinced that Holt was hiding out in that abandoned ranch house.

Forty minutes later, his suspicions were confirmed when they spotted smoke coming from the cooking pipe in the distance.

"He's in there, Lou!" shouted Ted.

"I see that, so shut up!" Lou yelled back.

They slowed down as they pulled their repeaters.

———

Doc was gaining on Bill Wheeler and had stopped scanning the sides or his back knowing that they were clear enough now and anyone coming to his aid would have to be in front.

He still didn't know what he was going to do with Wheeler, but he believed that there was a reason for his flight to the north.

They had passed the fort still riding north and then Doc began to worry about where he was headed. *Why would he be riding to the Circle B?* They wouldn't know that Rhonda was there, so they should believe that it was abandoned.

Then the only possible reason for Bill Wheeler to ride north rather than east to his ranch was that he expected someone to be there, probably his other two sons. He must have sent them to search for him after the other four didn't return to the ranch. Killing those men had put Rhonda in danger.

Doc set Trapper to a gallop, despite knowing he was three miles to the ranch house and Trapper had already been trotting for eight miles. It would be asking too much for his friend, but he had to demand it from him.

Bill Wheeler glanced behind him to make sure that Holt was still there and noticed his speed increase and kicked his horse into a matching gallop, hoping that Cajun Lou and Ted Frank were close. He knew his horse couldn't go much further.

———

Cajun Lou and Ted had circled wide around the ranch house and dismounted behind the barn of the Circle B. Lou then told Ted to take the front of the house, and he'd go into the kitchen.

They were just passing out from behind the barn when Ted spotted a dust cloud to the south, and it was moving fast.

He said, "Lou! Somebody's ridin' this way and he's comin' hard!"

Lou turned and stepped close to Ted and they both watched and soon noticed it was two riders, not one and the second rider was close to the first one.

"That's him! The second one is a pinto!" Ted said excitedly.

"The one in front looks like the boss's mare," Lou said, "let's wait for 'em to get close and then we open up on that Holt."

"Okay, Lou," Ted said as he cocked his Winchester.

Lou walked quickly over to the nearby bunkhouse to get a better firing angle.

Rhonda had heard the shouts, but just marginally before she stopped and tried to listen more closely didn't hear anything else, so she returned to her cleaning but still paid more attention.

————

Bill Wheeler's horse, frothing heavily and slowing, crossed the access road, then he glanced back at Doc Holt who was just a hundred and fifty yards behind him on his own laboring animal. He then began searching for Cajun Lou and Ted, hoping that they were nearby then spotted a horse's rump sticking out behind the barn and angled the horse in that direction, three hundred yards away.

Doc was doing his own scanning, and when Bill Wheeler suddenly veered to his right, Doc spotted the same thing that Bill had and turned Trapper to the left, heading toward the front of the house to hopefully have time to warn Rhonda that there was danger outside, unless they were already in the house.

Rhonda then heard the hooves set down her broom and looked out the front window, spotting Doc heading towards the house, but missing Bill Wheeler who had already turned away and was out of sight when she looked through the window.

She angrily turned, stormed back to the kitchen where she had left the Winchester, snatched her carbine, and cocked the hammer. She wasn't going to shoot him, but she wanted to show him that she was fine on her own now. Why he had returned didn't even enter her mind, just that he was there.

Her Winchester firmly in her grasp, Rhonda stomped back to the front room then stood in the doorway as Doc crossed into the front yard, and his horse collapsed under him, throwing him to the ground. She was startled by what had happened and dropped her pretense and her Winchester then raced from the house to make sure he was all right when a rifle shot rang out from the bunkhouse.

Doc was scrambling to his feet with his Winchester grasped in his left hand when he spotted Rhonda just as Lou's opening shot smashed into the ground just four feet in front of him.

"Get in the house!" he shouted to Rhonda as he ran up the steps.

But Rhonda was frozen in place as Ted took his first, hurried shot. The .44 rammed into Rhonda's left side, spinning her to the porch's floor with her blood already spreading over her dress.

Doc felt as much as heard two more bullets strike the porch, sending shards and splinters into the air as he reached Rhonda and slid her into the house then set his Winchester on the floor and ripped open her dress to look at the wound. She had been lucky it was Ted's shot and not Lou's. The angle from behind the barn had hit her side but had entered and exited just below the lower ribs. If it had been from Lou's bunkhouse position, it would have killed her instantly.

"Am I going to die, Doc?" she asked.

"Not if I can help it, Rhonda. Here, hold this in place over the wound," he said as he ripped off his shirt and pressed it against her side.

She laid on her right side and held it in place, wondering what was happening.

Doc, then cocked the hammer to the '76 and thought about angles for just a few seconds then ran back outside to the porch and looked for gunsmoke clouds.

He spotted Bill Wheeler riding a different horse as he left heading east, but he wasn't important now. The shooters were, but neither one was showing himself as they had moved from their previous spots to get better angles.

He wanted to go back in and help Rhonda but didn't have the time. His priority now was to keep her safe. He trotted down to the end of the porch, peered around the end of the house and spotted Ted Frank bent over as he left the far end of the barn to get to the kitchen.

Doc knew he'd be exposing himself to the second shooter, but had to make the shot, so he hopped down from the porch and shouted, "Hey!"

When Ted heard his shout, he swiveled his Winchester in that direction and was bringing it level when Doc fired, the bullet hitting Ted high in the chest just to the left of his breastbone, dropping him to the ground where he would die eleven seconds later.

Doc then quickly backed up two steps and turned toward the bunkhouse where he had seen the other cloud of gunsmoke. He hoped that the shooter was still behind the bunkhouse and decided to waste a few rounds to smoke him out. So, he aimed at the bunkhouse on the opposite end from the door then began to fire, walking his shots back toward the door, knowing that the bullets would blast through both sides of the bunkhouse with almost no loss of energy.

Lou had been distracted when Bill Wheeler had taken his horse and made his escape and had almost shot his boss, but when he heard Doc's shout then his shot, his attention was redirected back to Doc Holt. He had trotted to the other side of the bunkhouse, away from his smoke, and was planning on sneaking around the back of the bunkhouse and taking a clean shot when he could see the entire front of the house.

Then the board just nine inches from his right shoulder exploded when the .45 slug of lead exited the bunkhouse. He dropped to the ground and began to crawl around the back to see where Holt was. He felt better when the second round blasted through the bunkhouse further away, and he was sure that Holt was standing near the front of the house shooting into the bunkhouse.

He continued to crawl and was nearing the corner of the bunkhouse closest to the house as Doc continued his walking fire to the front of the bunkhouse.

Lou stood, took a breath and suddenly popped out, catching Doc Holt as he was getting ready to fire his fifth shot into the bunkhouse. He was momentarily startled seeing him without a shirt but still knew he had won the gunfight.

Doc picked up the motion and as he was bringing his Winchester to bear on Cajun Lou, he saw Lou's Winchester bloom with gunsmoke and his brain told him he was dead.

And he would have died if he hadn't been turning to shoot at Lou. Lou's .44 would have nicked his shirt's collar had he been wearing one, but instead the bullet buzzed just past the junction of his neck and his left shoulder.

Doc didn't take time to thank the god of ballistics but steadied his Winchester as Lou levered in a new round. He squeezed his trigger feeling the welcoming kick from the brass-plated Winchester butt knowing that he hadn't missed.

Lou felt as if he'd been kicked by a mule when the slug drilled into his chest after traveling the two hundred and forty-six feet. The bullet did extensive damage to his vascular system before exiting out his back between the sixth and seventh ribs, miraculously not breaking either, but it was the only break that

Cajun Lou received as he dropped to his knees when his lungs rapidly filled with blood, then fell onto his face.

Doc took a quick glance at Bill Wheeler riding off into the distance, but he was unimportant. He had to be Doc Holt now, not the avenging angel.

He ran back into the house, set his Winchester on the floor then knelt beside Rhonda, who just looked at him.

"Okay, Miss Brady, I need to sew up that wound. The good news is that the bullet went straight through the side of your gut, but it wasn't far enough in to hit anything. You're going to be sore for a while, but you should be okay. Where is your sewing kit?"

"In my bedroom on the bookshelf," she replied.

Doc stood and trotted into the bedroom and spotted it near her old cut-up dresses and wondered what she was doing but didn't dwell on it as he snatched the sewing kit and then returned to the main room.

"I don't have any whiskey to clean the wound of any infection," he said, then paused and said, "stay there."

Then he ran out of the front of the house and sprinted across the yard to the back of the barn where Ted Frank's horse was tied up. On the way, he'd spotted Trapper drinking at the trough and was relieved that he hadn't ridden him to death.

When he reached Ted's horse, he yanked off his saddlebags and hoped like hell that Ted as a drinking man. He dumped the contents onto the ground and was rewarded when he spotted a small, flat bottle of gin.

He scooped it up and trotted back to the house and took a knee next to Rhonda.

"I found some gin. This is going to hurt, so just get ready."

Rhonda didn't reply, so Doc first threaded a needle and set it aside.

"Here comes the sting," Doc said as he removed the blood-stained shirt and gently poured some of the gin onto her wound.

Rhonda screeched when the liquid touched the raw, open tissue, but then closed her eyes remaining still and quiet as Doc began to suture the wound.

He pinched the halves around the bullet hole together and began to sew quickly to reduce the amount of time that Rhonda would have to endure the pain. He put six sutures into each of the two holes, then splashed some more gin onto the wound.

"All done. You were very brave, Miss Brady," Doc said as he stood, "I'm going to get a towel to bandage the wound. I'll be right back."

Rhonda kept her eyes closed and heard his footsteps fade away and then grow louder when he returned.

Doc folded the towel twice and laid it on top of the wound, then ripped the sleeves from his shirt and slid them under her torso and tied them off to keep it in place.

"Miss Brady, did you want me to help you to your bedroom? You should try and relax for a little while after losin' the blood."

Rhonda said, "No. I can do it," then rolled slowly onto her back and tried to sit up, but the pain was excruciating, so she just grunted and laid back down.

Doc then slid his left arm under her knees and his right under her back and lifted her from the floor.

"Put me down! I don't need you or any other man," she protested.

"I can understand that, ma'am. But you can't just stay on the floor. I'll leave you on your bed and then I'm going to harness the wagon," he replied as he carried her into her bedroom.

Doc gently laid her onto her bed with her eyes still tightly closed. Then he turned and walked to the next bedroom where he removed the pillow and mattress from the bed and carried them out to the barn where he laid them on the wagon's bed.

After harnessing the two mules to the wagon, he saddled Bride, then drove the wagon out into the yard, hopped down and retrieved Trapper, leading him into the barn. He stripped his pinto and led him into Bride's stall, so he could eat. He pulled his spare shirt from his saddlebags and pulled it on quickly. The idea of riding two hours shirtless in summer sun in Texas didn't appeal to him.

Ten minutes later, Doc drove the wagon with Bride and Ted's horse trailing, Ted's horse now wearing his saddle complete with the Sharps and his '76. The two Bar W riders' pistols and Winchesters were in the wagon's seat well.

He set the handbrake and hopped into the house, then entered Rhonda's bedroom.

Rhonda heard him coming and turned her face away from the door and closed her eyes, keeping them clamped shut when she felt Doc's arms slide under her to pick her up again. She felt herself floating along then the brilliant sunshine passing through her closed eyelids told her she was outside again. She felt herself being lowered onto another mattress and then her head was being lifted onto a pillow.

Doc felt as if he was carrying a fresh corpse as Rhonda remained flaccid and didn't assist in being carried at all. She really must hate him for whatever he had done to offend her because she wouldn't even touch him.

Once she was on the mattress, Doc trotted back into the house and went through her drawers, taking all her clothes and other necessities and laid them onto her bedsheet and then grabbed the corners making a big sack.

He carried the sheet-sack out to the wagon, set it beside Rhonda then removed Bride's canteen and set it near her head on the side opposite the sack of clothes.

"There's a canteen next to your head, Miss Brady," he said before he clambered up into the driver's seat, released the brake and snapped the reins, getting the wagon moving toward the Adler ranch at a good pace.

Rhonda felt the wagon lurching and her stubbornness overrode her curiosity about what had just happened. *Why were those men shooting at her and why did Doc come back?* It took an enormous amount of obstinacy to keep her from asking those questions, but Rhonda had more than enough.

Doc kept the team moving and occasionally glanced behind him, first at his patient then at his backtrail, expecting to see riders at any moment. He figured that Bill Wheeler probably had reached his ranch before he had harnessed the wagon, so if they hurried back to the Circle B to find him, they could have reached the now-empty ranch less than an hour ago. Once they found he'd gone, unless they were really stupid, they'd notice the missing wagon and follow the fresh tracks that he was leaving.

But so far, he'd been lucky and every turn of those wagon wheels brought him closer to the Slash A. Once he left Rhonda in the care of Mrs. Adler or Martha, he'd take Ted's horse and go back to the Bar W. He needed to end this.

––––––

The reason that no one had come after him was that when he had returned to his ranch house, Bill Wheeler had called in his two sons and the last two ranch hands and as he pulled off his bloody shirt and wrapped a towel around his chest, told them what had happened, including the presence of that red-headed woman who they had believed to be dead.

He had seen Ted fall and was pretty sure that Lou was dead too, so he told them that he expected that Holt would be on his way soon.

Bill then dispatched Jim Porter and Larry Hooper to the west to follow the trail that he had made and set up an ambush for Holt and had Mo remain on the ranch and keep an eye on the access road in case Holt came from that direction.

He sent his son Al to Comanche to get the sheriff.

Because Bill Wheeler had shifted to a defensive mode, he had lost his best opportunity to kill Doc Holt.

––––––

Rhonda had drifted off to sleep shortly after the wagon began moving, but Doc couldn't tell the difference as she had never had her eyes open anyway.

The buildings of the Slash A were in sight about a mile away when the wagon bounced over a large rock, startling her awake.

She found the canteen, pulled off the stopper and swallowed some of the warm water.

Doc caught the movement and glanced back, saw her drinking and then looked forward again.

Rhonda didn't recognize where she was, so she finally asked, "Where are you taking me?"

"To the Slash A, ma'am. Mrs. Adler or Mrs. Lynch can keep an eye on you there and you'll be safe."

"Why is Mrs. Lynch at the Adler's ranch?" she asked.

"Because I moved her there, so she'd be safe until this was finished."

"Or maybe it was to give you some private time with your girlfriend," she snapped.

"What the hell are you talkin' about, Miss Brady? I don't have a girlfriend."

"You don't have to hide it from me anymore. I know now."

"Well, ma'am, you know more'n I do. Look, we're only a few minutes away from the Slash A. You were nice and quiet most of the way, so can't we make the last few minutes peaceful?"

"No, we cannot!" she shouted again, feeling a stab of pain from her side, then asked, "You slept with her last night, didn't you?"

"If you're makin' my Sharps a female then, yes, I slept with her last night. Now, stop sayin' such foolish things."

"Oh, so you think I'm a fool, am I? Well, I'm not. I know now. In my nightmare last night when those men were hurting me, I saw your face. You were there, weren't you? You've been lying to me ever since that night just to make yourself feel better, haven't you?"

He turned and looked down into her fiery blue eyes and angrily replied, "You can hate me all you want, Miss Brady, but I wasn't there, and no nightmare shoulda made you think that I could have been. But if believin' that I was one of 'em makes you feel better then you just keep on believin' it and keep on hatin' me," then he reached down into the footwell and pulled out one of the Winchesters and dropped it onto the bed next to her.

"Here, now you know how to use it."

Rhonda watched as the repeater thumped onto the wooden boards and knew she shouldn't have said what she had. She had wanted to hurt him for rejecting her, but she had gone too far and knew that her accusation as unfounded as it was, had hurt him terribly.

She looked up at the back of his head and pleaded, "I'm sorry, Doc. I didn't mean it. I'm just so angry and jealous, and I could never hate you. Please forgive me. Please?"

Doc kept his eyes straight ahead at the Adler ranch house just eight hundred yards away. He was much more than hurt by her accusation, he was crushed. *How could she even think of such a thing, much less say it?* He didn't know how to respond, so he didn't say a word.

Rhonda saw the buildings getting closer and became more desperate.

"Doc, talk to me! Please tell me you'll forgive me. I don't even care if you marry Beth anymore. Just tell me that you forgive me."

Doc was torn apart by hearing her begging for forgiveness, his own sense of loss, but when she said that she didn't care if he married Beth, then he realized that Fred must have been right.

So, without turning, he said, "Miss Blake, I'll forgive you for saying what you said, because I know you were angry at me. But I never was gonna marry Beth. She's like a little sister to me, but you sayin' it means that deep down, you still think that there's a chance that I lied to you. You'll never trust me, and I can understand that, too.

"I was ridin' for the Double L and I knew what they were doin'. Sooner or later, you'll be mad at me again for somethin' that I did, and you'd throw that at me again, and I don't think I could bear hearin' it. So, after I drop you off, I'm gonna go back and end this problem. Then, I'll move on and you and every other female around here can get on with your lives."

Rhonda closed her eyes knowing that he was probably right. Her temper would flare and no matter how much she loved him she'd use that as a weapon to hurt him again. Now that damned temper was driving him away forever, and she knew that there was nothing she could say to keep him from going.

He drove onto the ranch front yard and spotted Harold talking to Fred. He didn't shout but waited until they heard the wagon and turned then waved them over as he kept the wagon moving towards them.

"Doc, what happened?" Fred asked when he was within fifty feet.

He waited until he was closer before he pulled the wagon to a stop, pulled on the handbrake and stepped down.

"Bill Wheeler showed up at the Double L and we had a shootout. I hit him, but not too bad. He rode off and I chased after him to the Circle B, where he had two of his boys waitin'. One of 'em put a bullet through Mrs. Byrne before I got 'em both. I sewed her up, but she's gonna need help for a few days and I couldn't leave her there, not with Bill Wheeler probably sendin' someone over there again. I'm headin' back there now."

"Doc, you can't go right away. You need to hold off until the mornin' at least."

"No, Fred, I've gotta do this now. I can't let 'em come here. Just ask Mrs. Adler to help Mrs. Byrne. She's okay, but she's hurtin'. She'll have to have somebody take those stitches out in a couple of weeks, too."

"You'll be here, Doc. They ain't gonna get you," Fred replied.

"I'm leavin' right after this is all over, Fred. It's time I moved on, one way or the other."

Before Fred could reply, Doc turned and walked back to Ted's horse and mounted.

Rhonda had been listening and when she saw him mount, she shouted, "Doc, please don't go!'

Doc didn't reply but wheeled the horse back to the east and set him off at a trot.

Rhonda began to seriously cry as Fred approached the bed of the wagon and Harold walked to the house to talk to his mother.

"What went on between you and Doc, Mrs. Byrne? If you don't mind my askin'. We had a talk about you last night and I figured you and Doc would be headin' down the aisle pretty soon."

Rhonda looked at Fred and didn't care who she told anymore, so she replied in a shaking voice, "I was so angry that I told him that I thought he was one of the men who had attacked our ranch that night."

Fred said in a low voice, "You know that ain't true, don't you, ma'am? Doc never went on any of them night raids and felt real bad for not stoppin' 'em. That's why he's goin' over to the Bar W right now. Doc would never hurt anybody that didn't deserve it."

"I know that, but I was jealous and wanted to hurt him."

"Well, ma'am, I think you probably hurt him worse than any .44 could have."

Rhonda closed her eyes and said, "I know."

———

Doc rode away and instead of riding to the Bar W, headed for the Circle B, thinking it was more likely to find them there, and besides, he had to get Trapper out of there. If nobody was at the ranch, he'd lead Trapper back to the Double L and leave him with the remuda then move his tack to Fatty's big black gelding, who was probably the best of the bunch.

He had to return the Winchesters that he'd scattered about the place to the house, too.

As he rode, Rhonda's haunting plea for him to return kept rolling through his mind. He may be new to the man-woman game, but his refusal to even acknowledge her when he left wasn't right and he knew it. Yes, she'd hurt him badly, but at least he could understand why she did.

Rhonda had a horrible life since her teen years, being yanked one way or the other, being told one 'truth' then another conflicting one over and over. She'd made an understandable mistake when she was just sixteen and had been paying for it ever since. What had happened to her two months ago must have been a horror that had shaken her to her foundation, then she'd been left alone to deal with the constant terror of expecting a recurrence.

Every night, she'd had nightmares to remind her of that abominable event. *Who was he to put his own hurt feelings above her much deeper and almost constant pain?* He'd only felt that stab of pain for a few minutes, yet Rhonda had endured it much longer and much worse.

Suddenly, Doc wanted to turn around and ask for her forgiveness for not understanding enough. Fred had told him that he was smitten with Rhonda but smitten seemed so cavalier and so boyish. He felt much, much more for Rhonda. He wanted so badly to protect her and to let her push those demons from her past and give her a life where she could be happy and laugh again.

But he couldn't turn back. Not now. He was too close to the Circle B and knew he had to pick up Trapper and return to the Double L before sundown.

———

"He's at the Circle B?" asked Sheriff Olsen.

"That's what my pa thinks. He killed Cajun Lou and Ted Frank and shot my pa, too. He said you gotta arrest him or shoot him. You got a badge, so he won't shoot you like he did the others."

"Alright, Al, go and tell your father that I'll go up there, but if he's not there, I'm not gonna hunt for him."

"That's all he wants you to do right now. He thinks that Holt is gonna trail him to the Bar W, but we've got Jim and Larry set to ambush him if he does."

The sheriff snatched his hat off the peg and followed Al Wheeler out the front door. Deputy Lionel has already gone out on his rounds when the sheriff rode north out of Comanche. The deputy was walking out of The Shotgun Saloon when he spotted his boss riding past. Malcolm Lionel stepped out into the street and glanced to the east and saw Al Wheeler riding away as well. Something was up, and Deputy Sheriff Lionel wanted to know what was going on, so he forgot about his rounds and jogged over to the livery to saddle his horse.

———

Rhonda was lying in bed with Martha and Beth sitting alongside in straight-backed chairs. A kerosene lamp was burning on the bedside table, even though the sun was still up.

"That was pretty bad, Rhonda," Martha said, "you probably could have told him he was a coward and it wouldn't have hurt him as much and that's just about the worst thing you can say to any man."

"I know, Martha. I could see it in his eyes. This is all my fault, too. I was just so jealous of you, Beth. You're younger, prettier and have a much nicer figure, too. I couldn't compete with you."

Beth replied, "Fred told me on the way here. It was a long ride and I mentioned that I wouldn't mind hitching up with Doc and he explained to me what he and Doc had talked about. I suppose I should have seen it, but I just never talked to him that much."

"I know. He told me that he talked more to me in just a few days than he'd ever talked to any other woman, but I forgot all that and the night we sat out on the bedroll waiting outside of the Slash A, just talking for hours. I told him about my past and he made me feel free of guilt for the first time since I started down that path.

"He did all that for me and I treated him like I did just because I was jealous and angry. If I hadn't been so damned stubborn, I would have at least given him the chance to explain. But he's gone now, and he'll never come back."

Martha patted her on her hand and said, "Oh, I think he'll be back, Rhonda. He was just hurt by what you said. I've never met a better man than Doc Holt. Give him time to think about it and I believe he'll not only be back, but he'll apologize for how he behaved."

Rhonda asked, "Why would he apologize? I'm the one who did everything wrong."

"I just know Doc well enough to believe that he will think he was wrong, just like he believed it was his fault for what my husband and the others did because he didn't stop them."

Beth then asked, "Rhonda, why did you feel so guilty about your life before you talked to Doc? I can understand if you don't want to talk about it."

"No, that's alright. I can tell you now. I couldn't talk about it at all until I told him, but now I can. It started when I was twelve…"

———

Doc had reached the Circle B and had brushed down Trapper, who seemed to have recovered from his mistreatment, but Doc wasn't about to push him any further. He'd trail him down to the Double L and give him a few days off.

He was leading Trapper out of the barn as the sun was kissing the horizon when he spotted a rider coming from the south and trotted to Ted's horse and pulled his Winchester '76 from its scabbard. He didn't bother hiding from the oncoming rider as he knew he had the advantage in range and the rider didn't seem to care anyway.

Then he spotted a second rider about a half a mile behind the first one and wondered who was coming in such an odd fashion as neither rider was riding fast, and the first rider seemed oblivious to the second man.

He stepped toward the front of the ranch house and stood with his feet apart and the brass butt plate of the '76 on his right hip and soon spotted the star on Sheriff Olsen's shirt as it reflected the dying sunlight, so he dropped his Winchester's muzzle down, cocked the hammer, and returned it to his hip again.

Sheriff Olsen had seen Doc walk out of the barn, and only identified him when he saw Trapper. He kept watching him as he walked in front of the house with his Winchester and even saw him cock the repeater, so he pulled his own and cocked it as he rode closer and released his Colt's hammer loop, just in case. He was still counting on the badge on his chest, knowing that despite everything that had happened, Doc Holt was a law-abiding man.

Deputy Lionel was slowing his horse to match the sheriff's speed, still wondering what was going on. He'd recognized Doc Holt as well and had seen him ready his rifle, so he slid his own Winchester from its scabbard, but didn't cock the hammer. Soon he slowed his horse to a walk as the sheriff drew within fifty yards of the waiting Doc Holt.

"Evenin', Sheriff. What brings you out here?" Doc asked loudly when the sheriff finally stopped his horse twenty yards away, recognizing the second rider as his deputy.

"I've come to arrest you, Holt. You murdered two men today and you're coming back with me to face trial."

"I'll tell you what, Sheriff Olsen," Doc replied, saying it loudly enough for Deputy Lionel to hear, even though he wasn't sure why the deputy was there, "You give me another day, and I'll take away all your problems. I know that you were protecting those night riders who were killing and raping their way around your county to cleanse it of undesirables. Did you know what they were doin' before they did it? Did you sit in with Bill Wheeler when he gave them their marchin' orders?"

"I don't know what you're talking about, Holt. Just drop your Winchester, or I'll have to shoot you where you stand," he said as he quickly turned his '73 to bear on Doc.

Doc then took the biggest gamble of his life, which may be ending soon, when he dropped his '76's muzzle to the ground, released the hammer and let it fall. Then he used his left hand and unbuckled his gunbelt, letting the rig drop to his feet.

"Okay, Sheriff, I'm under your Winchester now. Are you so corrupt that you'd shoot an unarmed man who's been doin' your job for the past week? Yes, I killed those two a little while ago after they shot Mrs. Byrne. I found her near death last week after Charlie Lynch and his sons and the other ranch hands killed her husband and two ranch hands and raped her and beat her almost to death.

"She survived that only to get shot by Cajun Lou LaFontaine. I killed him and Ted Frank when they opened up tryin' to shoot me. Now, you can deny all that, and the attack on the Adlers just because some idiot thought they were Jewish, and the other ones if you want to, but I know better, Sheriff. You're in up to your neck in this and you oughta hang."

"Think I won't shoot you, Holt? Bill Wheeler isn't dead. You shot him, but he's back on the Bar W right now and he'll hire more men to replace the ones you killed and then we'll be rid of all the troublemakers in this county."

Doc saw Deputy Lionel raise his Winchester aimed at the sheriff's back and snarled, "You're the troublemaker, Joe. You and the rest of your like. You give us normal Texans a bad reputation."

Sheriff Joe Olsen opened his mouth to reply, but was startled when he heard, "Drop your rifle, Joe! I've got my Winchester aimed at your back!"

He didn't turn, but held his repeater off to the side and said, "Lionel? Is that you? I was just arresting Holt for murder. I'm glad you're here. Go ahead and tie up his wrists while I keep you covered."

"And let you shoot me in the back, Joe? I don't think so. I heard it all, and I kinda suspected there was somethin' fishy goin' on. Drop that Winchester to the ground."

Sheriff Olsen tossed his Winchester away and thought that he might be able to pull his Colt if he could distract Lionel somehow.

He ignored the disarmed Doc Holt for the moment as he wheeled his horse around to face Deputy Lionel, who still had his Winchester pointed at him.

"Now, Malcolm, you gotta know that I was just saying that to get Holt to confess. It's an old trick. You agree with everything a man says to get him to tell the truth. You make him trust you. I've told you that before."

Deputy Lionel's resolve slipped slightly as he said, "So, what is happenin', Joe? I kinda knew what was goin' on."

The sheriff had to act quickly before Holt picked up a gun, so he said, "Just ask Bill Wheeler," then he looked past the deputy and shouted, "Bill, tell Malcolm that's the truth!"

Lionel's head turned to see the non-existent Bill Wheeler and Sheriff Olsen ripped his Colt from his holster, cocking the hammer and bringing it to bear before Deputy Lionel realized his crucial mistake and turned back just as Sheriff Olsen's muzzle flared with a fourteen-inch flame sending the .44 into his deputy.

As soon as the sheriff had turned his horse, Doc had begun to bend at the knees, keeping his eyes on the sheriff as he felt for his gunbelt. Just as the sheriff shouted his bluff about seeing Bill Wheeler behind Deputy Lionel, he found the pistol, released the hammer loop and was bringing his gun level when Sheriff Olsen shot his own deputy.

Doc pulled the trigger and his .45 punched into Sheriff Olsen's back before he could turn around to shoot his prisoner.

Sheriff Olsen knew he'd been hit, but knowing he was going to die didn't provide him any solace as he dropped down to his horse's neck, blood pouring from the front where the bullet had exited his body, then sliding off to the side and plunging into the dirt.

Doc didn't worry about the sheriff but ran to where Deputy Lionel lay across his horse's neck with blood dripping from his sleeve.

He helped the deputy down from his horse and laid him on the ground before ripping open his shirt around the bullet hole on the right bicep.

"How is it, Doc?" Deputy Lionel asked with a grimace.

"Not bad, but not good, either. Let's get you into the ranch house and I'll see what I can do for you, Deputy."

"Call me Malcolm, will you, Doc? You just saved my life."

"I'll do that, but you should know that I was trustin' that you were an honest man. If you'd been some weak toady, then I'd be dead right now. So, you saved my life by bein' a good man."

Deputy Lionel smiled and just nodded, then let Doc help him stand.

When he gained his feet he asked, "What about the sheriff? Is he dead?"

"I think so. I'll kick him on the way past to make sure."

"Can I do it?" asked Malcolm.

"Sure, make it hard enough, so we'll know for sure that he's not fakin' it."

"You can count on that," he replied as they walked to the dead sheriff's body and the deputy administered a vicious boot strike to his head without any reaction.

Neither man said a word as Doc assisted Deputy Lionel into the ranch house where he'd sewn up Rhonda's wound just hours earlier. The sewing kit was still sitting on the table in the main room along with the flask of gin.

Malcolm's wound took twice as much time for Doc to close, and he noticed that the deputy made much more noise than Rhonda had.

When he was finished, Doc leaned back and said, "You're all set. I'll need to get those stitches out in a couple of weeks, and that arm is going to be useless for about a month or so, but you'll be okay after that, I figure."

"I can't help you, Doc, and I feel real bad about that. I shoulda done my job better."

"I think all of us shoulda done what needed to be done, Malcolm. You, me, the Adlers, everyone. There were too many folks hurt and we didn't step up. We were all wrong."

"Well, we won't be that way anymore. What are you gonna do now, Doc?"

"I was gonna ride down to the Double L, but it's too late now. I'll get to cookin' some food after I go out and clean up another mess. I still got those other two to put in the ground, too. So, after I bury the three bodies, I'll come back in here and fix us somethin' to eat. You can go into the bedroom and lie down for a while. You lost enough blood to make you a bit dizzy."

"Okay, Doc. Can you take care of Jasper, my horse, too?"

"I was gonna do that, Malcolm. Let's get you to bed."

After leaving Malcolm in Rhonda's bed, Doc left the house and began to clean up his latest disaster, taking care of the horses first before digging one grave for all three bodies. With the outside cleaned up, Doc took a short break by splashing into the shallowing creek and washing off the dirt and sweat.

An hour later, he and Malcolm were sitting at the table eating his not-so-bad supper and drinking coffee.

"How are you gonna handle Bill Wheeler, Doc?"

"I'm not sure, now. He's probably holed up waitin' for the sheriff to come and tell him what happened, but I don't know if that's gonna make him come after me in the mornin' or set up for my goin' to his place. I'll have to play it by ear."

"What can I do to help, Doc? I'm kinda useless with a gun now."

"You can do one real big favor for me, Malcolm. If I write a letter, can you ride it over to the Slash A?"

"Sure. Who is it for?"

"Rhonda Brady. She used to be Rhonda Byrne, but she's a widow now."

"She's the one you helped, isn't she?"

"But not enough, I think. That's why I gotta write the letter."

"So, what happened with her?" Malcolm asked as he sipped his coffee.

Doc spent almost a half an hour talking non-stop about Rhonda, leaving out her past because he felt that she had told it to him in confidence.

When he finished, Malcolm nodded and asked, "Why don't you just ride over there and talk to her?"

"It's too late, and she needs her rest, just like you do. I'll be gettin' up early so I can keep an eye out for any early visitors, and I'll saddle the horses, too."

"What do I tell the mayor and county commissioners about the sheriff?"

"Tell 'em the truth. It never hurt anybody that was doin' the right thing."

Then Malcolm asked, "What about Beth? You know, now that Ned is dead and all."

Doc smiled and said, "You figurin' on payin' her a visit, Malcolm?"

"Maybe, but I'm only a deputy sheriff, Doc."

"Well, I figure you'll be the sheriff soon, and I don't think she'd mind if you stopped by. Ned was a pretty poor excuse for a man, and you're real man, Malcolm. I figure she'll see the difference."

Malcolm grinned and even in the light of the kerosene lamp, turned red enough for Doc to notice.

After Malcolm went to the bedroom to lay down and get some sleep, Doc found a pencil and had to rip a page out of an old, almost unused ledger to serve as his letter paper.

Before he wrote, he looked at the ranch's ledger. He had wondered how the ranch survived with so few cattle which meant very little income. Rhonda had been there for ten years, and granted, they had been lean years, and her husband and the ranch hands apparently spent money in Comanche, so the question was how were they making money?

Doc studied the ledgers. They'd been selling a couple of head every few months, almost from the start. At the bottom of each year's entries was a herd count, and it always went up, despite the sales. The ranch had started with forty-two head of cattle, and they'd sold twelve animals that year, but finished with fifty, but only six calves, which should have given them thirty-six. *Where did the other fourteen come from?*

The pattern continued for the next eight years, until the herd counted up to a hundred and twelve critters. Then the numbers began to drop quickly until the herd numbered forty-eight. So, they lost forty-two head to the Double L, which he knew he could recover, but the nagging question of the growing herd over the years could only come from two sources: unbranded mavericks, which were probably available for the first year or two, but after that, they must have been rustling cattle from the big ranches, like the Double L or the Bar W. But because her husband and hands were only taking a couple from each ranch, and a perfect count was hard to obtain with strays, they wouldn't be missed. If they grabbed the animals before they were branded, then they could stick on their Circle B brand and increase the size of their herd.

It didn't really matter now, but it had reinforced Doc's already gutter opinion of Rhonda's common law husband and the two ranch hands. In his estimation, they got what they deserved that night and Rhonda had been the only innocent victim, as she always had been.

Doc straightened out the sheet of ledger paper, and for the first time in his life, he wrote a love letter, although to him, it was a letter of apology and explanation and the word 'love' was never mentioned.

He simply explained how unfair he had been in not truly understanding her and begged her to forgive him for being so thoughtless. He wrote that he was ashamed for treating her so poorly and that he wasn't going to leave, but he'd stay and, if she had no objections, he'd like to visit her.

When he finished the letter, he folded it and searched for an envelope, but didn't find one, so he just hoped that Malcolm wouldn't read it. But if he did, so what? He's already told him a lot about Rhonda and probably knew what was in it anyway.

He didn't have a mattress on the other bed, so after blowing out all the lights, he walked into the main room and tried to fit himself onto the couch, but failed miserably, so he finally just stretched out on the floor.

————

Bill Wheeler was in pain from the gunshot wound. He should have ridden into Comanche and had Doc Sylvester look it up, but he was worried about being bushwhacked by Holt, so he just laid on his bed with his homemade towel bandage wrapped around his chest. In addition to not having it sutured closed, he had also used a dirty towel from the kitchen. He and his boys hated doing laundry and towels were laundry. They hadn't had a woman cook or a cleaning lady for four years now because the boys tended to scare them away. So, they lived a man's life, which was plainly visible to anyone who set foot in the house.

His two boys had both returned as had Jim Porter and Larry Hooper, who had waited at their ambush site until after sundown. They were all eating in the kitchen, while Bill Wheeler waited for the sheriff to show.

He finally gave up on the sheriff, expecting that he had never gone to the Circle B, and groaned as he sat up then walked to the kitchen to tell the boys what he wanted to do tomorrow.

CHAPTER 6

Doc helped Malcolm into his saddle after telling him that his letter to Rhonda was in the saddlebag.

"Thanks, Doc. After I stop at the Slash A, I'll head back to Comanche and talk to the powers that be. Let me know how things turn out."

"I hope I'll be able to do that, Malcolm," Doc said as he squinted up at the deputy in the bright morning sun.

"You headin' down to the Double L before you ride over to the Bar W?"

"That's the plan, but it's probably gonna change. They always do."

"Okay, I'll tell them at the Adlers what you're doin', and I won't even read your letter."

"You'd better not, Malcolm, or I'll make your future hell," he replied with a grin.

Malcolm grinned back then started Jasper west toward the Slash A.

Doc watched him ride away then headed for the barn to mount Ted's horse and trail Trapper to the Double L. He was very familiar with the terrain, so he knew where all the ambush locations were but didn't expect to see them so early in the day. They would have had to get up at predawn and ride straight to the Circle B without breakfast to get there and he'd still spot them when they arrived.

But he still rode with his eyes peeled for anything that didn't belong.

———

"Are you sure he's still at that ranch, Pa?" asked Mo.

"No, I think that's the most likely spot. I saw that red-headed woman go down and he brought her into the house even with gunfire hitting nearby. I still don't know how those two missed him at that range. Anyway, I figure he's still in there taking care of her. If he's not there, he'll be at the Double L, and the only ones there are the two Lynch women."

"So, why don't we split up, Pa?" asked Al, "Two of us head west cross country to that small spread and two go to the Double L?"

"I want you to stick together, so you'll have a better chance at killing that bastard. Lou and Ted had him dead to rights at that ranch house and he still managed to kill them both. It's like he's got a protective bubble around him or something."

"We'll get him, Pa. Are you gonna be okay?" asked Mo.

"I'll be fine. I'll just sit in the parlor with a shotgun watching the access road through the window. If he comes down that road, I'll wait for him to come inside and let him have both barrels."

"Okay, Pa. We'll head out as soon as we get our breakfast."

"Get going, then," Bill snapped as the four men left his bedroom and headed to the kitchen.

Bill grimaced as he stood, then walked stooped at the waist to his office where he removed his twelve-gauge, checked its load then returned to the parlor and took a seat where he could stare down the access road. He should have had something to eat, but he didn't feel very good.

Twenty minutes later, he heard the back door close and he knew he was alone. It had been a long time since Bill Wheeler had been alone, and it was an eerie feeling.

———

Doc was arriving at the Double L as the four riders from the Bar W left that ranch and headed west toward Rhonda's ranch.

He didn't waste a lot of time as he unsaddled Ted's horse and left both animals in the corral with the large remuda and found Fatty's big gelding. He led the horse out of the corral, saddled him and then led him to the house and tied him off at the front hitchrail.

He spent the next forty minutes gathering all the weapons and consolidating them in the ranch house office. It was an impressive collection. Doc left his homemade bandolero, figuring it was now as useless as all of his plans that had failed. This was just going to be a straight shootout.

He then walked out to the porch and thought he'd wait for them to arrive, but he began to get antsy after just a few minutes, so he walked off the porch, mounted the tall black gelding, and rode north toward his fort. It was already stocked and would give him a better view of the area.

———

Martha and Nellie Adler were on the front porch talking and spotted a rider coming in from the sun.

"Who is that, Martha?" Nellie asked.

Martha shielded her eyes and said, "It's not Doc, he's too short. I think we'd better have one of the men come out here."

Nellie rose from her rocking chair, walked to the open door and shouted, "Leonard! We have a rider coming in!"

Leonard was repairing holes when she shouted, so he trotted to where his Winchester was leaning against the wall, grabbed hold of it by the barrel and walked to the doorway.

Rhonda was in her bed and heard the shout and hoped it was Doc, but knew it probably wasn't.

Leonard reached the porch looked at the rider and said, "I think it's Deputy Lionel. It looks like his horse."

Malcolm saw the Adlers on the porch and waved with his left arm to let them know he wasn't hostile and receiving an acknowledgement wave in return.

When he entered the yard, Martha, Nellie and Leonard all could see the blood on his right arm, and they would have been concerned if he wasn't smiling.

His smile widened when Beth walked out of the house.

"Mind if I step down, Mrs. Adler? I've got some news about Doc Holt."

"You don't have to ask, Deputy. You're the law."

Malcolm stepped down, reached into his saddlebag and pulled out the one-page letter before saying, "No ma'am, the law is the law, I'm just a deputy."

"Well, Deputy, come inside and tell us what happened."

Malcolm climbed the three steps to the porch, followed everyone inside and joined them in the sitting area, removing his hat before taking a seat.

"So, what happened with Doc? Is he okay?" asked Martha.

"Yes, ma'am. The last time I saw him was when he was headed for your place. I woulda helped him but I took a bullet last night and Doc fixed me up, but I can't shoot."

"Did Doc shoot you?" asked a startled Nellie Adler.

"No, ma'am. The sheriff shot me, but Doc shot him. He's dead."

"You were shot by the sheriff?" Beth asked with wide eyes.

"Yes, ma'am. I trailed him out of town, and he rode to the Byrne ranch where he found Doc and was gonna shoot him, but I had my Winchester on him, so he dropped his rifle. But he tricked me then shot me before the Doc finished him off," then he paused and asked, "Is Mrs. Byrne around? I have something to give her."

Rhonda had been listening intently to the deputy's explanation with a rising level of concern for Doc when she heard him ask about her and she jerked her head to the open door wondering why he had asked about her.

"Yes, she's in the first bedroom on the left, recovering from a gunshot she received last night," Martha said as she stood to show him the way.

Linda had caught enough of the conversations between Martha, Beth and Rhonda to add her name to the list of disappointed women as she watched Malcolm carry what was probably a love letter from Doc Holt to her room.

Malcolm rose and followed her to the room. Once inside, Martha stood aside to give room to pass.

Rhonda's eyes were glued to his face as he approached and was startled when he broke into a big smile.

"Ma'am, Doc said to give you this letter," he said as he offered her the folded ledger sheet.

"He wrote me a letter?" she asked as she accepted it.

"Yes, ma'am. He kinda talked about you for a while last night, and I can see why he did. I told him that I'd drop it off before I headed into Comanche to tell 'em what happened. I'll leave you to read it now. It's a real pleasure to meet you, ma'am."

Rhonda was staring at the piece of folded paper in her hand, but said, "Thank you, Deputy."

Malcolm was still smiling as he left and almost ran down Beth as he was leaving.

"Oh, excuse me, ma'am. I didn't see you there."

"Would you like something to eat or at least have some coffee before you leave, Deputy?" she asked.

"I wouldn't mind, ma'am. You can call me Malcolm. Doc calls me that now, too."

"Well, come into the kitchen, Malcolm. I'm Beth."

After they walked to the kitchen, Martha looked at Rhonda and said, "I'll leave you to your letter, Rhonda."

Rhonda nodded and unfolded the sheet of paper as Martha silently left the room, closing the door behind her.

Rhonda didn't know what to expect but was hoping it wasn't bad.

She had to wipe the moisture that was forming in her eyes before she began to read his surprisingly smooth handwriting:

My Dearest Rhonda,

I'm really sorry for leaving you the way I did. It was just that I felt bad and took it out on you, and that wasn't right. It wasn't fair.

You haven't had anything good happen to you for your entire life and I finally figured out that's why you are so afraid. Everybody cared more about themselves than you, and that included me. All I've been doing is complaining about how I was upset about not doing anything to stop what was happening, and I should have been spending all my time listening to you and trying to make your life better. I promise not to do that anymore. I want to understand you more.

I'm not going to go away, Rhonda. When I finish with this, I want to take as much time as I can to understand you and make you happy, even if it takes the rest of my life. You deserve to be happy. You are a wonderful person and I hope you'll give me the chance to make the rest of your life as happy as the first part has made you sad.

All I ask of you is that you understand that I'm an ignorant cowhand who needs to be told when he makes a mistake, because I'll never figure them out on my own. If you'll do that, then I'll try not to make any more of them, but I can't promise that I won't. I'll still be a man and we all say and do stupid things all the time, and it will be up to you to smack me on the head sometimes.

So, when this is all over, Rhonda, would you allow me to visit with you? It would make me happy if you'd allow me that privilege.

Forever Yours,

John Holt

Rhonda reread the letter three times before she set it down on her lap and closed her eyes, letting tears flow down her face.

She found it so incredibly like him. She had hurt him so terribly and unfairly yet, as Martha said he would, he was apologizing to her, but much more importantly, he was coming back to her. She vowed never to let her temper or stubbornness get between them again.

And there was one more thing she needed to do, so she called out, "Martha, could I have something to eat, please?"

———

Doc rode the tall black gelding north out of the Double L, the field glasses bobbing at his chest as he kept an eye out for other riders but only finding an empty horizon.

He reached the fort, walked the gelding inside and stepped down, then let the horse drink in the half-empty cistern before letting him graze on the stack of dried grass while he climbed onto the bottom boulder and stuck his head over the top, not seeing anything. So, he began climbing to the top of the fort, then when he reached the top of the tallest boulder, he stood and faced east looking for a dust cloud and wasn't surprised when he spotted one on the horizon, about five or six miles away.

He left his field glasses where they were because he didn't need them and there was the very good chance that the morning sun would reflect off the glass and let them know he was there. They were northeast of the fort and Doc thought it was all four of the remaining Bar W riders.

He sat on the rock, losing them when he lost the added height, but faced northeast until he expected them to reappear on the closer horizon.

If it was all four of them, he guessed they'd be heading back to the Circle B, and thought it was possible that they might not ride south after they did and might miss the fort altogether.

Doc slid down from the boulder to the lower rock then hopped onto the ground. He told himself to stop getting so antsy. He wanted this over and done so badly that he was worried he might do something stupid.

Despite his warning bells clanging furiously, Doc mounted the tall gelding and walked him out of his fort heading north to intercept the four riders.

———

Mo Wheeler was in charge of the Bar W riders and had them riding at a medium trot. It wasn't baking hot yet, but the thermometer was creeping close to ninety degrees already and each of the men could feel the sweat rolling down his back as they rode west. They were all highly alert, not wanting to feel the bite of Doc Holt's Winchester.

The fear of a sudden slug finding its way into them had a significant impact on Jim Porter. He began to wish he'd never heard of the Bar W, much less Doc Holt. He wasn't being paid enough for this. The only reason he didn't turn around and head back was because the other three were going and he didn't have the sand to leave.

They rode for another thirty minutes before Larry Hooper picked up some movement to the southwest.

"Is that him?" he shouted as he pointed at the distant dust cloud being churned up by a lone rider.

"It ain't a pinto, but it looks like Fatty's horse," yelled Jim Porter.

Al then shouted, "I don't want him runnin'. Jim, you swing south and get behind him. Larry, you go with Jim, but come at him from his right. I'll go straight at him and Mo, you go north and attack him from his left. Let's go!"

Their orders given, the other three men all peeled off to surround Doc Holt.

————

It wasn't as if Doc wanted to be seen, but he had fallen into a trap of his own making. He'd been targeted by so many guns over the past few days that he was beginning to believe in his own invulnerability, whether he knew it or not. There were only four of them trying to kill him, and his desire to finish this and that unwarranted belief that he had nothing to fear by their shots made him ride straight toward the oncoming riders.

When he saw them suddenly break apart, he initially thought it would be to his advantage because he'd have the firepower edge on each of them and wouldn't have to engage them all at the same time.

So, just fifteen seconds after they raced apart, Doc snapped his heels against the big gelding's flanks and shot toward Al

Wheeler, pulling his Winchester as the horse flew across the open ground.

———

As Jim Porter rode south with Larry Hooper, his link of having to follow the group was broken, and when Larry began making his turn to the north, he kept going south rather than head west to get behind Holt. Jim was running away as fast as he could. He'd get to the Bar W, take what he could, and get the hell out of Comanche County.

None of the others noticed that he was leaving.

———

As Doc closed the gap to Al Wheeler, the gelding began having problems with his footing when they entered the shallow sandhills that ran along an almost non-existent gully that had once been a wide creek. His hooves were losing purchase and making him unsteady, but Doc didn't notice as he finally realized the mistake that he had made by charging at Al when he saw two of the others turn to close on his flanks faster than he had expected. He had made their jobs much easier by riding straight at Al.

He suddenly pulled the gelding to a dusty halt and fought the panic that was rising inside him. Al was about four hundred yards away and still coming at him and when he checked the other two, he estimated that neither was closer than eight hundred yards, so this might work out after all. He just didn't know where that fourth rider was, and that made him even more nervous. Yet even as anxious as he was, he still sat on the black and cocked his Winchester waiting for Al to get within range.

But Al wasn't stupid. He could see that he was a lot closer to Holt than either Larry or Mo, so he began slowing down to give them a chance to get closer.

"Damn!" Doc said out loud when he noticed Al slow, so he nudged the gelding forward again to get to Al before the others arrived and locked him in their trap.

Al noticed, then stopped his horse, dismounted and dropped to the ground on his belly, assuming a prone shooting position with his Winchester aimed at Holt as he approached, knowing that they had him. He couldn't do anything to escape now.

Doc was a hundred and eighty yards away from Al Wheeler when Al opened fire, mainly to keep Doc in place so the others could get within range.

Doc thought he was safe and was preparing to open fire with his '76, expecting to make short work of Al before facing the others who were probably less than four hundred yards away. So, he brought the tall gelding to a stop and pulled his Winchester level.

Then Doc's shield of invulnerability left him when Al's second .44 struck the saddle's left jockey right near his thigh, but because of the angle and range, didn't penetrate the heavy leather, but did scrape the inside of Doc's upper leg and much more critically, it spooked the gelding.

Doc felt the horse rear and with his hands grasping the Winchester, he didn't have time to grab the reins or even the saddle horn as he lost control of the animal, and found himself flying backwards over the horse's rump as his cocked Winchester seeming to float in the air with him.

Everything seemed in slow motion as he was falling to the ground and kept his eyes focused on the rifle just three feet away. He wondered if he was going to be shot by his own gun as he braced for the impact on the hard ground.

But when he struck the earth, it may not have been pleasant, but the sand broke his fall much better than the normal sunbaked ground he would have hit just a half a mile away. With the gentle curve of the sandhill also making for a better landing spot, Doc didn't have any serious injuries when he crashed to the surface.

He may not have broken any bones, but he knew he was in real trouble now. He scrambled to his feet and lunged to pick up his fallen Winchester as the gelding raced away with his Sharps.

With the Winchester in his hand, he duck-walked to the other side of the sandhill and plopped down on his chest to evaluate just how bad things were as Al's bullets continued to pepper the ground around the hill.

Al still had to be the first target and that graze shot had done enough damage to hamper his mobility, but he knew he couldn't stay where he was, so he took a second to inspect the Winchester to make sure it didn't blow up in his face when he needed to fire, found it clean enough, then took a deep breath and jumped to his feet and charged over the top of the sandhill toward Al Wheeler.

It was like one of those nightmares when you're running away from some horror and your feet just slip and slide and you can't go anywhere as Doc's boots sunk into the sand when he tried to sprint.

Al was stunned to see him appear, expecting that he was either shot or seriously injured when he'd been thrown and would just hunker down and wait but after that initial shock, he continued his fire in earnest.

Doc had him pinpointed easily as he zig-zagged as best he could on the other side of the long sandhill's downslope. But he didn't want to get to the bottom of the shallow dune because he wanted the extra height to make Al an easier target.

After making a sudden turn, Doc stopped and took quick aim as Al's .44s searched for him where he should have been. Doc only took one shot, knowing he only had a least ten more rounds and three more shooters.

His first .45 exploded the sandy ground directly in front of Al, throwing dirt and dust into his face, effectively blinding him.

Doc saw the shot and then Al's wild attempts to clean his eyes, so he stopped zigzagging and ran straight at Al with his eyes glued to the prone shooter for the first sign that he was preparing to fire again.

While Doc ran, Larry Hooper was the first of the flanking riders to open fire at two hundred yards when he saw that Al was in trouble, but his shot and the two others he fired at long range were ignored by Doc Holt as he concentrated on Al.

Al's tears from his blinking eyes and wiping fingers finally cleared his vision enough to allow him to fire, so he blinked once more as he sighted on Doc Holt, but it was only long enough to see the gunsmoke cloud erupt from his Winchester's muzzle. It was the last piece of information his eyes ever passed to his brain when the .45 smashed into the frontal bone of his skull.

Doc was less than a hundred yards out and knew he was still in a lot of trouble. It would take him about thirty seconds to reach Al's horse, and the others would catch up to him by then.

He didn't know that he didn't even have half of that time left as both Larry Hooper and Mo Wheeler began to fire in earnest, and Doc could see the bullets either smashing into the ground nearby or hearing them buzzing past. But the two shooters were still on their horses and moving at a decent speed to close the distance, so it would be a miracle if either of them managed to score a hit. But Doc no longer believed that he was protected by some invisible shield, and he needed to kill them both soon.

He suddenly went into a roll, hoping that they'd believe that they'd hit him for even a few seconds and stop firing, but he was only half right. They both thought he'd been hit, but they kept firing their Winchesters.

Doc had barely stopped rolling when he brought his Winchester to bear on Larry Hooper, who was the closer of the two shooters. He waited for just a couple of seconds to make sure of the shot and squeezed the trigger just before the dirt to his right burst into a small volcano from one of Mo's shots.

If it had hit just a half a second earlier, Doc would have probably jerked his trigger finger, throwing off his shot, but it hadn't arrived in time to affect the bullet's trajectory as it plunged into Larry Hooper's gut, just below his diaphragm, but bursting his abdominal aorta. Larry slumped forward and then fell face-first into the dust.

Mo had seen Larry go down, but still believed that Jim Porter had his back and kept firing as he drew within a hundred yards.

Doc had to radically alter his aim after shooting Larry and was bringing his Winchester almost a full half-circle to his right as one of Mo's .44s clanged off the top of the Winchester's barrel, knocking the repeater from Doc's hands. He knew he couldn't trust the weapon now. It could have survived the hit without any serious damage, but it was just as likely that it had become a grenade now.

As Mo continued to come at him, Doc pulled off his Colt's hammer loop and brought it to bear on Mo, who had seen Doc's Winchester fly away and knew that he'd won. He actually smiled as he began to slow his horse for a more accurate shot, not concerned with Doc's pistol at sixty yards.

Doc steadied his aim and fired, the .45 caliber lead missile blasting from his Colt's muzzle but missing its target. He then fired again as Mo's Winchester's muzzle pointed straight between his eyes.

He rolled to his right suddenly just before Mo fired then even as the ground where he had just been standing exploded like a small stick of dynamite had been set off, he scrambled to his feet and raced as fast as the bleeding thigh would let him to close the range to Mo Wheeler.

Mo had him now as he watched the limping Doc Holt come into his sights. He squeezed the trigger and waited for the kick, but all he got was a surprisingly loud click as the hammer fell on an empty chamber. He was out of ammunition.

He began scrambling to pull cartridges from his jacket pocket as Doc pulled to a stop at forty yards and fired. His third shot missed as well, but as Mo was jamming a .44 cartridge into his Winchester's loading gate, Doc fired his fourth shot, the .45 Long Colt cartridge doing its job as the bullet spun down the seven-and-a-half-inch barrel, the gases from the burning powder accelerating it to nearly the speed of sound. It crossed the one hundred and seventeen feet between the muzzle and Mo Wheeler's chest in a small fraction of a second with enough energy to drill through his breastbone, sever arteries and then lodge in his spine.

Mo Wheeler lived long enough to watch the ground coming up to his face, but not long enough to feel the pain he would have felt when he hit.

Doc watched him fall and immediately scanned for the fourth rider and not finding him anywhere. *Where the hell did he go?*

————

Jim Porter had reached the bunkhouse of the Bar W, rushed inside and grabbed his things then ran back to his horse and stuffed his clothes and shaving kit into his saddlebags.

He was getting ready to mount his horse again to make his escape, when he looked at the ranch house. Bill Wheeler was the only one inside and he was still hurting from being shot yesterday, so Jim figured he might as well take what he could. He knew where the boss kept the payroll money, so he decided to help himself.

He forgot that Bill had said that he'd be waiting in the main room with his shotgun in case Holt made it to the house. It wasn't a good time for a memory lapse.

Jim was grinning when he walked to the front of the Bar W ranch house, his Colt drawn and cocked, just in case Bill objected to Jim helping himself to his money.

Inside the house, Bill Wheeler was sitting in an easy chair facing the front door, the twelve-gauge on his lap. But it had been a long, boring morning and he wasn't feeling all that well as his chest throbbed. It had also robbed him of some much-needed sleep last night, so Bill had found himself nodding off periodically, then when he snapped back out of it, he'd curse himself for dozing.

He had just finished cursing himself when he heard bootsteps on the porch, and he quickly cocked both hammers and aimed the twelve-gauge at the front door, anxious to pay back Holt for the damage he'd done to his chest.

Jim swung the door open, saw Bill Wheeler with the shotgun pointed at him then reacted automatically and brought his Colt to bear.

Bill Wheeler identified Jim Porter and was beginning to lower the shotgun when Jim fired, the .44 hitting Bill's left shoulder, causing him to jerk his trigger finger, setting off two barrels of #4 buckshot.

At fifteen feet, Jim Porter felt the full impact of the blast, sending him reeling backwards out of the open door, his feet still churning as he crossed the porch and fell onto the steps, his face pointing up into the late morning sky.

Bill Wheeler dropped the shotgun and reached for his left shoulder to see how badly he'd been hit. He couldn't see it, but his fingers could feel the blood beginning to soak his shirt.

He stood and struggled toward the bathroom to get some towels and staunch the flow of blood, knowing it was only going to be a temporary fix. He needed help.

———

Doc's wound wasn't nearly as bad as he climbed into Al's saddle and turned his horse toward the Bar W. The blood had clotted and stopped the bleeding from what amounted to a shallow flesh wound. He had picked up Al's Winchester, loaded it with spare cartridges he'd found in his saddlebags and had it in the scabbard as he set off straight to the ranch at a fast trot.

While he refilled his Colt, he still scanned for the fourth rider as he rode, wondering where he had gone. He was tired of shootouts and wanted this over. He didn't know if Bill Wheeler had gone to Comanche to have his wound treated or if he was still in the house, but he knew he'd find him. If Bill went to

Comanche, Malcolm Lionel would deal with him. If he was in the house, Doc would take care of him himself.

Fifteen minutes later, Doc neared the back of the ranch house, and decided to go in through the back door.

He walked the horse to the house, stepped down with a grimace, then tied off the horse before pulling his pistol.

He stepped quietly onto the back porch and slowly opened the door. When he stepped inside with his Colt entering first, he was stunned to see a bloody Bill Wheeler sitting at the kitchen table with a blood-soaked towel pressed against his shoulder because he knew he'd hit him on the right side of his chest.

Bill wasn't nearly as surprised when Doc walked into his kitchen. He was almost expecting it, but all he could do was glare at him.

"Are you going to shoot me now, Holt?" he asked.

Doc released his hammer and slid his Colt back into its holster as he replied, "No, Wheeler, it looks like someone already beat me to it."

Bill Wheeler laughed and said, "Jim Porter walked in the door and I thought it was you and had my shotgun ready. The bastard shot me, but the two barrels of buckshot made short work of him, too."

Then after a short pause, said, "You have to fix me up, too. Doctors have to do that."

Doc replied, "If I was a doctor, I would, but I'm not, so I don't have to do a damned thing to help you. I can just stand here and watch you bleed to death."

Bill Wheeler knew he would if he did nothing and shouted, "You've got to help me! You can't let me die! I'll pay you! I'll give you a thousand dollars!"

"Nope. Sorry, Wheeler. You caused too much pain around here. You're all alone now. Everyone else that you had livin' on this ranch is dead. I just couldn't bury the other three 'cause I got shot myself."

"You killed my boys?"

"Every last one, but all of them were shootin' at me when they died. Sheriff Olsen died when he shot his deputy and I got him. So, you have nothing anymore, Wheeler. This ranch is worthless to you now. You're going to stand before God in a little while and have to try and talk your way into heaven, but I don't think He's gonna buy what you'll be sellin'.'"

Bill Wheeler, like many powerful men, didn't envision his own death, at least not like this. At the very least, he expected that his sons would take over. Now, he really did have nothing, and he felt incredibly empty.

"You have to help me, Holt. I'll give you anything you ask. Anything."

"It's too late to give me anything, Wheeler. Besides, you wouldn't want a Jew to sew you up, would you?"

A look of total shock exploded on Bill Wheeler's face as he exclaimed, "*A Jew? You're a Jesus-killing Jew?*"

"Now, Wheeler, if you weren't so damned ignorant, you'd know it was the Romans that killed Jesus, not the Jews. Some Jews in power may have convinced them to do it, but it was the Romans who pulled the trigger, not that it matters any. So, if you had to have a Jew-boy fix that shoulder, would you let me do it?"

Bill Wheeler glared at him and snarled, "No damned Jew is ever going to touch me! Go to hell!"

"I'm really not a Jew any more than I'm a Catholic or even a Protestant. We never went to church of any kind 'cause my father lost my mother when I was born, and he blamed God. Blamin' God is a waste of time, just like blamin' Jews, or Catholics, or coloreds for just bein' what they are. You just couldn't see that, could you, Wheeler? What a man is born with isn't what marks him as a man, it's what he does, and you don't even qualify as a man."

"You lied to me! You're nothing but a liar and you're going to die alone, too."

"No, sir. I'm not going to die alone. I'll have my red-headed wife and a passel of children that will call me papa and mourn me when I'm gone. And when I pass beyond, I won't have to lie to God about what I did, and I hope he forgives me for what I didn't do."

"You bastard!" Bill Wheeler growled.

Doc just looked at him then walked past him toward the front of the house to find Jim Porter's body to make sure he was dead, and Bill Wheeler wasn't exaggerating.

When he reached the porch and spotted the body, he didn't have to get close to make his diagnosis.

So, he turned and walked back into the house, down the hallway and re-entered the kitchen as Bill Wheeler continued to glare at him.

"I'm gonna make some coffee and somethin' to eat. You want any?"

"Go to hell," Bill Wheeler replied weakly.

Doc shrugged, opened the cookstove's firebox and lit some kindling. After he'd tossed in the last piece of wood onto the blazing fire, he slammed the door closed then filled the coffeepot with water.

As he was slicing some bacon, he said, "You know, Wheeler, this house is a real pig sty. You boys all lived like animals. How come you didn't keep it cleaner?"

Bill Wheeler was growing foggy from loss of blood and asked, "What?"

"Your house is a mess. How come you lived like this?"

Bill didn't reply as he stared at Doc as he slid the bacon into a frypan. *Who was that man standing at the stove?*

Doc glanced over at Bill Wheeler's glazed eyes and knew he didn't have long to live. He was only cooking to pass the time and remain in the kitchen. As he cooked the bacon, he kept taking peeks at Bill Wheeler as his head began to nod as if he were falling asleep which he was, but it was the never-ending sleep that faces every living creature.

He had just pulled the bacon from the pan when he heard a loud thump as Bill Wheeler collapsed onto the floor with the chair following his body.

Doc sighed, then limped over to him and laid him flat on the floor because he knew that rigor mortis would take over before the Farley brothers could put him in the ground.

He then returned to the cookstove, slid the frypan from the hot plate and grabbed a strip of bacon before walking out of the kitchen and heading for his office, hoping to find something that would clarify Wheeler's motive for doing all this. He knew it really didn't matter, but he wanted to know.

He chewed the last of the bacon, wiped the grease off his fingers on his shirt, then entered the office. The rest of the house might be in shambles, but the office was surprisingly neat.

Doc took a seat behind the desk and began pulling the drawers open. There were two accounting ledgers that he pulled out of the top left-hand drawer and found that they were simply well-kept records of expenses and income from the ranch, which showed that if nothing else, Bill Wheeler was a good businessman.

On the bottom right hand drawer, he found a metal cash box that he pulled out and set on the desk. There was a lock on the box, so he ran his fingers under the center drawer, found a leather pocket and slipped his fingers inside. He pulled out the key, opened the box and pulled out the operating cash of the Bar W.

At least, he thought it was the operating cash, which should have been about five hundred dollars to pay the ranch hands and probably dole out to his sons for their trips to Comanche, but it wasn't. Either Bill Wheeler had much more operating expenses than a normal ranch, or he didn't trust banks, because when he counted the cash, it amounted to almost six thousand dollars.

He checked the ledgers again and guessed that he didn't trust the bank at all, because he surely couldn't have had that much cash on hand if he had.

Doc stared at the cash and suddenly knew what he'd do with it. He took most of the bills out of the box, closed it and returned it to the drawer. He then walked back out to the kitchen, set the cash on the table, grabbed his last strip of bacon, then poured himself a cup of coffee.

When he finished, he spent a few minutes cleaning his thigh wound, then picked up the currency, left the house and returned to Al's horse. He put the money into the saddlebag and then rode out of the Bar W and headed for Comanche.

———

Rhonda was in the main room, sitting for the first time since being shot and talking to Martha and Beth. Linda had joined them as an observer. Rhonda had told them about Doc's letter but didn't let them read it because she felt it was personal.

"I don't believe I've earned this," Rhonda said as she clutched the letter, "I've treated him terribly and unfairly despite everything he's done for me. I just don't understand why he wouldn't hate me."

Martha replied, "When you told me and Beth about your life, Rhonda, it was plain to me that you never loved or were loved in return. Your jealousy about Beth was because you were afraid of losing the one man you had come to love, nothing more. You were angry and hurt and lashed out at Doc because you believed he was the one who hurt you.

"The problem was that Doc is so completely lost when dealing with women that he couldn't see what was bothering you and you were too angry to explain it to him. When he returns, I'm sure that you'll both be able to get past what happened."

"I hope so. I can't imagine my life without him anymore."

———

Doc stopped at the sheriff's office and found Malcolm with his arm in a sling behind the desk. When Malcolm saw him entering, he grinned and stood.

"Doc! It's good to see you!"

"Howdy, Malcolm. I've got some more deaths to report and I need to have the Farley brothers head out to the Bar W."

"Have a seat, Doc, and tell me what happened."

Doc limped over and sat across from the desk and explained what had happened since he and Malcolm had parted company.

When he finished, Malcolm leaned back and whistled.

"He was shot by Jim Porter and then blasted him with his shotgun?"

"Yes, sir. The three I shot are all northwest of the ranch about two miles. I can show them where if they need the help."

"I think the buzzards will point 'em to the right spot. I dropped off your letter to your girl, and she seemed real happy to get it."

"How was she, Malcolm? Was she okay?"

"She was sore, but for somebody getting a .44 in the gut, I think she's doin' real good. I think your letter was pretty good medicine, too."

"Malcolm, what will happen to the Bar W? The Wheelers are all gone, and there might be some problems with the ownership of some of the cattle and horses."

"The county will do some checkin' to see if there are any relatives, and if they're aren't, then it'll go up for auction."

"How long before that happens?"

"A month or so, maybe. Why? Are you interested?"

"I'm kinda thinkin' that way. Rhonda's place is small, but that's not the problem. The ranch just isn't a good place for her with all that happened there. I figure if I can buy the Bar W, then we can start fresh."

"Can you afford a place like that, Doc? Even at auction, the place would go for almost five thousand dollars."

"Well, I've been savin' for years, so I've got more than fifteen hundred in the bank, and I figure the bank could hold a mortgage for the rest."

Malcolm leaned back and said, "I'll tell you what, Doc. I'll go and talk to the county commissioners. I talked to 'em earlier and they were kinda relieved when I told 'em what happened to the sheriff. I think they knew what was goin' on and were a bit afraid of him and Bill Wheeler both. I figure with them helpin' and me bein' the new sheriff, we might be able to avoid that mortgage altogether."

Doc smiled and said, "I appreciate any help you can give me, Malcolm. I'm gonna head over to the Farleys and let 'em know about the five bodies up there, then I'll head over to the Slash A and talk to Rhonda."

"You do that, Doc. And tell Beth 'howdy' for me, will ya?"

"I'll do that, Malcolm," Doc replied as he stood.

Malcolm looked down at his bloody pantleg and said, "You gotta get that looked at, too."

Doc looked down and said, "It'll hold for a while," then limped out of the office and mounted the horse not even remembering who had been riding it earlier that day.

————

Two hours later, Doc spotted the Slash A ranch house in the distance and began to pick up the horse's pace. He had been growing more excited each mile after leaving Comanche, knowing that Rhonda was waiting for him. He hoped that Malcolm had been right, and she was happy to have received the letter and not mad at him for leaving without saying a word, so he just wasn't sure which Rhonda would be waiting in the house for him.

He didn't even reach the access road when that question was answered when he spotted a red-headed lady waving wildly at him from the porch. He waved just as crazily from the back of the horse, grinning widely as he did and setting the horse to a canter.

Martha had kept everyone else in the house, allowing Rhonda to have the porch by herself as soon as Doc's dust cloud was spotted.

Doc wondered just how she could be standing on the porch when she'd been shot not two days earlier. She still was thin and should be in bed, but he'd worry about that later. Right now, he was simply overjoyed at seeing her smiling face.

Rhonda totally forgot about her wound as her side throbbed when she waved. She had never been so completely happy in her entire life and was fighting to keep her eyes dry as Doc drew closer

Then she saw the blood on his leg and her smile disappeared.

But Doc still was grinning as he pulled the horse to a stop in front of the house, stepped down gingerly then tied off the wealth-laden horse and gimped up the steps to face a concerned Rhonda.

"John, what happened?" she asked as she looked at the bloody pants.

Doc noticed that she had called him John, rather than Doc, and replied, "It's nothing much, Rhonda. Sit down, please. You shouldn't be standing."

He reached over and took her hands and led her to one of the rocking chairs and let her sit before sitting next to her.

"I read your letter, John," Rhonda began before Doc managed to sit, "I can't begin to describe how happy it made me, but you shouldn't have apologized. I was the one who was at fault and I should be asking for your forgiveness."

Doc said, "Rhonda, let's do this right now. Today is the first day. None of those bumps that we made for ourselves before matter. No more apologizin' or worryin'. I'm gonna be here for you now. You are more important than anything else. You need to get better and know that from now on, I'm gonna make you happy. Okay?"

Rhonda smiled and said, "Okay."

Doc smiled back and asked, "When do you want to leave? I have a lot to tell you and I suppose we need to talk to everyone else, too."

"Can we leave today, John? I'm doing better, but I think that my nightmares scare everyone, especially the children."

"We can do that. Let's go inside and I'll tell everyone what happened. It's over now, Rhonda. It's finally over."

"They're all dead?" she asked.

"Yes, ma'am. I'll explain when we get inside."

Doc stood, took her hand and then they entered the ranch house and found every adult in the place, even Lenny, waiting for them, but had managed to leave the couch unoccupied.

After Rhonda and Doc sat closely on the couch, he told everyone what had happened since he left the Slash A after dropping off Rhonda.

Fred stood grinning as he listened to Doc, noticing that Rhonda was simply looking at him and smiling as they held hands. He had heard about the letter but didn't need to know what he had written. It was pretty obvious to him and everyone else that its contents had cleared the air between them.

When Doc finished, he had to answer questions from everyone, which included questions about the Bar W.

The only secret he kept from them was the money in the saddlebags. He would reserve that piece of information for Rhonda later.

When everything wound down, Doc said that he'd be taking Rhonda back to the Circle B for a few days to help her recover while everything was sorted out. Doc was the only one in the room who believed that was all he and Rhonda would be doing at the Circle B.

After an early dinner, Doc harnessed the mules to Rhonda's wagon, and helped her onto the mattress again. He hitched Bride to the back of the wagon along with the money horse, then waved to everyone as they pulled away in the early evening light.

Once they were heading east, Doc turned to Rhonda, who was looking at him and said, "Rhonda, I didn't tell anyone about something else that I found at the Bar W. When I was going through the desk, I found a box of cash. Most of it is in the saddlebags on the horse trailing the wagon. I was planning on using the money to buy the ranch, so you didn't have to live on the Circle B anymore.

"I don't feel the least bit guilty about taking the money because of all the hurt that Bill Wheeler caused you. I talked to Malcolm about the ranch and he's gonna see what they can do about gettin' it for us. I don't want you to think I'm stealin' the money just 'cause I wanted it. If you want me to, I'll give it to the county or just burn it. I don't care, Rhonda. I just want you to be happy."

Rhonda smiled up at him and said, "Burn it, John? Did you really say that? How much money are you talking about, anyway?"

"Um, about five thousand dollars."

"Five thousand? Who keeps that kind of money in a desk drawer?" she asked, astonished at the idea.

"Bill Wheeler, I guess. He must not have trusted the bank in Comanche. So, you can live with what I did?"

"Yes, Mister Holt, I can live with what you did. I'm also pleased that you're worried about me. I wasn't really overjoyed about living on that ranch again anyway. But what can you do to help Martha and Beth?"

"Oh, I figure I can help them, too. I'll have to hire a bunch of ranch hands for both places, and they have Fred and Juanita there already. Just to warn you, though. The Bar W is a dirty house. It's a big, strong house, but those boys didn't have a woman to keep them from livin' like pigs, so it's gonna need some serious cleanin'."

"I guess you're going to have to do some work then, Mister Holt. I've been shot and need to recover, according to my doctor," she said as she grinned up at him.

Doc laughed and said, "I suppose I can do that. But maybe, if we get the ranch, I can hire a cleaning woman to take care of that. I mean, you're gonna be too busy gettin' better and gettin' some of that weight back on so you can feed our babies."

Rhonda then grew serious and asked, "John, I don't know if I'll ever have babies. I must have something wrong with me because I've lost three of them and each one broke my heart."

Doc realized he'd made a mistake in mentioning babies and didn't know how to recover, so he just drove for a minute while he thought about it.

Then he let the mules drive themselves as he turned and knelt on the seat and leaned over Rhonda's face. He was upside down as he looked into those dark blue eyes that were gazing up at him.

"All we can do is try, Rhonda," he said quietly then, with his head swaying and bouncing from the wagon's motion, he leaned down and kissed her on the forehead, not risking trying to kiss her anywhere else in that awkward position.

Then he smiled at her and resumed his seating position while Rhonda closed her eyes and tried to think of something else other than babies.

Rhonda allowed herself to drift off to a nap as Doc drove and thought about what he could possibly do to help Rhonda rid herself of the worries that still simmered inside her.

By the time they rolled into the Circle B's yard, he had come up with a plan. It would take some time, but he believed that Rhonda deserved it. He just hoped it wasn't as big a failure as his other plans.

He pulled the wagon to a stop and hopped down to assist Rhonda out of the back of the wagon. Once she was on her feet, she walked better than he did as they stepped up onto the porch and they walked into the house.

"I'm going to go back outside and put the horses away and unharness the team. I'll be back in about thirty minutes, okay?"

Rhonda nodded and then asked, "John, where are you sleeping tonight?"

Doc smiled and answered, "I'd planned on sleeping with you, Rhonda. Is that okay?"

She hesitated before replying, "John, you know that I can't, you know, do anything."

"Of course, I know that. I'm here to help you get better, Rhonda, not pop those stitches loose."

She smiled and touched his face with her fingertips, "I'm sorry, John. I shouldn't have even mentioned it."

"No, you should have. It makes sense, too. You may need to put on a few pounds, lady, but you're still a very pretty woman. It'll take a lot of ignorin' that for me to make it through the night, but I will."

His answer could not have been any better for Rhonda as she smiled and said, "I'll eat as much as I can while I'm getting better, John."

Then he leaned over and kissed her softly on the lips, surprising them both, and Rhonda simply melted, making Doc catch her, thinking she was fainting.

"Are you okay, Rhonda?" he asked as he held her.

Rhonda smiled up at him and replied, "I'm wonderful, John. I just got weak in the knees."

Doc smiled back and escorted her into the bedroom and let her lay down before going back out to the wagon and leading it and the horses into the barn.

———

The sun was down, and Doc had Rhonda snuggled in against him, and as he anticipated, it was difficult for him to think of anything else, but knew he had to. They had talked for two and a half hours while they lay close to each other with Rhonda wearing one of her nightdresses, making it even worse for Doc. They'd talked about many things, mostly about their future, but none touching Doc's plans for helping Rhonda.

She had finally fallen asleep, and Doc held her against him waiting for her to wake up screaming from her nightmares. As he lay beside her, he began to break his plan down into details. It wouldn't matter if they got the Bar W or not, as the ranch wasn't critical to what he wanted to do for her but having the ranch would make the logistics much better.

Doc held her until he finally succumbed to sleep after another hour.

————

He and Rhonda both awakened when a loud clap of thunder shook the house, as the subdued light of a cloudy day filled the room.

Rhonda looked at Doc and said, "Good morning, John."

"Good morning, Rhonda. I think we're about to hear the pounding of rain on the roof."

"I think so, but I need to get to the privy before it hits."

Doc slid out of bed, helped Rhonda stand and walked with her down the hallway. Before they reached the kitchen, the clouds opened up and a downpour began drumming on the roof, making Rhonda turn back around and head back to the bedroom to use the chamber pot while Doc continued to the door, walked onto the porch and added his own downpour to Mother Nature's as lightning flashed nearby followed almost immediately by a huge clap of thunder.

Doc turned quickly back into the house, pumped some water into the coffeepot, set it on the stove and then built a fire in the firebox.

He was preparing breakfast when Rhonda returned and sat down at the table, knowing that Doc would tell her to sit down if she tried to help.

"John," she asked, "if we get the Bar W, what will I do with the Circle B?"

Doc slipped the bacon onto the frypan and said, "Whatever you want to do with it. It's yours. You don't have to think about that for a while, though. We have a lot of things to do, now."

"Okay. How is your leg?"

"Not bad. I checked it last night and I'm not even gonna stitch it up. I cleaned it and covered it, so that should be enough. It'll scar, but not too much. I should be walkin' okay in a couple of weeks."

"When will I be back to normal?" she asked.

"It all depends by what you figure is normal. I don't know if I've ever seen a normal Rhonda."

Rhonda laughed, knowing that she would probably have thrown something at him two days ago.

"You know what I mean, Mister Holt."

"I know. If we can get some of your weight back over the next couple of weeks then after I take out the stitches, you'll be sore, but you should be able to get around okay. I think you'll be able to be yourself again in another month or so."

"A month?" she asked in surprise, *"We can't do anything for a month?"*

"We can do a lot of things. We probably will have to move, and I'll have to get all the horses together and figure out what to do with all the guns and other stuff. We're gonna be pretty busy, ma'am."

"Don't play Mister Ignorant Cowhand with me, John. You know what I mean."

"I suppose so, ma'am. But I think you'll have to remain chaste for a month or so. I don't want to risk you gettin' hurt, Rhonda. I can survive for another month, and I think it'll be a good way for us to just figure each other out better, too."

"Why do I think you're just making up an excuse?"

"I wish I was, but I'm not. You took a bullet to your gut, Rhonda. You were really lucky that it was so far off to the side that it didn't do anything really bad inside. Of course, you coulda been a might luckier and had it miss altogether, but it didn't. I don't want to take a chance on causin' you any more pain."

Rhonda sighed and said, "I understand, John, but I do wish we didn't have to wait. I've never really had a man make love to me before and I want you to love me, John."

Doc turned and said, "I do love you, Rhonda, and when I make love to you, you'll know how much. I'm holdin' off on that because I do love you so much. You mean that much to me. Did Fred tell you my biggest confession?"

"He told me that you didn't talk to women at all and that you were smitten with me and not Beth. Is that what you mean?"

"No, my confession that I've never been with a woman at all. It's a bad thing for a man to tell another man, but I did. I'm tellin' you so you can understand just how much I care about you."

Rhonda didn't have the same reaction as Fred had because she suspected that it was true after they had their long talk the night of the Adler raid, but she did understand how difficult it would be for him to deny himself while he laid close to her.

"John, did you want to sleep in a different room?"

"No, ma'am. That would be worse, 'cause my imagination would go crazy. I do like holdin' you close, though. I feel like I'm talkin' to you without sayin' anything."

She smiled and said, "Me, too."

———

They stayed together alone on the Circle B for another four days before they had their first visitors when Sheriff Malcolm Lionel and Beth rode to the ranch just before noon and found Doc chopping wood behind the house.

He waved and stepped over to them with only a slight limp and sweat pouring across his shirtless, woodchip-covered chest.

"Mornin', folks," he said loudly as they dismounted, and he began to brush off the pieces of wood that clung to him.

"Where's Rhonda?" asked Beth as she tied off her horse but stared at Doc.

"She's in the bedroom sewin'. She's doin' a lot better already, but I'm makin' her take it easy."

"Thanks," Beth replied as she trotted into the house but took one last look at Doc before entering.

Doc turned to Malcolm and said, "Beth seems happy."

He grinned back and replied, "Yup. I think so. I figure you're gonna be happier, too. The county commissioners got together and after they appointed me sheriff, they kinda did some fiddlin' with the rules, and put the Bar W up for auction and yours was the only bid. So, you need to go to the county land office, pay the agreed to price and they'll sign the deed over to you."

Doc couldn't help grinning back and asked, "How much arm-twistin' did that take, Malcolm?"

"None at all. I told 'em what had happened, and they were so happy that all those raids were stopped that they were more than pleased to make it happen. You know that Will Hatfield is one of the commissioners, don't ya?"

"Nope. I don't care about those kinda things. What was the price they came up with?"

"Five hundred dollars."

Doc stared at him with wide eyes and raised eyebrows for thirty seconds before asking, "How much?"

"They wanted to make it a dollar, but then they figured it woulda looked bad. So, when you go to the county land office, you give 'em five hundred dollars and you've got the Bar W."

Doc shook Sheriff Lionel's good hand and said, "Thanks a whole lot, Malcolm. You gotta hire some more deputies, though."

"I do. They're letting me hire two deputies."

"That's great, Malcolm, but I need to go and tell Rhonda. Beth isn't tellin' her the news, is she?"

"Nope, I think she's askin' about you two, and tellin' her that she's spoken for now."

"Meanin' the new sheriff is visitin' Beth now?"

"That's the truth of it. She wants Rhonda to know that you're all hers now."

"I figure Rhonda knows that by now."

"So, did you two, you know, figure somethin' out?"

"Believe it or not, Malcolm, I'm just helpin' her to get better. It's kinda bad at night for me, but it's more important that she gets strong."

Malcolm stared at him and said, "You're serious, ain't ya?"

"I can't hurt her, Malcolm. She's just too important to me."

"I gotta admit, Doc, I'm kinda impressed."

"Glad to hear it. Come on inside and you and Beth can be there when I tell her."

"Now, that'll be fun," he said as he followed Doc into the house.

Doc grabbed his shirt from the porch rail as he passed and pulled it on, buttoning it as they entered the kitchen where they found Beth and Rhonda sitting at the table in deep discussion.

Both looked at the men as they entered, and Beth gazed at Doc with even more respect than she had held before, which was considerable. Rhonda had told her what he had just told Malcolm.

As Doc filled a glass with water, he said, "Rhonda, Malcolm told me I have to go to the county courthouse tomorrow. Now, I don't want to leave you alone, but I think you can ride Bride now. Did you want to come along?"

"What do you have to do at the courthouse?" she asked.

"I've got to give them five hundred dollars for the Bar W ranch then get a new brand."

Rhonda was almost as stunned as Doc had been but replied, "I can ride with you."

Doc smiled at her and winked before saying, "Good. You stay there, and I'll cook some lunch."

Beth rose and said, "You will do no such thing, Mister Holt. I'll handle lunch while you sit down and talk to Rhonda."

"Yes, ma'am," he replied before glancing over at Malcolm and grinning.

———

After they'd gone, Doc and Rhonda sat at the table and talked for a while about the ranches and what they planned to do with them.

Then Doc surprised her by asking her if she could stay with Martha and Beth while he prepared the Bar W for her, promising to have it all done in time for their wedding, which they had set for September 9th.

"I'll come over and visit every day, Rhonda, but I want to keep you safe and trust me when I say that the house isn't fit for folks to live in."

"Will you sleep with me, John?" she asked.

"Every night, sweetheart," he replied.

She nodded and laid her hand on his.

———

The next day, Rhonda and Doc rode into Comanche and Doc paid the county then they signed the paperwork and became the new owners of the Bar W. They had to go through the book of established brands to find one they could use as theirs and applied for the Diamond H, would work out as a good overbrand if they decided to do that, but the Bar W was still registered to the ranch, so the cattle could be sold with that brand on their hides.

They didn't return to the Circle B, but stayed at the Double L, and Rhonda was moved into her new bedroom. Doc did as he had promised and slept with her tucked in close that night, but left early the next morning to ride to the Bar W, or Diamond H.

He didn't want to leave all the cash in the metal box in the drawer because he wouldn't be spending much time on the ranch, so he put the money into the box, then took the box out to the barn and slid it behind the bundles of hay in the loft.

Then he rode into Comanche and put out the word that he was hiring fourteen ranch hands, six for the Double L and eight for the Diamond H. He also needed a cook and a cleaning woman for the Diamond H.

He also bought all new bedding and some furniture that he needed replacing as well as all new kitchenware and linen for the house and filled up the large wagon that was in his new barn.

While the word was circulating for the new employees, Doc returned to the Diamond H and began to do basic cleanup and put the new kitchenware in place and tossed out anything he couldn't use. He brought anything useful that he couldn't use back to Comanche and donated them to the Methodist and Baptist churches in equal proportions for them to distribute to the needy.

As the house became cleaner, he began hiring. The cleaning woman, Elise Humphrey, would live in the big house while he was there and then move into the small house that Doc assumed was originally meant for either servants' quarters or if one of his slob sons was lucky enough to find a woman who would accept him.

He found a good cook when Fred recommended a friend. Hiring the ranch hands was difficult because there were so many qualified applicants and Doc hated turning any of them away, but he soon had fourteen men that he knew he could trust. Not surprisingly, the stories of what he had done helped to ensure that they would limit their activities to ranch duties.

Doc had removed everyone's stitches and because of his use of alcohol, no one showed a hint of infection. His own wound had scabbed over and then was cleaned leaving a scar. Rhonda's scar was less noticeable as she began putting on weight.

But the biggest advantage to having the Diamond H was its location on Comanche County's eastern border with Erath County.

It was that proximity that had inspired Bill Wheeler to decide to go add the Mulligan family to their list of targets but had never been able to carry out the attack. Doc was taking advantage of the ranch's nearness of the town of Dublin, Texas to carry out his own plan that had nothing to do with guns, but everything to do with Rhonda's Irish heritage.

It only took only a little more than an hour to make the ten-mile ride to Dublin, which although it was a small town, still had a Catholic church…St. Patrick's, naturally. He met Father Jim Duffy at the church and explained what he wanted to do. Doc was surprised how understanding he was as his expectations were based on what Rhonda had told him about her life and the priests she had known. By their third meeting, he counted the young priest as much a friend as a spiritual counselor and began to look forward to their meetings.

He continued to sleep with Rhonda, who was making great strides in her recovery and her weight gain, both of which made Doc's nights even more troubling.

Rhonda spent her days with Beth and was using the money that Doc had given her when he had first left the Circle B, buying a lot more clothes that showed her swelling figure to advantage. Even Beth complimented on how she looked, which helped Rhonda's confidence.

The new ranch hands were doing a great job getting the cattle sorted out, and even moved the six cattle from the Circle B to the main herd. They sorted out all the brands that didn't belong there, and those that could be returned were, as were the illegally obtained horses in the remuda. Even then, when everything was sorted, the herds numbered just over eleven hundred animals and the down-sized remuda contained an even sixty horses.

The house was perfect, and Elise had moved into the small house by the first of September. Rhonda was getting excited about their upcoming wedding and kept asking Doc if she could move into the new house because she felt normal, but as difficult as it was to deny her requests, Doc did.

———

Early on Friday morning on the eighth of September, Doc rode to the Double L on Trapper, stepped down at the back of the house and tied off his horse before stepping onto the back porch and knocking on the door.

Doc hadn't shown up in the morning at the ranch in quite a while, so Rhonda wasn't even in the kitchen when Beth opened the door and smiled at Doc.

"Is everything ready, Doc?" she asked as she let him inside.

"Yes, ma'am. Is Bride saddled?"

"She is. I'm so excited! I wish I could be there today, but we'll be happy to be there tomorrow."

Rhonda heard Doc's voice from the main room and trotted quickly into the kitchen wearing a big smile.

"John, this is a surprise. Is there some reason why you're here so early?"

"I've come to take you away, Rhonda. Bride's saddled and ready to go."

"Do I have to come back to the Double L?" she asked excitedly, hoping she could stay at the new house...their house.

"For one more night, then we go home."

"I suppose I can last one more night. Where are we going?"

"East," he replied mysteriously.

Rhonda latched onto his arm and Doc winked at Beth as he and Rhonda left the house. She had taken to wearing her new riding skirts every day in anticipation of the day when Doc would take her home.

As they rode east from the Double L, Rhonda asked, "Where exactly are we going, Doc?"

"Erath County."

"I've never been there. What's there?"

"Nothing much except for a few small towns. It still has more people than Eastland County where the Circle B is. What have you decided to do with the place now that it's empty?"

"I don't know if I should sell it or just keep it. What do you think, John?"

"I say we keep it. It's not worth that much and we're pretty good with money."

"I can't wait to see the house. You should have let me pick out the curtains, though."

"I let Elise do that, so you didn't have to suffer."

"John, I've never met Elise. What's she like?"

Doc laughed and asked, "Jealous?"

"No, of course not. I was just curious, that's all."

"Elise is a very nice lady. She's about forty and a widow. Her son, Jake, is one of the ranch hands, by the way. I think you'll enjoy having her around the house."

"I'm sure I will," she replied.

Doc managed to keep the conversation away from their destination until they crossed into Erath County.

"So, where are we going, John?" she asked as she spotted some buildings in the distance.

"That town right there, Rhonda. I've been visitin' the town for the past month, and it's time that you visited it, too."

"Why? What's there to see?"

Doc looked up at the familiar town and pointed, saying, "There."

Rhonda looked at the buildings and squinted asking, "What am I looking for?"

"You'll see in another minute or two," he replied.

A minute later, she spotted a sign that read DUBLIN, and she started to laugh.

"You brought me all the way here to show me a sign?"

Doc shook his head and said, "No, my love, I brought you here to bring you to church."

Of all the possible responses Rhonda had expected, his answer was nowhere on her list.

"Church?" she asked, "I didn't think you ever went to church."

"I didn't until a few weeks ago, but I've been goin' a lot since then, but not for me, for you, Rhonda."

"Me?" she asked, in confusion as they reached the outskirts of Dublin.

Doc smiled at Rhonda and nodded, then pointed to the almost unnoticeable St. Patrick's church across the street.

Rhonda panicked and said quickly, "No, John, I can't go in there! I can't. You don't understand. I'm not allowed to go in there."

John turned Trapper to the hitchrail in front of the church and waited for Rhonda to pull Bride next to him.

"John, please don't do this! I beg you!" she exclaimed, almost in panic.

Doc put out his hand and said, "Rhonda, you know I'd never hurt you, and I'm askin' you to join me."

Rhonda looked down at Doc, glanced at the church and then back into Doc's light blue eyes. It was one of those defining moments as Rhonda had to trust him now or she never would.

She took his hand, stepped down from Bride and kept her eyes focused on her soon-to-be husband and asked quietly, "Why, John?"

"You'll understand soon, Rhonda."

Instead of leading her into the church, Doc walked with her around the side of the church to a small house that served as the rectory.

They stepped onto the small porch and Doc knocked on the door. It was opened just a few seconds later by Father Duffy, who took one look at Rhonda's deep red hair curling down around her face and broke into a big smile.

"Now, sure this is the pretty lassie that you'll be marryin' tomorrow, John. Come in, come in," he said as he ushered her into the rectory.

Rhonda's fear had shriveled to nothing as she had heard the almost laughing brogue of the young Irish priest.

Doc held a chair for Rhonda who took a seat before Doc sat next to her.

"Now, Miss Brady, that heathen that is sitting next to you came here a few weeks ago to ask a favor of me, and would you believe that this non-believer actually tried bribing yours truly with a bottle of Irish whiskey? I thought it would be a true sin to waste the gift, so I tried a wee bit and absolved him of his sin, but he persisted, and we've been having long talks ever since. He told me what he had done and how he finally understood that he was his brother's keeper after all, and I believe that you'll be marrying a fine man. But now, I would like to talk to you.

"John has told me that you feel as if you have sinned by not going into the convent and other things that shamed you, and I agree with him that most of them were not sins at all, but the pain of a lost soul. Tomorrow, I will be marrying you and John, and before the ceremony, I will need to hear your confession. If you feel it is a sin, then tell me. I will absolve you of the real sins and those that may not be sins but still haunt your soul.

"When you and John wed tomorrow, you will be as free from sin as the day you were baptized. You and John will enter into your new life together with nothing to concern you other than filling each other with joy."

Rhonda looked over at John and tears began to flow down her face before she turned back to Father Duffy and whispered, "Now, Father?"

"If you feel ready."

Rhonda bowed her head and began the confession, and despite his dismissal of the things she had done in her life years earlier, she recited everything in a shaking voice as she continued to cry.

Doc just watched her, hoping that he had done the right thing.

When she finally finished, even confessing how poorly she had treated John, Father Duffy absolved her and assigned her penance.

When Rhonda finally looked back at Doc, she seemed transformed. All the weight that she had hung on her soul for all those years was gone. When she had confessed to John that night and he had explained that he didn't think she was a sinner at all, she thought that it had been enough. But the guilt had still been buried deep within her, and now she felt truly free, finally forgiving herself as well.

She smiled at John and said softly, "Thank you, John."

Doc smiled back at Rhonda and just nodded.

Then she turned back to Father Duffy and asked, "Father, will I have babies now?"

He smiled at her and said, "Aye. John tells me I'll be baptizing lots of wee Holts over the coming years."

She turned back to John and beamed a big smile at him.

After she finished her penance, which was lengthy simply because Father Duffy knew that she expected it, they stayed and talked about tomorrow's wedding, finally leaving the rectory just after three o'clock.

Doc and Rhonda walked to the only eatery in town for a late lunch, and as they waited for their food to be delivered a radiant Rhonda smiled at Doc.

"John, I can never fully express how much that means to me. I thought I was better when I told you what happened, and you told me it wasn't my fault, but I was wrong. It was still deep inside eating at me. How did you know? You told me that you didn't understand me, but you knew even if I didn't."

"When I told you that you needed to gain the weight to feed our babies and you told me that you lost three babies and it broke your heart, I saw how much it hurt you to say that. That's when I figured out that you still felt guilty about things. It was kinda hard for me to understand the religious part of it, so I rode out to Dublin 'cause I knew there was a Catholic church there.

"I was kinda expectin' the priest to toss me out on my ear or tell me that you shoulda felt guilty for what you thought were sins, but when I talked to Father Duffy, he surprised me. He was really understandin' about what happened to you and so, I went back a few times to see if he could help. I count him as a good friend now, even if he does wear dresses."

Rhonda laughed, then asked, "Are you going to become a Catholic now?"

"No, Rhonda, but you are and that's why I had to find Father Duffy, and he understands that. You grew up bein' told what is good and what is bad, what you had to do and what you couldn't do. All religions do that, which is why there are so many of 'em. I grew up without anybody tellin' me those things, so I made my own rules, and they were pretty simple.

"I never hurt anyone unless they're tryin' to hurt me, and what didn't concern me wasn't my business. Now, that second one I finally figured out was wrong, so I changed that rule, but I can't see joinin' a church, just so some priest or preacher can start tellin' me a whole bunch of rules that will keep me from doin' what I think is right. Can you understand that?"

"Of course, I can, John. I wouldn't ask you to stop being you. It's not important to me. You are."

John looked at her enchanted face and said, "You know you look different, don't you? Your eyes are smilin' at me."

"So is the rest of me."

"Did you want to stop and see our house on the way back to the Double L?"

"I can see it now?"

"Yes, ma'am. I told Elise that I'd be bringin' you by this afternoon. She's really kinda anxious to meet you 'cause I talk about you all the time."

———

Rhonda didn't talk much on the ride home as she just reveled in the light feeling of her pure soul and riding with the man who made it and her new life possible.

They arrived at the Diamond H ranch house just after five o'clock, and Doc introduced Rhonda to Elise then each of the ranch hands and the cook.

She was thoroughly pleased with her new home and with Elise's selections for the woman's touches that the house had never seen when it had been occupied by the Wheelers. But she was most pleased with the addition that John had put in. She thanked him profusely when she spotted the large bathtub and said that she'd tell Beth just to make her jealous for a change as her new tub was even bigger than the one at the Double L.

Doc and Rhonda then made the thirty-minute ride to the Double L and joined them for dinner. Rhonda was bubbling the entire time and both Beth and Martha could tell the dramatic change that the visit to Dublin had made in her.

That night, as Doc and Rhonda lay close together, Rhonda didn't say a word on the eve of her wedding, but just felt the absolute tranquility of feeling John close to her and basking in the depth of the love that he had given to her that day.

———

The wedding itself was like a continuation of the day before, and John surprised her again when he produced wedding bands. When Father Duffy pronounced them man and wife, Rhonda knew for the first time in her life that she was truly married.

Beth and Malcolm had been their witnesses, but Martha and the entire Adler family had made the trip to Dublin for the ceremony.

They filled the café afterwards for a celebratory lunch, then the large convoy of riders made the long ride back to their respective ranches.

Doc had given all the ranch hands and Elise the day off, so when he led Rhonda into the house at the Diamond H, they knew that they were alone and intended to make the most of it.

For a month, they had laid closely together, and Doc had restrained himself as had Rhonda but now, there was nothing holding them back. It was nothing short of chaos as the couple consummated their marriage progressively around the house.

Rhonda's lost weight had returned, and Doc made sure that she understood how much he appreciated the full Rhonda.

That night, as they finally were able to relax and Mister Holt held Mrs. Holt close to his chest with her red curls covering most of his chest, Rhonda whispered, "John, for an ignorant cowhand who doesn't understand women, you've made this woman happier than you'll ever know."

Doc kissed her on her forehead and said, "I think you'll be even happier in two years when you have our daughter on your lap, and she looks at you with her big blue eyes and says 'mama'."

Rhonda closed her eyes and prayed that her husband was right.

———

A month and a half after their wedding, Doc and Rhonda acted as witnesses for Malcolm and Beth when they married at the First Baptist Church in Comanche.

That night, Rhonda told her husband that she was expecting, and despite her expressed confidence in having a healthy child, her worries began again. She and John would ride to Dublin each Sunday, and Father Duffy did his best to set aside her worries, but she still couldn't shake her fears even as she began to swell.

Doc bought a buggy in February for the Sunday trips, so Rhonda didn't have to ride to Dublin, and she seemed happy, but he could tell that she was very worried.

On the first of June, just after seven o'clock in the evening, Rhonda went into labor. Because he was so concerned for his wife, Doc defied tradition and stayed with her the entire time, talking to her telling her how beautiful their daughter would be, just like her mother. Rhonda never questioned why he had always told her that they would be having a daughter and not a son.

Rhonda worried between contractions well into the night, but Doc was still with her at 2:27 a.m. when Elise, who was also a midwife, slapped the behind of their baby, and little Mary Frances Holt's first cry filled the room.

Rhonda began to cry herself when Elise laid her very healthy baby on her chest and she held onto the small, squealing, pink human that she had brought into the world.

She felt such rapturous joy as she felt her baby squirming against her that for just a few moments, she forgot about Doc who was sitting near her head beaming at her.

When she did turn her face towards her husband, all she could say was, "Thank you, John."

Doc leaned over and kissed his wife on the forehead before kissing their daughter on hers.

He then sat back and let out a long sigh before Elise finally was successful in kicking him out of the room.

————

On March 27, 1879, Doc was in the ranch office working on the ledger after a recent cattle sale. The Diamond H was becoming a very successful operation, and he found himself spending more time in the office than out on the ranch with the herds but had to live with it.

He had just finished making an entry when Mary Frances toddled into his office and put out her arms. Doc smiled at their first daughter and scooped her into his lap.

"Howdy, ma'am," he said as he tickled her tummy, "come to see your old papa?"

Mary giggled and poked her father's nose before she opened her small mouth and spoke her first word.

Doc rolled his chair back, stood up and carried Mary out of the office and walked to the parlor where a pregnant Rhonda sat with one-year-old Jake at her feet playing with some colored blocks.

"I see Mary found you," she said as she smiled at the common sight.

"She did. She poked me in the nose too, so I figured I'd let her poke you this time," he replied as he plopped Mary onto her mother's lap.

On cue, Mary smiled to her mother, her blue eyes twinkling as she jabbed her small index finger into Rhonda's nose and said, "Mama."

EPILOGUE

The question of the Circle B was resolved that year by an unexpected change in their lives when Rhonda received a letter from her oldest sister Mary Sullivan, the one who had altered her life by explaining how wonderful marriage was. There had been upheaval in the Brady household after the ouster of Boss Tweed in '74 had finally trickled down to Alderman Jimmy Brady, and he lost his election to a reformist, which stripped him of his power. Mary's husband, Jack Sullivan, hadn't been part of Tammany Hall, but his father had, so he lost his job and couldn't find one, so in desperation, Mary had written to her long-lost sister asking for help.

Rhonda had explained Mary's situation and Doc knew his wife well enough now to know what she wanted to do before she even finished.

So, the Circle B became the home of a large, Irish Catholic family that required a lot of help in adapting to the alien lifestyle of being Texas ranchers. The boys in the family all took to the new way of life rapidly, of course, and Rhonda was more than just a little pleased to have Mary nearby.

Over the next nine years, Doc and Rhonda added their own crowd of youngsters to the community, finally finishing with seven healthy, active children. Mary was followed by Jake, then Beth, Martha, Lauren, Robert and finally little Amanda.

Only the first three were baptized by Father Duffy who had been reassigned to a parish in Missouri after his church was finally closed and Dublin disappeared from the maps. But Santa Miguel was opened in Comanche the following year, so the

Holts and Sullivans could make use of the new church. Doc would attend, but never did become a Catholic or anything else other than a Texan.

———

After having her seventh child, Rhonda was grateful that the spigots somehow were turned off as she struggled to keep those lost twenty pounds from becoming the discovered thirty. But Doc never complained and went out of his way to prove how much he appreciated her figure.

Jake was thirteen now and was entering those horribly wonderful years of confusion that confronts most teenaged humans and was having one of those moments that was torturing him.

He had been moody all day and approached his mother as she was sewing on her new machine.

"Mama, can I talk to you?"

Rhonda stopped the machine, looked at Jake's troubled face and said, "Yes, dear, of course. What is the problem?"

Jake looked down at his shuffling feet and said, "Well, it's um, it's about Penelope Franklin. You know Penny, don't you, Mama?"

Rhonda smiled and replied, "Yes, Jake, I know Penelope."

"Well, you see, Mama, the other day, I was talkin' to her, and, well, I don't know, I kinda…well, it just seems…I don't know…I think I…"

Rhonda smiled and said, "Jake, why don't you go and talk to your father."

321

Jake looked up at his mother and said, "Papa? But it's about a girl, Mama."

Rhonda started up her machine again, saying, "I know, but your father knows more about women than anyone else I know."

BOOK LIST

1	Rock Creek	12/26/2016
2	North of Denton	01/02/2017
3	Fort Selden	01/07/2017
4	Scotts Bluff	01/14/2017
5	South of Denver	01/22/2017
6	Miles City	01/28/2017
7	Hopewell	02/04/2017
8	Nueva Luz	02/12/2017
9	The Witch of Dakota	02/19/2017
10	Baker City	03/13/2017
11	The Gun Smith	03/21/2017
12	Gus	03/24/2017
13	Wilmore	04/06/2017
14	Mister Thor	04/20/2017
15	Nora	04/26/2017
16	Max	05/09/2017
17	Hunting Pearl	05/14/2017
18	Bessie	05/25/2017
19	The Last Four	05/29/2017
20	Zack	06/12/2017
21	Finding Bucky	06/21/2017
22	The Debt	06/30/2017
23	The Scalawags	07/11/2017
24	The Stampede	08/23/2019
25	The Wake of the Bertrand	07/31/2017
26	Cole	08/09/2017
27	Luke	09/05/2017
28	The Eclipse	09/21/2017
29	A.J. Smith	10/03/2017
30	Slow John	11/05/2017
31	The Second Star	11/15/2017
32	Tate	12/03/2017
33	Virgil's Herd	12/14/2017
34	Marsh's Valley	01/01/2018
35	Alex Paine	01/18/2018

36	Ben Gray	02/05/2018
37	War Adams	03/05/2018
38	Mac's Cabin	03/21/2018
39	Will Scott	04/13/2018
40	Sheriff Joe	04/22/2018
41	Chance	05/17/2018
42	Doc Holt	06/17/2018
43	Ted Shepard	07/16/2018
44	Haven	07/30/2018
45	Sam's County	08/19/2018
46	Matt Dunne	09/07/2018
47	Conn Jackson	10/06/2018
48	Gabe Owens	10/27/2018
49	Abandoned	11/18/2018

Made in the USA
Las Vegas, NV
28 November 2022

60570425R00194